UNEXPECTED *Love*

ERIN GRAVES

To anyone who forgot who they were for a little bit.
We all need a little help sometimes.

AUTHOR'S *note*

Unexpected Love is an open-door romance intended for mature readers, containing sexually explicit and adult content. While this story is filled with friends, family, and love, and a happily ever after is guaranteed, it does touch on some sensitive subjects. Please see the back of the book for a complete list, or visit my website for a detailed list, should you need it.

Additionally, the timeline of Unexpected Love does overlap slightly with Shuttered Hearts. While both stories stand on their own and can be read as complete standalones, there will be minor spoilers for Shuttered Hearts in this book.

www.eringravesauthor.com

Playlist

"Until I Found You" – Stephen Sanchez
"The Adventure" – Angels & Airwaves
"That's Life" – Frank Sinatra
"Slow It Down" – Benson Boone
"Everything We Need" – Wilfred
"Too Sweet" – Hozier
"Light On" – Maggie Rogers
"No More Bad Days" – This Wild Life
"How Do You Feel?" – The Maine
"Love is Dangerous" – blink-182
"Lost & Found" – Daren Kiely
"Better Love" – Eisley

Prologue

AVA

MY PARENTS HAVE NEVER BEEN the most loving, but I never believed they could be so unfeeling. I stare at the two of them, stunned and unable to form a coherent thought, let alone words.

My mother sits on the couch in the formal sitting room—don't even get me started on how ridiculous it is that we have a formal sitting room while living in our small town of Harborview, Massachusetts—an air of conceit surrounding her.

My father stands behind her, a tumbler of scotch in one hand and his other resting on the back of the couch, his brows pinched in a stern look. One that would normally have me agreeing to whatever they want me to do.

"I will not marry that man. No way in hell, and the fact that you're asking me to after what I just told you…" I shake my head, unsure how to finish that statement.

My heart breaks thinking about what they're asking of me.

I've always known that my parents care about appearances. It's why they were so upset when my brother, Declan, got a divorce. But they seemed to come to terms with that, and

I thought, when it comes down to it, they care more about our happiness than anything else.

Now I know exactly how Declan felt before he left and moved to Ashford Falls, Maryland. It's not the same; what happened with Declan and what they're asking of me, but I understand it all the same.

I'm left wondering how I can face them after today. Especially if they truly expect this from me—how am I supposed to continue living in this town, pretending we're some happy family when that's the furthest thing from the truth?

"I'm done." I turn away from them, knowing there's no hope I'll change their minds. I need to get out of this house, away from them and this life they've so carefully curated for me—a life I thought I'd been choosing for myself this entire time.

"Ava Margaret Day." My father's voice booms from behind me. "You will not walk out of this house without having a civilized conversation with your mother and me."

My father's words stop me in my tracks. "A civilized conversation? You call this civilized?" I turn to them. "We live in the twenty-first century, and you're talking about an arranged marriage. To a man who tried to force himself on me."

"Oh, Ava. Don't be so dramatic." My mother scoffs, unbothered by everything. She and my father exchange a look, communicating something silently before turning back to me. "Brian comes from a good family. There's no way he acted even remotely like you described."

I stare at her, trying to figure out how she became this way. I can't remember ever feeling unsafe in my parent's presence; though, we were never close. They always pushed me to "do more" and "be better," but never to the point that I questioned my safety and well-being.

"Dramatic?" I ask, my voice going flat. I was angry before

—furious, really. But now I feel numb. "How the fuck am I being dramatic? He—"

"Ava," my mother interrupts, "I taught you better than that. We don't use that kind of language in this house."

"Who are you?" I don't mean for that question to come out, but I can't stop the words. I don't recognize this woman before me.

"Ava, that's no way to talk to your mother." My father moves around the couch, taking his place beside her.

My mother continues as if I never said anything. "His assistant said nothing inappropriate was happening in that office. From what she could see when she walked in, she said *you* were the one coming onto Brian—not the other way around."

The disgust on my mother's face makes me want to run to my room and hide like I've done something wrong, but I know I haven't done anything to warrant any of this. Unless it's work-related, I never talk to Brian. We may work at the same firm, but he's a criminal defense attorney while I'm in family law. We rarely have the same cases or clients.

"Of course she did! She can't afford to lose her job!" I shout, turning my back on them.

Are they so far removed from the real world they don't know what it means to need a job?

I know I've lived a privileged life. Being born into one of the founding families of this small town afforded me so much, on top of having parents who were very successful in their careers. But I've always worked for everything I wanted. It wasn't something my parents required, but I saw what they did to my brother when he accepted any kind of assistance from them. It was always held over his head like there was some quid pro quo to all of it, and I didn't want that for myself. I avoided taking anything from my parents—unless I truly needed it. The only big thing I accepted from them was their help paying for school.

"Ava. This is important to your mother and I. I don't know what happened between you and Brian, but I know it can't be as bad as you're making it out to be." I hear the exasperation in my father's voice and I want to be hurt by it, but this whole conversation has drained me. I'm too exhausted to feel much of anything.

I don't know if it's because I'm an adult now, but my parents have never been so hardheaded—so inconsiderate of my feelings. Maybe the issue is that I always follow what they want, no questions asked. This is the first time I've pushed back.

I played the sports they wanted me to play, and I did the extracurricular activities they required of me. I studied pre-law in undergrad and graduated from law school at the top of my class. And most recently, I got the job at the big fancy law firm like they pushed me to.

But this? Telling me—not asking me—to marry Brian Wellsley, a man who couldn't take no for an answer, is just too far.

I turn back to my parents sitting on the couch. "I don't know how to make you understand me, but there is nothing you can say or do to get me to marry that man."

"Ava, you don't have a choice. Everything has already been decided. The contracts are signed." My father sounds like he's discussing any other business deal, not selling his daughter to the highest bidder.

"You can't be serious. You can't legally force me to marry this man. At the very least, I have to sign the marriage certificate, and I can promise you, I will *never* do that." I stare at them for another minute before I turn and walk away.

This time, when my father calls after me, I ignore him.

CHAPTER

One

AVA

I KNOCK on the open door in front of me, nervous about this conversation with my boss. Things have been off for the last two weeks. They've been bringing on additional staff to help with coverage on some of my cases and removing me from others.

I have a good idea of what's about to happen, and if I'm being honest with myself, I don't think I'm that upset about it.

My boss glances up and waves me into the office as soon as he sees me. "Ava, come on in. Thanks for staying late to meet with me. I know it's not news to you that when a judge calls you in you go without question."

"It's no problem." I sit in the chair Mr. Henry gestures to as I walk into his office.

I know small talk is the appropriate response, but I don't have it in me to pretend I'm not about to be fired. Brian Wellsley is the son of one of the partners at this firm and is set to become a partner within the next six months.

When I rejected him and then told my parents about what

he tried to do as a result of that rejection, I have no doubt he ran to his parents. Add to the fact that his parents have a contract with mine to ensure we would marry—which I refused—and it's no surprise I'm about to get fired. But I'll be damned if I let my parents force me into "fulfilling my purpose" by marrying that man.

Mr. Henry sits behind his desk, studying me for a few minutes before finally speaking. "You've always been a smart woman. I don't think it will shock you why I asked for this meeting."

"No, Mr. Henry. I feel confident I know what this is about."

"I wish we lived in a different world. The fact you're about to be punished for rejecting a man is..." Mr. Henry sighs, clearly at a loss for words, but I don't step in to help him. I understand where he's trying to take this conversation, but at the end of the day, he's not wrong. If anyone should be fired in this situation, it *should* be Brian.

When he doesn't continue, I break the silence. "Just say it, Mr. Henry." I may understand what he's trying to say, but I won't help him. He's part of the problem.

"I'm afraid we're going to have to let you go. Immediately." He pauses again, taking a breath before continuing. "You've been a valuable member of the team for the last five years. I *am* sorry to see you go." I see him swallow as if preparing to lay another blow. "Unfortunately, this will be a for-cause termination, meaning there's no severance package, and you'll need to leave the premises as soon as we're done here. Someone from HR will pack your personal belongings, and you can either pick them up or we can mail them to you."

"I don't have any personal items at my desk, just my purse, which I can't leave without." I may have been here for five years, but putting a personal touch on my space never felt right. Maybe that should have been a sign I wasn't meant to be here long before now.

"Of course. I'll escort you out as soon as we're done." He pauses again, studying me.

I don't know what he expects, but I've never been an overly emotional person. My parents never would have accepted that. It was instilled in me from an early age that you do not express any intense emotions in the presence of others.

"Do you have any questions for me?" His voice is quiet, a little hesitant, as if he's waiting for me to argue with him about my termination.

Even with Massachusetts being an employee-at-will state, it's clear I'm being fired due to everything that happened with Brian. Without a single negative mark on my employment record at this firm, it would be quite easy to prove wrongful termination in this case. But I don't have it in me to fight.

I don't want to work at this firm—in this building— knowing that Brian will always be around the corner. Even if I prove wrongful termination and keep my job, Brian will never be fired—not with his father being one of the founding partners.

I didn't report what happened to anyone. The only people I told were my parents and I don't think they would corroborate my story, not when they want me to marry the man.

And recently I've realized—I hate my job.

Part of it could be working for this particular firm. Henry, Wellsley, & Ford is a prestigious firm that only takes on the wealthiest of clients and only takes on cases they know they can win. I'd been content going into law because I thought I would be helping people. But most of the time, I don't feel like I'm doing anything worthwhile here. I don't want to spend my life working in this kind of environment. It's not who I am.

I see the shock in his eyes when I finally respond. "No, Mr. Henry, I don't have any questions."

"All right. Then I just need you to sign this stating you understand everything we've discussed." Mr. Henry pushes a document toward me.

I don't pick up the document. He might be telling me the truth, but I also suspect there is some fine print saying I forgo the right to sue them for wrongful termination. While I have no plans to move forward with that, I won't take that chance away from myself, should I need it. "I won't be signing anything."

"Ms. Day—"

"No, Mr. Henry. You can't force me to sign that, and I won't be doing it." I give him a moment to see if he'll say anything, and when he doesn't, I continue. "If there's nothing else, I'd like to go."

"Yes, of course. I'll take you to get your bag from your desk."

I MAY HAVE KNOWN what was coming, and I may have realized I hate my job, but I've still spent the last twenty-four hours wallowing in self-pity.

I've never been fired from a job. And while I logically know this has absolutely nothing to do with me and everything to do with Brian, I hate that I was fired.

I know I'm going to be okay. Fortunately, I didn't pay for my education, so I don't have loans to worry about, and I've always been smart with my money, so I have plenty saved up. I'm not in danger of losing my home or anything, but I hate the idea of starting again somewhere else. If I even want to continue practicing law.

Going into law isn't something I wanted. It was something my parents pushed me into—like they tried to do with Declan and a business degree. Though, he convinced them his dreams would still bring the prestige they expected from someone with our last name.

I'll never understand how my parents came to think our last name was synonymous with clout, power, and prestige to everyone in our small town. My grandparents were some of the most loving and down-to-earth people I've ever known. The love they had for their family was endless, always wanting us to be happy—no matter how we went about accomplishing that.

They hated all the attention they received whenever they were in town helping out—as if they were more important by simply being part of one of the founding families. They never wanted to be viewed as better or more important than anyone else in town. They understood that what made small town living unique was how everyone came together to make it a special place. Not one person or family was more important than another.

I can remember overhearing the arguments my father would have with them when I was in high school. They didn't like how he constantly pushed Declan and me into certain activities. They fought tooth and nail to make sure my parents let Declan have his art, and they were so proud of him when he sold his first piece.

Unfortunately, they died a year later, and my parents had no one to curb their behaviors when it came to pushing me into whatever box they were trying to make me fit into. For Declan, he had already proven he could make a name for himself with his art. But when it came to me? I was fifteen, impressionable, and, like most teens my age, just learning about all the opportunities available to someone like me—I had no idea what I wanted to do.

By that point, I'd joined the debate team—at my parents' insistence—and while I didn't love it, I didn't hate it either. And I was good at it. Seeing my potential, law became the thing my parents steered me toward. It likely helped that their close friend, Paul Wellsley, was a founding partner at one of Boston's most prestigious law firms. And knowing what I know now, my becoming a lawyer and working at that firm would have made it very easy to convince the world Brian and I had fallen madly in love while working together.

Well, that plan is officially thrown out the window, no matter how much my parents say otherwise. Hell will have to freeze over ten times before I agree to marry that man. Even then, I'd run away and change my whole identity before doing that.

I know I'm going to have to get my ass in gear and figure out what I'm going to do now, but I'm giving myself the weekend to wallow. I'm camping out on this couch, comfy in my robe and blanket cocoon, eating all the ice cream and junk food I want while watching *Veronica Mars*.

All while ignoring my constantly ringing phone.

I know I could just turn it off, but something in me won't let me. Maybe it's me hoping my parents will change. But more than likely, it's the obedience my parents drilled into me peeking through—at least in part. I am disobeying them by simply refusing to answer their call. Growing up, if I refused to do anything they requested of me it resulted in the silent treatment, but to the extreme. It was truly like I didn't exist if I disobeyed them. I learned quickly to suck it up and do what they wanted. It was always easier in the end.

It's been about an hour since my phone last went off, and it's officially after ten in the evening, so I think I'm safe for the rest of the night. That optimism quickly fades when my phone starts ringing just as I've hit play on the next episode. I contemplate completely ignoring it, but a glance down shows my brother's face instead of one of my parents. It's not strange for my brother to call, but ten o'clock on a Saturday evening is definitely out of the norm.

Pausing the show, I answer his call. "Big brother? What are you doing calling me this late on a Saturday? You know I'm hours away, and you'll have to sit in that jail cell for quite some time if you made me your one phone call."

"Hey, Ava." Declan's tone is far too serious for the joke I just made, and I instantly regret it.

"What's going on?" I sit up on the couch, my back going taut. Declan has been through a lot over the last six years, but even with everything, he's always been one to go along with my jokes. Something serious is going on for him to ignore everything I said.

"Scott just got served legal papers from Nicole. She's suing for custody of Max."

I stand from the couch, throwing the blankets off, and move to the laptop I left on the dining room table. There's no way I can sit here at home when I could be helping Scott and his family. My time for wallowing is over.

The Marks family quasi-adopted my brother when he moved to Ashford Falls five years ago. Obviously, he was a grown adult when he moved, but he met Caleb Marks, the oldest son, one night at a bar, became fast friends, and was dragged to family dinners shortly after. His father, Scott—one of the best men I've ever known—pulled Declan into the fold, never letting him go.

"When were the papers served?" I ask as I pull up flights to Baltimore, Maryland, the closest airport to Ashford Falls.

"Just a few minutes ago."

"Okay, I'll get on the next flight and we'll figure out next steps when I get there."

"Ava, I didn't call so you would fly here. I just—I feel help-less, and I know you could give them some advice on what they should do."

"I know, but this is literally my job. I'm not going to let Scott go through some horrible custody battle when I can do something to help." Especially not when he needs to focus on himself and the rest of his family.

Scott was diagnosed with lung cancer five years ago, and three years ago he went into remission. Unfortunately, during his routine check-up in August, they found that the cancer was back, and this time it was likely he wouldn't win the battle.

"That bitch doesn't deserve a second of anyone's time. She definitely doesn't deserve custody of Max."

After doing a number on Caleb and Quinn during their childhood, Scott's ex-wife, Nicole, went and abandoned all of them when Max was still an infant. When I say that woman doesn't deserve a moment of anyone's time, I mean it with every fiber of my being.

I hear Declan sigh before he finally responds. "I love you, squirt. I really was just calling for some advice, but having you here will be so much better."

"I'll text you my flight information as soon as I have it. Tell Scott we're going to figure this out."

"I will. Be safe, and I'll see you soon."

CHAPTER
Two

AVA

FINDING DECLAN in a crowd of people is easy. At six-foot-six, he's generally one of the tallest people around. And even though I'm his sister, I can admit his features are striking, causing most people to pay attention to him. He's tall and fit, has shaggy brown hair, and wears glasses. He exudes a confidence and grace that's always made me a bit jealous, but I couldn't love him more. So the second I see him waiting for me at baggage claim in his worn jeans and cable-knit sweater, I rush toward him.

"Hey, big brother," I say as I pull him into a hug.

"Hey, squirt." His hug is tight and long, but I let him get away with it. Boston and Baltimore really aren't that far from each other, but we don't get to visit each other often, so these moments are rare. "Thanks for flying down so quickly," he says as he takes my bag.

"Of course. You know I love Ashford Falls. I would take any excuse to visit. Plus, Scott has loved your mopey ass for years now. He deserves my awesomeness in his life for a little bit."

He laughs and throws his arm over my shoulder. "Did you check any bags?"

"Yeah, just one. I'm not sure how long I'll be here."

"You're welcome as long as you want, but don't you have to get back to work?"

I hesitate for only a moment. I know I should tell Declan exactly what happened back home, but I'm not ready to talk about it with him. I know how disappointed he'll be—not with me, but with our parents.

Declan always went out of his way to keep me away from all the problems he had with them when he got divorced. He didn't want his relationship with them to impact my relationship with them. I know it's already so strained, but I won't be the reason for more stress in his life. Not when I can handle this myself.

"I've got plenty of saved up PTO, and I'm between cases at the moment, so this really couldn't have happened at a better time for me." He looks at me curiously, and I know he doesn't totally believe me. "So, anything new going on here?" I ask before he can say anything else.

"No." Now it's my turn to doubt his honesty. I stare at him, waiting for him to break. "What?"

"You seem a little fidgety."

"Fidgety?"

"Yeah, I don't know how else to describe it." I cross my arms, giving him a stern look. "What's going on?"

He studies me for only a moment before finally telling me. "I may have kissed Quinn last night. And by kissed, I mean made out with."

"You may have? You don't know?" I ask, a smile tugging at the corners of my mouth. It's been a long time since I've seen this look on my brother. Ever since his divorce from Melissa, Declan hasn't shown much interest in anyone—at least not in a serious way. And I know if he's making out with his best friend's younger sister, he's taking it very seriously.

"No, I definitely did. In the middle of the town square at the Fall Harvest Festival. Where everyone could see." I can see him looking at me from the corner of his eye. He clearly has some feelings about this, but maybe he isn't entirely ready to share all of it.

"Go big or go home, huh?" I tease. But the annoyed look on his face has me second guessing myself. "Okay, sorry"—but I'm me and I can't help myself—"wait, one more. You've really got a thing for your best friends' little sisters, don't you?" I laugh so hard and loud people stare.

"You got it out of your system now?"

"I'm sorry, but you have to admit, that was a good one. First Ryan and now Caleb?" I'm still laughing when I see my bag come around the carousel and rush forward to get it before it passes.

I don't know how Caleb would feel about his little sister dating Declan but I know Ryan hadn't cared one way or the other when his little sister and Declan started dating. It wasn't until Melissa and Declan had gotten engaged that Ryan showed any real emotion toward their relationship, and at that point Ryan was just happy Declan would be his brother for real.

The divorce complicated things, but Ryan understood why they were getting divorced and ended up supporting both of them. While Melissa and Declan weren't the closest of friends after, they were cordial with each other, and the rest of our friendships went back to exactly how they were before they started dating.

"If I were in a joking mood, I would probably agree with you, but I'm not there yet," Declan says when I get back to him, taking the suitcase from me. "Come on, let's get out of here."

"Okay, I'm sorry, I'll be serious." We're quiet as we walk to his truck. I can't help but wonder how I've missed whatever is happening between Declan and Quinn. We talk at least once a week, and we've talked about Quinn, but I had no idea he had feelings for her. "I know I've heard about Quinn from everyone, you included, but you've only ever talked about her as a co-worker and friend. What changed?"

"Nothing changed. She's still very much those things." He puts my bags in the back of his truck and opens the door for me.

"Okay, but it's more than that now." I know it's not a question, but I expect some kind of response from him. He closes the door and moves around the front of the truck, climbing into his seat before saying anything else.

"I think it's actually meeting and seeing her with her family. Hearing her talk about her students, even the ones that piss her off." He pauses for a moment. Whatever he's thinking has the goofiest smile forming. "She really cares. Like in her soul, she cares about all of them." He glances at me, and the smile falls, his eyes taking on a serious look. "After everything she's been through, and not just with her mom, but everything in her life, the fact she still cares so deeply blows me away."

I don't think I've ever seen my brother look this way when talking about anyone—even Melissa. He's a man who is falling madly in love with a woman, and I couldn't be happier for him.

"I knew she was a great woman based on how Scott and Caleb talked about her, but you've made me a little jealous. I'd love to have someone talk about me the way you just did Quinn." I reach out and squeeze his hand. "I can't wait to meet her." I turn forward in my seat and buckle myself in. "As for kissing her in front of the whole town, if it's meant to be it'll all work itself out. I have no doubt you'll fight to make sure that happens if that's what you want."

My brother has always been a man to go after everything he wants. Take his art, for example. Even when my parents told him no, he still did it. He may have caved to many of their demands, but he still made his art a priority.

Declan will respect whatever Quinn wants, but he'll only accept defeat when he truly believes it's what she wants. Declan is one of the best men I know. I have no doubt he'll make it very hard for her to say no.

He studies me for a minute before finally buckling his seatbelt. "Thanks, Ava."

"Of course. Are we going straight to Scott's now, or are you taking me to the inn to get settled?"

"In what world am I letting you stay at the inn? You're staying with me. If you're good with it, we'll head straight to Scott's. It's Sunday, so everyone will be there for breakfast."

"Yeah, you know I don't need much sleep to function. As long as they have coffee I'll be good to go."

Declan is quiet for a moment, his gaze focused on the road in front of him before he finally responds, his voice quiet. "I'm really glad you're here. I'm not happy about the reason, but I love when you visit, and it's been a while. I've missed you."

"I've missed you, too." I reach over and squeeze his forearm, resting on the center console. "I wasn't kidding about all the time off I have saved up. I could stay through Thanksgiving. We could celebrate with the Marks instead of going home." I shouldn't continue with this lie, but thinking about going home and trying to act like nothing's going on with my parents makes me exhausted. I just can't do it—not yet.

He glances at me, concern evident in his eyes. "What's going on?"

I look out the passenger window, avoiding his line of sight. I've never been a good liar, not when it comes to him. "Nothing. Like I said, I have a bunch of saved up time."

"Ava, you can talk to me."

I hate the worry I'm causing him, but I'm just not ready to get into all of it again. I know he'll believe me and support me however he can, but I don't want to see pity in his eyes when he learns the truth about my situation. "I know, but I'm not ready to talk about it."

"Okay, but you'll let me know when you are?"

"Yeah, I will."

"THANK GOODNESS YOU'RE HERE." Caleb rushes to pull me into a hug the second he opens the door. "Quinn is driving me crazy with her pacing. I don't know what's gotten into her. She's normally so calm under pressure—like, scarily calm."

I pull back but keep my hands on his shoulders, squeezing slightly. "Custody battles are always scary, even when the other person doesn't have a leg to stand on. We'll get this all figured out."

"Well, come on in, everyone's inside." Caleb turns and leads Declan and me into the house. "Ava and Declan are here," he announces as we enter the kitchen.

"Ava! Did you bring me anything?" Max asks as he rushes over to me.

"Max! That's so rude!" A woman, I assume Quinn, stops pacing and looks at her brother in shock.

Everyone else laughs, used to this interaction between Max and me.

"It's fine." I chuckle, looking at Quinn before turning back to Max. "This was such a spur-of-the-moment trip I didn't have a chance to get anything good, but I did bring you this cool deck of cards I found at the airport in Boston. They've got fun facts about the city on each of them." I reach into my bag, pull the cards out, and hand them to him.

"Awesome." Max turns for the living room, tearing into the pack, mind now focused on the playing cards.

"Hey, Ava. Good to see you," Emily, Caleb's wife, says from the stove.

I give her a wave before catching Scott trying to stand from his seat at the kitchen table. A few weeks ago, Scott fell while coming down the stairs and broke his leg, requiring surgery to fix it. He's been in a cast since and shouldn't be moving around more than necessary.

"Sit back down. I'll come to you." I make my way over to him, bending to hug him. "How much longer are you in that cast? I can't imagine you're enjoying it much."

"Just a few more weeks in this one before I can switch to a walking boot, but you're right, I'm ready to be done with this thing," he says, reaching out to squeeze my hand. "It's wonderful to see you." A look of gratitude crosses his features. "Sorry for the circumstances."

I offer a small smile and squeeze his hand in return. "I'll take any excuse to be here. I'm thinking about making this an extended trip. Maybe crash your Thanksgiving dinner."

"You could never crash something in this house. We would love to have you and your brother with us."

I squeeze his hand one more time before releasing it and turning to Quinn. She's gorgeous. I understand why my brother is so twisted up about her. Her brown hair is down in waves, falling to her shoulders, and her eyes are so blue I'm struck by their brightness. I'm only five-foot-four so most people are taller than me, but she seems taller than normal. She's fit but curvy and giving off a very nervous energy that I can only imagine is due to the circumstances.

I never doubted my decision to come here to help, but knowing how everyone in this room feels about Quinn and seeing in this brief moment how concerned she is, I'm even more sure I made the right decision.

"Hi, I'm Ava, Declan's younger and much more outgoing sister."

Quinn chuckles slightly, making her way over to me. "Nice to meet you, I'm Quinn." Quinn puts her hand out for a handshake, but I quickly push it away, pulling her into a hug.

"Oh no, I feel like I've known you forever with how much this group talks about you. I'm hugging you."

Quinn is tense for a moment before she returns my hug, but when she does, I feel her entire body relax into me.

"I promise that we'll figure all of this out. I won't stop until we know Max is safe," I whisper in her ear before pulling away. Quinn offers me a small nod before we both turn back to the group. "So, what's for breakfast? And can I help with anything?"

CHAPTER
Three

GAGE

I ROLL over and check the time on my phone—5:55 a.m. It's not a surprise. It's been years since I actually slept until my alarm goes off. I'm sure it has something to do with my days in the army and never really relaxing, even in sleep.

Being in the army is nothing like they show in movies or TV, but it's still an intense experience. And being prepared for anything is definitely a reality of any branch of the military.

I lie there in the dark, giving myself a few minutes to just *be*. Life is hectic and unexpected as it is. Most days I never have time to be still and exist in the moment. Giving myself these five minutes might be all I get for the day.

Monday mornings have always been my favorite. I'm not entirely sure why, but there's something about a new week and starting fresh—almost like the start of a new year—endless possibilities.

I would've thought, as I got older, that outlook on Mondays would change, especially after becoming a police officer. The shifts that come along with being a deputy, even in a small town like Ashford Falls, mean my weeks don't always start on

Mondays. But I still love them, always excited to see where they might take me.

The alarm sounds, and I shut it off as I sit up in bed, throwing my legs over the side and stretching. The cracks along my spine are audible in the silence of the room. I give myself a moment, absorbing the sting of pain in my lower back. It's always at its worst first thing in the morning. Once I get up and start moving around, it'll become a dull ache that's second nature and easy to ignore.

Striding to the dresser, the chill in the air causes goosebumps across my skin, and the picture frame on top catches my eye. I don't know why I put it there—every time I see it I'm reminded of how my life isn't what I thought it would be.

Today marks three years since I was honorably discharged from the army. While I still talk to the guys from my unit, it's not the same. There's a sullenness that comes over me as I stare at the picture—a pit in my stomach, a feeling that comes with being around the same group of people day in and day out, trusting they have your back the same way you have theirs, and then all of a sudden you rarely see them.

I don't blame any of them for how we've grown apart. Even if I stayed with the army I wouldn't have been serving with them anymore. My options were to sit behind a desk or be discharged, and I couldn't sit behind a desk for the rest of my career. Not when I knew I still had some good years left in me. Sitting behind a desk would have killed me slowly.

I grab a pair of shorts and a shirt from the drawers and turn away, moving to the bathroom to start my day.

I've had the same Monday morning routine since I became a deputy, and a run through town with a pit stop at my mom's before heading to work sounds like exactly what I need.

Ten minutes later, I step outside and stretch, taking in my surroundings. Ashford Falls is slowly waking up for the day.

It's still early, no one is out in the neighborhood quite yet, but I see the lights starting to flicker on in windows.

I turn left out of my front yard and begin a slow jog, warming myself up. I'll slowly make my way toward town before veering off to the farmland on the outskirts. To the farm I grew up on and where my mother and sister still live.

Ashford Falls is the definition of a small town. Right in the center is a gazebo where all major town celebrations start and end. Surrounding the gazebo is a large park where the town sets up for our quirky festivals. Around the park are all the shops and restaurants. A little further out from the shops and restaurants are a few different neighborhoods, and just past them is all the farmland surrounding our little town.

Despite being on the outskirts of the town, the run to my mother's house is only about five miles—something I can run in just over half an hour.

As I jog down the road to my mom's, my little sister steps out onto the front porch, coffee mug in hand, eyes searching for me, exactly as she does every week.

My family tree has some complicated roots. My parents had me when they were young, and while they tried to make it work, they realized they weren't meant for each other. In hindsight, I'm forever grateful my parents realized it when they did. Yeah, I was ten when they divorced, and I didn't understand any of it at the time, but they never spoke ill of each other in front of me, and they always made sure I knew they were both around if I needed them for anything. Even when they got remarried—or, in my father's case, both times he got remarried —and had other kids with their partners, I was always a priority to them.

I love all three of my younger siblings and feel lucky to have a close relationship with each of them. I enlisted in the army when they were all still so young. Asher was five, Leo was about to turn two, and Liv had only turned one a few months before I left for basic training. And while I visited and called when I could over the twelve years I served, I still missed out on a lot of moments in their lives.

When I get closer to the house, I can't help but smile when I see the scowl on Olivia's face. "What's with the face, Pickle?"

Olivia and I don't look much like siblings—understandably so. She's my half-sister, and I look more like my father than our mother, but if you look closely, you can see the resemblance. Her eyes are where you can tell we're related. She and I have the same striking aqua-blue eyes as our mother.

Olivia stands at about five-foot-five, though her slender frame and long legs make her seem taller. She'll always be the baby of the family to me, but now at sixteen it's easy to see the young woman she's growing into.

She hasn't gotten dressed for the day yet. Her light brown hair is thrown up in a messy knot on her head, and she's still in her flannel pajama pants, an army sweatshirt to ward off the chill in the air, and a pair of fuzzy socks. She looks cozy, exactly how you want to be on a fall morning.

Liv rolls her eyes at the nickname. "You're late."

I glance down at my watch and see it's 6:52 a.m. I guess I am a few minutes later than normal. "Sorry. Walt had a question for me when I ran past the bar."

"What was he doing there so early?" she asks as I walk up the porch stairs, pulling her into a hug and ignoring her when she pushes at me. "Disgusting! You're all sweaty!" She squirms out of my hold, and I can't help but laugh.

"Murphy's gets their deliveries early Monday mornings. He was there dealing with those." I chuckle as we walk into the house. "Hey, Ma," I say when I see her in the kitchen at the end of the hall.

While Liv is still getting herself ready for the day, I know Mom has been up for a couple of hours by now. She's already dressed in worn jeans, a thick flannel shirt, and a pair of work boots on her feet. Her hair is falling in its natural waves past her shoulders, and I have no doubt her hat is close by to throw back on before she gets back to her farm chores.

"Hi, honey." She smiles and offers her cheek for a kiss. "What does your day look like?" she asks as she hands me a cup of coffee and turns back to the stove where she's making breakfast.

I sit at the kitchen island, Liv plopping into the seat next to me, and watch Mom move around. Closer to her now, I see the light strain on her face, the wrinkles a little more prominent than normal. At fifty-one, she's still more than capable of managing everything on her own, but I know it's got to be wearing on her more each year.

While the farm isn't a working farm anymore and doesn't produce anything on a major scale, Mom does have a vegetable garden, and goats, cows, and chickens. All of which produce far more than she and Liv need. While she gives a lot away to neighbors, she also sells a decent amount at a few different farmers' markets in the area.

"I'm due at the courthouse this morning, so I got a little bit of a later start to the day," I answer her.

She glances at me quickly, but I still see the look of concern cross her face. "You're working today?"

"What else would I be doing?" I know I'm being intentionally evasive. I wasn't in a great place when I first came home after my discharge from the army, and Mom saw that first-hand. She was worried and had every right, but I bounced back quickly—mostly because that's what was expected of me.

I've always been the "good time guy," the person you go to for a laugh, the comedic relief. It's a person I like being. I don't enjoy staying in the negative moments; I'd much rather find a positive spin to any situation. But sometimes it's hard to find the positive when your life takes a different turn than you were expecting—and one you didn't want.

I wanted to retire from the army, not be honorably discharged. It was going to be my career. But after a failed mission that resulted in an injury causing chronic back pain, making it impossible for me to meet the fitness requirements expected of a special forces operative, my responsibilities changed. I appreciated they still found me valuable enough to want me behind a desk, but I was never good at sitting still. I could have retired from the military if I wanted, but it wouldn't have been the *way* I wanted.

Coming home had been a change. Things weren't the way I left them. My mom had divorced her second husband, and my dad had divorced his third wife. My siblings were all teenagers with new personalities, interests, and lives of their own. Finding a place for myself in all that was hard—especially while coping with the loss of a career I truly loved.

I moved in with Mom when I first got back to Ashford Falls. I love my father—he truly tries his best—but Mom has always been the more settled between the two of them. And when I first got home, I needed settled. But moving in with Mom meant she saw my transition back to civilian life the most. After twelve years in the army—three with special forces —I was allowed to be a little less cheerful.

Mom was more than understanding and never pushed me more than I needed. I appreciated that she let me figure it out on my own—it would have been so easy for her to push me back into "normal" life, especially on the weeks Liv stayed with Mom.

But *I* hated my mental state—it wasn't who I was used to being and it wasn't who I wanted to be.

So I pushed myself to find a new purpose in life, something I could be proud of doing. Law enforcement felt like the right place to be. I might not be helping the country at large, but I'm still helping people, and that's what I want most.

Living with Mom for those six months while I was in the

police academy was probably the best thing I did for myself. She pushed me while also supporting me—both mentally and emotionally. She knew when I needed space and when I needed attention. And Liv had been the perfect distraction when I needed one.

I think those six months in this house are why Liv and I are as close as we are. While I missed most of her childhood, I got to be here for all the big moments since, and I honestly wouldn't pass that up for anything, even being back in the army.

"Well, it's the anniversary of your discharge—three years since you lost your dream," Liv says all nonchalant next to me. "So, I mean, I think it's reasonable to question if you might want to take the day off and do something else. Like wallow on your couch while binging your favorite TV show and eating a whole bunch of junk food."

I see the look in Mom's eyes, ready to reprimand Liv for the flippant way she's talking about my discharge, but I appreciate Liv's realness. "Isn't that what you're supposed to do when you break up with someone?" I ask.

"Well, yeah. But wouldn't you say your discharge was like a break-up? They wanted to keep you. You were the one who wanted out, the one who walked away."

"Olivia Grace." Mom's voice is stern, a clear warning she's toeing the line, but I laugh because Liv's not wrong.

"Maybe that first year wallowing would have been acceptable, but it's been three years. Besides, dreams can always change." I nudge her shoulder lightly. "We can't stay the same, and if we do then we're doing something wrong."

"That might be a little too profound for seven o'clock in the morning."

"Have I told you lately that you're my favorite sister?" I chuckle.

"That line doesn't work on me anymore. I'm not five. I

recognize that I'm your only sister and, therefore, the only option."

"Well, I still love you," I say, pulling her back into my side.

"Gross!" she shouts, pushing me away. "I'm going to get ready for school. Love you, loser." Liv presses a quick kiss to my cheek before she rushes out of the room.

"You sure you're doing okay?" Mom asks as she sets a plate of eggs in front of me.

"Yeah, Ma, I'm fine." I smile at her and dig into the food. "What about Liv? She not eating breakfast again?"

"She is. She just doesn't want the big breakfast anymore. She made herself a fresh bagel this morning."

"You didn't need to make all this for me. I can take care of myself, you know." I keep my tone light, wanting to make sure she knows I'm joking.

"I know, but I like taking care of you." Mom turns back to the stove and starts cleaning up the mess.

I watch her for a few minutes before asking her about her plans for the day and the rest of the week. It's a simple conversation—nothing out of the norm—but it's a comfort all the same. This farm has always been a comfort; one I took for granted.

I may not have wanted to leave the army when I did, but there are definitely worse things that could have happened. If I can't be there, there's nowhere else I'd rather be.

CHAPTER
Four

GAGE

"ARE YOU READY FOR THIS?" Reid, another deputy and my good friend, asks as I walk up to him outside the courthouse later that morning.

"It's a routine traffic stop violation. Nothing to get nervous about."

"I always get nervous when dealing with a judge. It doesn't matter how often I do it or who the judge is," I hear Reid's voice as he continues talking, but my attention is dragged away by a woman I've never seen before.

Ashford Falls is far from a tourist town. While we get the occasional person driving through, it's not very often you see them walking up to the courthouse. My traffic violation is indeed an out-of-towner, but she isn't this out-of-towner.

No, this woman is impossible to forget.

She's dressed professionally in a matching pantsuit and blazer, with heels that make it seem like her legs go on for days. Though, it's clear she isn't tall, definitely no taller than Olivia. Her hair hangs loosely down her back in soft waves, framing her small, heart-shaped face.

She glances over toward Reid and me briefly, and I'm

struck by the look in her eyes. Even though she's looking right at me, I can tell she's not seeing me—but I see her. I know absolutely nothing about this woman, but her stare is empty as if she's haunted by something, and I'm instantly curious about her.

Reid pushes my shoulder, bringing my attention back to him. "Have you heard anything I've said?"

"No," I answer honestly, my eyes following the woman as she enters the building. I contemplate leaving her alone for the briefest moment, but realize I can't ignore the look I saw on her face.

"You're due in court in ten minutes, Gage!" Reid calls after me as I walk away from him.

"I'll meet you there," I say over my shoulder.

I immediately start searching for the woman the second I step into the courthouse and find her easily. She's standing in the small center atrium, looking at the signs, definitely trying to decipher where to go. And now I don't have to come up with an excuse to talk to her.

"Can I help you find what you're looking for?" I ask as I step in front of her.

She doesn't even glance at me before responding. "No, I'm fine. Thank you, though."

While she continues standing there, studying the signs around the atrium, I study her. I was right about her appearing taller than she is. Even in her heels I still tower over her, and up close I can see her eyes more clearly now. They're a pretty hazel color, with a golden ring surrounding them—familiar to me somehow, but I can't place it.

That emptiness I thought I saw outside is even clearer while standing this close. There's also a stiffness to her posture, as if she's waiting to wage war against someone.

Something in me wants to cause physical harm to whoever caused the look in her eye, but I don't know why when I don't even know this woman. Maybe it's just the principle of the whole thing—being in the army and now law enforcement, I always want to find justice when deserved, and anyone who can put a look like that in someone else's eyes deserves the worst kind of justice.

She still hasn't moved, and now I've been standing here studying her for way too long. I know I'm coming off like a creep, but, even knowing that, I can't turn away.

Slowly, her eyes move to mine. "You going to stand there staring at me all morning? Or do you have somewhere to be?"

I shake myself from my trance and answer with a partial truth. "Sorry, you look familiar, but I can't figure out why. I wouldn't forget meeting you."

"Does that line normally work for you?" She holds her hand up, stopping me from responding. "Wait, I already know the answer to that." Her eyes track down my body slowly before coming back up to mine. "Of course it does. I mean, look at you—attractive and in law enforcement—who wouldn't fall to their knees for your attention?"

I hear the sarcasm in her voice but decide to run with it, a smirk forming on my lips. "You think I'm attractive?"

"Of course, that's what you focus on."

"What man ignores when a beautiful woman calls him attractive? That's not very smart, and I like to consider myself a smart man."

"Is that so?" Her tone suggests she thinks I'm the farthest thing from smart, but I see her shoulders drop from her ears, her body relaxing the slightest amount. Even if she never gives me the time of day, knowing I gave her a moment's reprieve from whatever is troubling her will be a win.

"Well, I *did* graduate high school a year early and at the top of my class, so that's gotta count for something."

"Book smarts don't always equal street smarts."

"That's true. But life experience typically brings street

smarts, and I think I've had my fair share of life experience." I lean closer to her, lowering my voice. "You never pass up an opportunity to talk to a beautiful woman, even if she turns you down. You only regret the opportunities you never even try to take." I stand straight again, giving her back the space I invaded. Though, I note she never backed away from me, leading me to believe she might not have minded me invading her space too much.

"A Lewis Carroll fan?"

"I don't think that's exactly what he said, but I'm a fan of anyone who offers a positive way to look at the hard moments in life." I can't be sure, but she seems a little impressed I know who Lewis Carroll was and that I misquoted him. I'm honestly a little impressed she knew my words resembled the famous quote. Most people might recognize it, but I don't think they would know exactly who said it.

We both stand there studying the other, and I'm sure we would have continued to if it weren't for Reid walking up to us.

"Gage, man, we're gonna be late for court." Reid offers a polite smile to the woman in front of me. "Sorry, ma'am."

I ignore Reid, and reach my hand out toward the woman. "I'm Gage Flynn."

She hesitates, her eyes bouncing between my offered hand, my face, and Reid behind me, but it's only a moment before she places her hand in mine. "Ava Day. You might know my brother, Declan. Maybe that's why I look familiar."

It's a peace offering, her giving me that information, and I gladly take it, a genuine smile forming on my lips as I squeeze her hand lightly. "Nice to meet you, Ava." I pause momentarily before offering her my help again, "Can I help point you in the right direction?"

I don't release her hand from mine, but I loosen my grip so she can retract her hand if she wants.

"I'm looking for the county clerk's office." Even though she has to tilt her head, she looks me straight in the eye, leaving her hand in mine.

I gesture to our left with my free hand. "It's straight through that doorway there. You can't miss it."

"Thank you." I hear the genuine gratitude in her voice and offer her a small smile in return.

"I hope to see you around, Ava." I squeeze her hand once more, giving her a slight head tilt, before releasing her and walking away. I want to glance over my shoulder, but I keep my focus straight ahead.

"What was that?" Reid whispers at my side.

I don't answer him right away, trying to figure that same thing out for myself.

It started as me wanting to talk to a gorgeous woman but quickly morphed into something else. What that something was, I don't know. That haunted look in her eye and that stiff posture stood out to me. Maybe it reminded me a little of myself when I was first discharged from the army, and I wouldn't wish those feelings on anyone.

I remember feeling lost and alone when I first came home. People constantly tried to reach me, but I never wanted to burden anyone with my problems. So I kept it all inside, burying it deep, until I couldn't ignore it anymore, and it all came crashing down around me.

"Gage?" Reid places a hand on my shoulder, bringing my attention back to him. "You good?"

"Yeah, I'm good." I offer him a small smile, reaching over and squeezing his shoulder in return. "Just got caught up talking to a beautiful woman. You know how that is?" I joke, brightening my tone to prove everything is good.

Reid chuckles, patting me on the back before heading into the courtroom. I glance back the way we came. I can't see the atrium from where I stand and I know I won't be able to see if

Ava's still standing there, but I hope, more than anything, I see her again.

I shake myself from my thoughts and enter the courtroom. Now isn't the time to focus on any of that, now is the time to focus on the job.

CHAPTER

Five

AVA

I STAND THERE after Gage walks away, forcing myself not to look over my shoulder at his retreating back. It's more of a struggle than I want to admit. I have no doubt the view from the back would be just as good as the view from the front.

I wasn't lying when I told him he was attractive. That man definitely doesn't fit the stereotype of the donut-loving cop many movies and television shows always portray. No, that man clearly takes care of himself and takes his job seriously.

He wasn't in his uniform, but the badge was clear as day hooked to his belt. He wore dark pants that hugged his hips and thighs like a second skin, a dark button-down with the top button undone, and a sports coat. I would have expected a police officer attending court to dress in a suit, but small towns typically allow for a more casual appearance. I'm sure I stand out dressed as formally as I am in my sleek and tailored black pantsuit with a matching blazer.

It took me a moment to really take him in when he came up to me, but it was difficult to look away once I did. His height was the first thing I noticed. Being five-foot-four means almost everyone is taller than me, but Gage towered over me.

His aqua-blue eyes got me next. They were so bright, and while initially filled with an emotion I couldn't quite decipher, they quickly shifted to one full of mischief. It was hard to look away. But his high cheekbones and chiseled jaw covered with the lightest amount of stubble grabbed my attention—another thing that didn't fit the court appearance I had come to expect from my time with the firm in Boston.

His honey-brown hair, shorter on the sides and longer on top, was tousled slightly, causing it to fall along one side of his forehead, giving him a rugged look.

He's the definition of an attractive man, at least for me, and that is more than dangerous, especially with how he flirted with me—and how my body responded to that flirting.

One too many men have let me down when I thought I could trust them. Being attracted to a man as good-looking as Gage Flynn is just asking for more heartache.

Besides, I'm not in Ashford Falls for anything other than helping the Marks family. They have to stay my primary focus.

Gage is long gone by the time I glance over my shoulder in the direction he walked. I have no doubt, if I'm in town long enough, I'll run into him again. That's the hazard of being in a small town—you can't avoid anyone for very long.

***

AFTER FINISHING up at the courthouse, I make my way back to Declan's house, planning on hanging out there until he gets home from work. Even after changing into leggings and an oversized sweatshirt, I can't sit still—I'm too antsy.

I know there's nothing else I can do with Scott's case right now—I've done all I can.

After getting home from breakfast yesterday morning, Declan and I had a chill day, just catching up and spending time with each other. I went to my room at the same time as

Declan last night, hoping to sleep, but sleep hasn't been easy for me since everything happened with Brian and my parents.

When I finally gave up trying to sleep, I worked on the return suit for Scott's case. That man loves those he cares for with his whole heart, and to try and rip a child from his home when he has limited time left in this world is the worst kind of human.

Filing the return suit this morning was the next step. There's literally nothing else I can do until we hear back from the courts.

No, my unease comes from the number of unanswered notifications on my phone—all from my parents.

I still haven't spoken to them since the night at their house over two weeks ago. As far as I know, they still think I'm at my apartment in Harborview. I want to be shocked they haven't reached out to Declan, concerned about my well-being, but I'm not. After everything that's happened, I'm more surprised they keep calling.

The silent treatment Declan and I received as children wasn't in the casual or playful way most parents do, pretending the sound of our voice was the wind or something equally silly. No, they treated us like we didn't exist. There was no acknowledgement that we were there at all. Meals weren't made for us, we weren't tucked into bed, we weren't directed to take a bath or brush our teeth. For all intents and purposes, we simply didn't exist.

It sounds harsh—and it was—but it was also all we knew when it came to punishment. Our parents weren't the kind to come talk to us about what happened, to allow us to explain ourselves, to help us process the situation or our feelings. They would wait for us to apologize for not listening or doing what we were told before acknowledging us and allowing us to move forward.

Declan and I learned at a very young age that it was easier

to do what they wanted than fight them and deal with their version of punishment. Mom and Dad also altered how they communicated with us, manipulating us into believing whatever they wanted us to do was our idea—though, I didn't realize that until just recently.

Looking at the clock, I realize it's close to Declan's lunchtime. Sitting here thinking about everything that happened back home will only drive me insane. I know I need to figure out what to do in the long run, but I can avoid it for a little longer.

I'm a little early when I get to the school—but luckily, the staff in the front office remember me from the few times Declan has brought me to school with him, and once I finish signing in they let me head to Declan's classroom.

As I walk past the first classroom in the art hallway, Quinn catches my eye. This must be her room now, but I don't see any students in there. This might be the perfect opportunity for me to get to know her a little better.

"Hey!" I say from the doorway, making her jump slightly from behind her desk.

"Hey, your brother's classroom is one more door down, but he's got a class right now." Her voice is friendly enough, but I've made my career on being able to read people, and I can see from her tense shoulders and the way her eyes bounce around slightly that she's nervous.

"Oh, I know. I got here a little early, but thought I could bug you for a little." I step into the classroom easily, trying to show her I mean nothing but getting to know her. "Unless you're busy."

"No, I'm not busy. Come on in." Her shoulders fall a bit, and she waves me further into the room, standing behind her desk.

"Are you enjoying teaching so far?" I ask as I look around, taking in the artwork she has hung on the walls.

"You know what? Surprisingly, I am." She hops onto the edge of her desk, taking a seat. "It's not what I expected, but I love watching when a technique or concept clicks in their brains. It's fun."

I can't help but smile when I turn to look at her. "You sound like my brother."

"I'm going to take that as a good thing."

"Oh, absolutely. I love my brother. Like you said yesterday, he's a good man." I turn back to the photos on the walls again and mumble the next part. "Better than most."

"Everything okay?" I hear the concern in her voice, making me smile again—she really is just like Declan.

"There you go, sounding like my brother."

The bell rings, signaling the end of class and saving me from her response.

"That's lunch." Quinn hops down from her desk, grabbing something from a drawer. "Did you bring something with you?"

"Yeah." I hold up the bag I brought with me from the house. "Where do you normally eat?"

"Your brother normally meets me here, but we can head to his classroom."

Before we have a chance to turn for the door, Declan comes barreling around the corner, heading straight for Quinn. "Okay, I've calmed down, but it took way longer than—" Declan stops talking abruptly when he sees me in the room with Quinn.

"I'm sorry?" A brief feeling of confusion flashes through me, but the second Quinn starts laughing and a look of horror passes over Declan, I know something is going on between them.

"Nothing," he mumbles. "I didn't know you were coming to the school today," he says louder, pulling me into a hug.

"Yeah, I finished writing the return suit and filed it this

morning, so I thought I'd come bug you for lunch before I look for something else to occupy my time," I say a little flippantly. It's a brush-off, and we both know it.

"You wrote and filed a court document all in one morning?" he asks in disbelief.

"Well, I wrote the brief last night, but I had to wait for the courthouse to open this morning to file it." I avoid looking at him. I know he can see right through me, but I'm still not ready to talk about everything.

"You wrote it last night? You must have been up all night."

I hear Quinn shift from her spot by her desk, but I don't look at her—or Declan. "I haven't been sleeping well, so I figured I would just get it done." I finally look at him, trying to silently tell him to leave it alone.

"Ava, I don't—"

"Big brother," I interrupt when he clearly doesn't receive the message, "I told you yesterday I didn't want to talk about it."

Quinn walks up to Declan's side, placing her hand on his back. He startles slightly, glancing at her before turning back to me. "You're right." He studies me for only a moment before turning back to Quinn and kissing her lips quickly. "Let's sit."

I follow Declan to the table placed in front of Quinn's desk and take a seat across from the two of them.

"How's your morning been?" Quinn asks Declan, changing the subject for me.

"It was good. Nothing out of the norm to report." He glances at Quinn out of the corner of his eye, and she laughs, making me wonder exactly what I'm missing.

"What am I missing?" I ask out loud.

"Nothing," Declan rushes to answer, and I think it might be better that I don't know. "How was your morning?" he asks Quinn. "Anything else from Tyler today?"

"No, he wasn't in class. I checked and he was marked absent from school today."

"Weird. I don't think he's ever missed a day of school."

"Tyler's the kid you told me about?" I ask. "The one who acts out a little in class?"

If I'm right, Tyler is one of Declan's favorite students, and while he's always had a bit of a rough home life, he's always been a good kid. This year, though, things have changed for him. Tyler's become more withdrawn and acts out in class—things he's never done before.

"Yeah. It's normally not serious, but he was a little more disruptive than normal on Friday," Declan tells me.

"Why not write him up?" I don't know anything about being a teacher—at least not more than Declan has told me—but it seems like writing a student up would be the quickest way for them to learn a lesson.

"He's so smart and doing well in his classes, but his behavior has him on the cusp of being expelled. I don't want to be the reason for that," Quinn answers. "I don't want to ruin his chances of doing whatever he wants after high school."

"Not everyone is worth saving," I mutter under my breath. I know I'm being harsh, but I've been burned one too many times to offer more chances after people let me down.

"Do you know what you want to do with your time in town since you'll be staying longer?" Quinn asks, changing the subject and saving me yet again.

"I honestly don't know." I know I need to figure it out, but I have plenty of time since I don't have a job to get back to.

"Do you know how long you're staying?" Declan asks as he picks at his lunch.

"Well, I've got a little over a month saved up. So I was thinking about staying through the new year."

Declan stiffens in his seat, and I see Quinn place her hand on his back. "Ava." He closes his eyes briefly before opening them and looking at me. "I know you don't want to talk about it, and I want to respect that, but I need you to give me something to stop me from worrying."

He's right. I know I'm causing him more stress by making him imagine worst-case scenarios, but I'm not ready for the look of worry and sadness I know he'll have when he learns the truth.

"I was fired from the firm." I offer him a partial truth.

"What?" Declan breaths out.

"That's all I'm going to say on it. I'm not sure I'm upset about it. Practicing law hasn't made me happy for a while now." I look at Quinn. She's clearly someone my brother trusts and leans on for support, and I'm glad he has that.

I look back at Declan and give him as much as I'm ready to. "I just need a little time to figure it all out. I promise, when I'm ready I'll tell you everything."

Declan takes a deep breath before responding. "Okay. You're welcome to stay as long as you want."

"Thank you."

I look back at Quinn and realize she and I aren't all that different. Until recently, she was living in New York City as a big-time photographer with no plans of returning home. The only reason she's here now is because of Scott's cancer returning.

"I know you're still in the same general field, but you did technically change careers. Would you recommend it?" I ask her.

"Ava!" Declan shouts, but Quinn laughs.

"You know what? I absolutely would. Sometimes, being forced to change one aspect of your life leads to a domino effect of wonderful things falling into it."

We smile at each other, and lunch continues without issue.

CHAPTER
Six

GAGE

THREE DAYS LATER, and while I now know why Ava was at the courthouse—small town living has its perks—I can't stop thinking about her or that look in her eyes. I haven't seen her, but I've thought about her almost constantly.

It's new for me, thinking about someone as much as I've thought about her. I've been turned down before—not that Ava actually turned me down—but I've never cared about it. Many would say I didn't care enough with how quickly I moved on from rejection in the past.

The way I see it, love doesn't exist. Infatuation? Lust? Like? Absolutely. But romantic love? I just don't see it. So why waste time thinking about someone who doesn't want to be with you?

I can admit my perception might be warped from seeing my parents in and out of numerous relationships with people they always claimed to love. But if love was real, wouldn't at least one of those relationships have lasted? Wouldn't those people have stuck around? I sometimes question whether any kind of love exists.

I do love my parents and my siblings—more than life. And

in the past I would have probably said I loved my unit when I was in the army. But you go out of your way to stay in the lives of the people you love. It hurt to be so far away from my unit when I first got home, but if I'm honest with myself, that pain wore off quickly.

On the other hand, while I loved being in the army and serving my country, it physically pained me to be so far from my family and to have such little contact with them. I was in the army for twelve years and I never got used to being away from my family.

I think that's what love is—when it hurts to go long periods without interacting in some capacity with those you love.

Each time my parents remarried, their spouses claimed to love me. But when their marriage ended, they'd be gone, never to see me again. That is, of course, unless they had kids. Then, I would see them when they came to pick up my half-siblings for holidays and special occasions. But I was rarely acknowledged—barely a blip on their radar.

I know I'm in the minority when it comes to my beliefs about love, but I've never seen it in real life—not up close. And it's hard to believe in something you can't see or feel. Outside of my parents and siblings, I can't say that I've ever felt love—definitely not lasting love.

I tried the serious relationship thing in high school but never felt anything deep for the girls I dated. And once I joined the army, getting into a serious relationship never felt right when I didn't know exactly when I would be home. Casual has been the way for me since I was eighteen, and it works. I don't have to worry about putting my heart on the line —the way I've seen both of my parents do multiple times—and I don't have to worry about hurting anyone else or myself.

And yet, even knowing all this, I still can't figure out why Ava is constantly in my thoughts. Maybe one could argue it's the chase, but I've never been one to chase a woman. I lean more toward the belief that Ava's a mystery I can't help but want to solve. I need to know what caused that haunted look, that stiff posture, the look of always being prepared for battle.

I wonder if Declan's noticed it, and if so, what he's doing to help her.

I met Declan a little more than two years ago, shortly after I graduated from the police academy. I happened to be at the bar, Murphy's, with my dad when I overheard Declan talking to Caleb Marks about one of his students.

Declan was worried his student might be in an unsafe environment at home and didn't know what to do. I'd jumped in to ask a few questions and determined—while it was a shitty situation—legally, there wasn't anything he could do. Though we all agreed to keep a close eye on the kid, none of us liked that we couldn't help him. But we could always make sure he knew there were people in his corner if he needed them.

Declan's a good man; one you want in your corner. I can't imagine—if he knew what was going on with Ava—that he's just letting it go. But, then again, maybe he isn't seeing what I do when he looks at her. Sometimes, being so close to a person keeps you from seeing the trouble lingering inside.

My phone rings, bringing me back to the present. I glance quickly at the screen to see who it is before answering. "Hey, Dad."

"Hey, son. What are you up to? You're off today, right?" My father's smooth voice comes across the line.

"Yeah, I'm walking into Murphy's now to grab a quick bite."

"Mind if I join you? Leo's with his mom this week, and you know Asher's back at school."

I smile but try to swallow back the amusement in my voice. "Still can't get used to the empty house, huh?"

"I've never been good at being alone, you know that."

"Yeah, Dad, I know." There's a certain level of resignation

in my voice, I know it, but his inability to be by himself is a major reason for his three marriages. "Of course, you can join me. Are you still at Harvest Hills?"

Harvest Hills is the pick-your-own farm Dad started managing after he and Mom divorced—when they decided it would be better if they didn't work together to co-parent me successfully. It's on the opposite side of town from Mom's farm and isn't far from Murphy's. But if he's still there now, it means he'll be there a bit longer before he'll meet me.

Dad doesn't know how to be alone, which means he finds anything to keep himself busy, including working ridiculous hours. I have no doubt he was at the ranch by six this morning.

"Yeah, and I need to finish up a few things. I'll probably be here another thirty minutes."

I glance at my watch and see it's just after six. "I'm about to walk in now, but I can grab a drink and hang out. Take your time. I'll be here."

"I'll be as quick as I can. Love you, son."

Knowing my dad, I still have at least an hour to kill before he shows up. Dad has never been good at stopping mid-task, and I have no doubt he's in the middle of something now. "Love you, too. See you in a bit."

Murphy's, the local—and only—bar in town, is owned by Walter Murphy, the father of an old friend and a man who takes great pride in the business his father started back in 1965. Murphy's has the feel of an old-school Irish pub mixed with the warmth of being home. Whenever I walk through the doors and see Walt standing behind the bar, I know I made the right decision to come here instead of going to The Diner for dinner.

"Gage! Good to see you, kid." Walt smiles as I take a seat at the bar.

I can't help but return the smile. "Hey, Walt, how're you doing?"

"I'm all right. Spoke to Jude today, you know that always brightens my day."

"He's doing good?" Even though Jude is two years older than me, our dads were close friends, making it so Jude and I grew up together, becoming close friends ourselves. But shortly after graduation, Jude left town and hasn't returned since, not even for a quick visit.

I know it hurts Walt not having his son close by, but Walt seems to understand why Jude stays away, even though no one else does. Jude's absence is the town's biggest kept secret. Absolutely no one knows why he left.

When Jude left, he cut ties with everyone but his dad. I know from talking to Walt that Jude made sure to call at least every other day, if not more often. And I know from Walt that Jude has spent the last sixteen years traveling. He says Jude is happy, and even though they talk often, finding time to see each other in person is hard. With Jude not willing to return to Ashford Falls and Walt being stubborn and unwilling to leave Murphy's for long periods, Walt always has to wait for the wind to bring Jude closer to Maryland before they can actually visit each other. I think it's been about five years since Walt has actually laid eyes on his son, and that time is starting to wear on him. He doesn't carry himself with the same carefree manner he used to.

"Yeah. He should be in DC in the next few months, so I should be able to get down to see him soon. Maybe in time for Christmas."

"That's great, Walt." I offer him a small smile. I'm genuinely happy for him, but I also feel for him.

Walt looks more haggard every time I see him. The dark circles under his eyes are growing, he's losing weight, and the wrinkles on his face are getting deeper and more pronounced. I don't know what's going on with him, but I can't imagine it's only the stress of owning a business.

Walt has been running Murphy's on his own for almost twenty years—ever since Walter's father gave it to him when he retired. The stress of running his own business isn't new to Walt. Murphy's is also a well-established bar in a small town— it practically runs itself at this point.

There's something else going on, and I just wish I knew what it was. I've asked Walt, and he continues to tell me nothing is wrong, which I'm sure is what he's telling Jude, too. If I could contact Jude and tell him about my concerns, I would, but when Jude cut everyone out, he made it very hard for anyone to find him.

"Oh, stop looking at me like that. You and your father worry too much. I'm fine." Walt turns to walk away before I can respond. Which is probably a good thing, because I have no idea *how* to respond.

Before I can simmer on those thoughts much longer, a cool breeze blows in from the open door. I turn to see who's holding the door open long enough for the air to reach me in the middle of the bar, and there stands Ava. It seems fitting that the only person who can take my mind off the worry I'm feeling for Walt is standing in the open doorway of Murphy's.

I fight the urge to get up and greet her. Instead I stay where I am and watch as she studies her surroundings, clearly deciding if this is where she wants to stay. I would have thought Declan would be with her, but as she continues standing there, the door still held open, it's obvious he isn't.

"Can I help you, miss?" Walt asks, standing at the end of the bar closest to the door. "You're letting in the chilly November air." His voice is kind as he speaks to her, but her entire body still goes taut as she steps further into the bar, letting the door fall closed behind her.

"Oh! Sorry. I didn't—I didn't mean to." Her voice sounds hesitant, and I'm instantly on edge. She may have been guarded when I met her, but she wasn't hesitant. She'd been strong, ready to stand her ground against anything.

"It's all right." He offers her a soft smile. "You're Declan's sister, right?"

"How do you—never mind." She steps forward, sitting at the end of the bar in front of Walt. "Small towns, right?"

"Afraid so. But also, your brother speaks very highly of you. I've seen your picture plenty, and it's in your eyes. You and your brother share the same eyes."

As I watch Walt and Ava interact, I see her start to relax, a soft smile forming on her lips. It's strange how *my* body starts to relax as I see the tension slowly leave her body.

Walt has always had that effect on people. Looking at him, you would think people would be afraid, but it's his easy manner and welcoming nature that quickly win people over. He's a tall and well-built man. The type of build that comes from hard work, not a gym. And when his sleeves are rolled up like they are now, you can see the tattoos covering his arms. His hair is still mostly dark, though salt and pepper is starting to show on the sides. But I know it's the smile that really takes the cake. Even behind his full beard, the dimples are hard to miss.

I find myself smiling right along with Walt when a soft laugh breaks free from Ava. I know I'm being the biggest creep —watching them as closely as I am—but even knowing that, I can't look away.

"I'll go put that order in for you." Walt offers Ava another smile as he pats the bar in front of her before turning away. He catches my eye as he passes me, giving me a knowing look, and I can't find the energy to care about the shit he's going to give me later.

I stand from my seat, grab my beer, and make my way toward Ava.

CHAPTER
Seven

AVA

I MADE the mistake of answering the phone. I knew it the second I hit accept, but I just wanted them to stop. I *needed* them to stop. The notifications from missed phone calls and text messages I refused to answer were driving me crazy.

I don't know what I thought I would accomplish by answering, but I should have known it would be absolutely nothing. I think I hoped that in a one-on-one conversation with my mother, she would finally hear me and offer me the shoulder I needed. I held out hope that, at least as a woman, she would believe and support me.

Unfortunately, nothing about her opinions or attitude has changed since that first conversation in their living room. She demanded to know where I was and what I was doing, and I refused to tell her anything.

I'm done following the road they laid out for me and caring about the way they view me. I'm taking a page from my brother's book and doing what makes me happy.

I have no idea what makes me happy anymore, but I'm determined to figure it out. I've spent too long focused on the school and career they guided me to, and I lost myself along the way. I don't have hobbies or friends anymore, and I miss those things. I want to be able to pick up the phone and just word-vomit all my thoughts on someone, and right now it feels like there's no one.

I know Declan would be that person for me in a heartbeat, but if I had called him that night he would have been on the next flight. He would have been breaking down doors and probably would've ended up in jail. I can't be the person taking Declan away from the life he's building here. He deserves everything that's happening with Quinn. Seeing their interactions at breakfast and lunch earlier this week makes me so happy. If there's anyone who deserves to find their person, it's Declan. He's always putting those he loves first and going out of his way for them, and I love seeing him have someone there supporting him.

Sitting around this empty house, stewing in the words my mother threw at me, is making all of it so much worse. Without really thinking about it I bundle myself up and make my way into town.

At this point, I've been to Ashford Falls a few times, but more often than not, it was only for a weekend, and Declan and I spent our time hanging out at his place or with the Marks family. While we've driven through town and eaten at The Diner, I never really paid attention to the shops or anything else on those trips.

It's just after five as I leave the house, the sun barely peeking over the horizon on its daily descent. I've never minded how the days get shorter this time of year. And in a place like Ashford Falls—surrounded by farmland—the shorter days and longer nights mean you have more time to enjoy the evening sky.

I have no idea where I'm going, but I need to move and the town square isn't far from Declan's house. The only thing I'm sure of when I walk out that door is that I can't go to The Diner. Not if I want to avoid Declan.

Thursday nights have become a quasi-date night for him and Quinn at The Diner after his pick-up soccer game. And I know if he saw my face, he would push me for all the information I have yet to give him.

While he's still respecting my wishes to let me figure it out before I tell him everything, I see the look in his eyes every time he looks at me and he's worried. Declan has always been a fixer, and by not giving him all the information, I'm keeping him from fixing everything.

It takes me a little over thirty minutes to reach the center of town, but when I get there I still have no idea where to go or what to do with my evening.

The stars are so bright here. On nights I'm unable to sleep—which is every night—I find myself sitting on the porch swing studying the stars. I've never paid much attention to them before, but there's something kind of amazing in the vastness of space and how we can see stars that are millions of light-years away from us.

I glance to my right and see Quinn sitting in one of the windows at The Diner. She doesn't even seem to notice the world around her, focused entirely on her laptop. I could stop in to say a quick hello, but I know she'll invite me to join her, and Declan will be there soon. I'm pretty sure they haven't had much time to themselves since I arrived, and things have gotten a bit more serious since the Fall Harvest Festival last weekend.

Facing the street in front of me, I see the town market and a line of shops that look to be closing up for the night. It's early, but in a small town these shops won't stay open much past dinner, especially not at this time of year once the chill in the air becomes more frigid.

Turning to my left, I see another row of shops. The building in the middle stands out from the rest. The wooden exterior creates a warm atmosphere, drawing me in, and, as I get closer, I realize it's a bar. The hanging sign above the door reads *Murphy's,* and I'm instantly reminded of a few conversations I've had with my brother about this place. Most people will tell you The Diner is the only restaurant in town—which isn't necessarily wrong—but The Diner isn't the only place that serves food. From what Declan has said, Murphy's doesn't have a large menu, but the items they do have are "fucking delicious."

It seems as good a place as any to spend my evening, but as I walk past one of the shops, I'm distracted by a *Help Wanted* sign in the window. I stop in my tracks and take in the shop, Falls Book Haven, and through the window it looks like a haven indeed.

The lights inside emit a warm glow, creating a cozy atmosphere. A woman stands behind the checkout counter, her elbow resting there and her hand propping her head up as she reads a book lying open in front of her. Around her, the shop is filled with bookshelves from floor to ceiling on almost every wall, not an inch of open shelf space. In front of the shelves, there are several chairs that look like they would be perfect for reading. The shop looks like it was designed to invite people to spend the day there, not just as a pit stop along the way.

I step inside and a bell rings, making the woman behind the counter glance up.

"Sorry, you're probably getting ready to close, but I saw the sign in the window..." I trail off, not really knowing where I'm going with that train of thought. I know I need a job, I can't sit at home—or Declan's house—doing nothing, but working at a bookshop? It would be a massive change from what I've been doing for the last five years, eight if I count my three years in law school.

"Oh." The woman studies me for a minute before continuing. "It's just part-time. Stocking shelves, keeping the place clean, that kind of thing."

"Gotcha."

We're both quiet after that.

I don't know what to say or do. It was a spur-of-the-moment thing for me to step into the store. I honestly didn't even realize I was doing it until I heard the bell ring. Now that I've asked about the job, I think I'm interested.

"Are you new in town?" the woman asks, closing her book but staying where she is behind the counter. She has a kind look. Her face is free of makeup, and she has a natural beauty about her. Her hair, clipped back at the base of her neck with a few pieces falling in natural waves around her face gives off a laid-back vibe. Even dressed in an oversized sweater, I can tell she has a small frame, though the look in her eye makes me think she's much stronger than she appears.

"Technically, I'm only visiting," I tell her as I step closer to the counter.

"Technically?"

"I'm visiting my brother, but my situation back home has changed, and I think it might be time for something new." I offer her a small shrug.

"Change can be good." She glances away briefly before looking back at me, offering me her hand. "Abbey Selbey, the manager here at Falls Book Haven."

I shake her hand and smile. "Ava Day."

"Nice to meet you, Ava." She studies me some more before letting my hand go. "That sign has been up for a few weeks now, and you're the first person to ask about it. So I think it's safe to say the position is yours if you want it, but it won't start until January. The owner is making a few changes to the place and doesn't want to bring on new staff until then."

I nod my head, looking around the shop some more. I

thought it looked like a haven from outside, but being inside the store brings it to life in a whole new way. The exposed brick wall behind the counter, the leather chairs, the dark shelves, the soft amber lights—all of it creating this cozy atmosphere that sucks me in.

I turn back to her. "Can I think about it?"

"Absolutely."

"Thank you." I give her a small smile before turning and walking out the door toward Murphy's as I planned before getting distracted.

I feel a little lighter. I know I didn't do anything, but just stepping into that store and asking about a job makes me realize I can do that. If I'm really done caring about what my parents want, then I can take that job or any other job I want. I'm *actually* free of them.

Of course, that light feeling comes crashing down the second I hear my phone ring and see that my father calling me. Just seeing his face on my screen has my entire body going tight. I'm frozen in place, half in the bar and half out, just staring at my phone for a moment before I ignore it and shove it back in my pocket.

When I glance up, I pause for a different reason. This bar feels exactly like walking into an old Irish pub, and I'm instantly in love with it. The warm, dark tones of the place create a welcoming atmosphere, and even though I've never been here, it feels like home. There's a warmth in the air that somehow makes it easier to breathe—something I've only ever experienced with my grandparents, Declan, and the Marks family.

"Can I help you, miss?" a man asks from behind the bar. "You're letting in the chilly November air."

I feel my body tighten more, preparing for the harsh comments I assume will follow, but before they can, I step further in, letting the door fall closed behind me. "Oh! Sorry. I didn't—I didn't mean to."

"It's all right." He offers me a small smile, his voice kind. "You're Declan's sister, right?"

I look at him, confused. "How do you—never mind." I step up to the bar, taking a seat in front of the man. "Small towns, right?"

"Afraid so. But also, your brother speaks very highly of you. I've seen your picture plenty, and it's in your eyes. You and your brother share the same eyes."

I notice the tattoos on his fingers first, and I think I should be nervous speaking to him, but something about him has me relaxing slightly. I feel my shoulders fall from my ears and that light feeling I had only moments before starts to return.

"He's a bit of a teddy bear, that brother of mine."

The man laughs, deep and hearty, dimples easy to see even behind his beard. "That he is. He can't seem to help himself."

I laugh quietly, knowing truer words have never been spoken.

"I'm Walter, but most people call me Walt."

"Nice to meet you, Walt. I'm Ava."

"Lovely to meet you, Ava. Do you need a menu?"

"Can I just get a cheeseburger? I haven't had one in far too long and a burger sounds really good right now." I sag in my seat, letting some of the weight of everything lift, at least for a little while.

"Sure thing. Fries okay with that?" Walt's smile is kind, though I think there might be a little pity peeking through in his eyes.

"Yeah, and a Guinness would be great."

"A woman after my own heart," he jokes, placing his hands over his heart.

He drops his hands after a moment, placing them on the bar in front of me, almost as if he wants to give my arm a comforting squeeze but decides against it. "I'll go put that order in for you."

Walt isn't gone long before I feel someone take the seat next to me. I'm getting ready to tell them to leave me alone when I realize it's Gage Flynn, the deputy from the courthouse earlier this week, a charming smile quickly growing on his face.

CHAPTER
Eight

GAGE

I CAN SEE in the way she holds herself that Ava's not open to a conversation at the moment—something is clearly weighing on her. But even seeing that, I can't walk away. I want to help lessen the load, even if only for a little while.

With a smile I'm not entirely sure I feel, I plop onto the seat next to her. "You know, I honestly thought I would run into you around town sooner than this, but somehow it never happened." I turn to her, taking in her guarded eyes when she looks at me.

She scoffs, facing forward. "Been looking out for me, have you?"

"Oh, definitely." I can't take my eyes off her, even if she refuses to look at me. "Especially after learning about what brought you to town. Anyone who helps Scott Marks keep that bitch of a woman away from Max is a person I want to shake hands with."

"Gotta love small towns," she mumbles under her breath, releasing a deep sigh before speaking louder. "You already shook my hand." She fiddles with the napkin Walt placed in front of her.

"Maybe, but that was before I knew what you were doing here." I turn in my seat, angling my body toward her.

She lifts her head to look at me, studying me for a moment before mirroring my position. "Well, I wouldn't want to let you down."

She holds her hand out between us, offering me a handshake. Her eyes are still guarded, but there's something else in them, too. Maybe sadness? Or resignation? I feel the smile fall from my lips as I take her hand in mine. It's soft and warm. I'm not surprised by the softness, but I'm surprised by the warmth.

"You decided to come introduce yourself, did you?" Walt's voice breaks through the moment as he places a pint in front of Ava.

I turn to Walt, quickly coming back to the moment. "We actually met earlier this week. I just wanted to commend Ava on helping Scott. That man deserves the best, and we all know from Declan that Ava's the best."

"Right, I forgot about Nicole being back in town." Walt turns to Ava. "I'm sure you can't talk about it, but Scott won't lose that boy, right? He's too good of a father and she's too much of a...well, I don't know the right word for that woman."

"Bitch?" I offer.

Walt taps the side of his nose before pointing at me, signaling I'm right but he won't be saying it himself.

One side of Ava's lips tip up in a half smile as she shakes her head slightly. "No, I don't think Scott has anything to worry about. I think any judge looking at the evidence will leave things exactly how they are."

"Good," Walt says right before the door opens, letting in another gust of cold air. He lifts his head, looking to see who entered, lifting his hand in greeting before looking back to Ava and me. "I'll be back with your burger as soon as it's ready." He taps the bar twice before walking away again.

I turn back to Ava but don't say anything. I've got so many

questions running through my head, but there's no reason for her to answer them. We don't know each other, and something tells me she's not really in the mood to change that.

I've always been good at reading people—it's one of the things that makes me good at my job. But this woman clearly has a shield around her keeping herself safe, and I can't read anything else. It's driving me mad.

Her phone rings before I can open my mouth to say anything else. She pulls it out of her pocket, looking at the screen quickly before ignoring the call and placing it face-down on the bar. It's only a minute before it starts ringing again.

Ava's entire body deflates, her elbows falling onto the bar and her hands cover her face. The phone stops only to begin again, and her shoulders start to shake slightly.

As gently as I can, I place one hand on her back and reach around her to silence her phone. She jumps slightly at my touch. Trying to soothe her, I bring my mouth to her ear and whisper, "Just breathe. You're safe here." I don't know what makes me tell her that, but something in my gut says she hasn't felt safe in a while. Her body sags a little more, but I feel her take a deep breath.

I press the power button on her phone, shutting it off. I'm sure that's crossing yet another line, but whoever keeps calling has caused enough stress. A few hours' reprieve is something Ava seems to need—desperately.

"I know it's a stupid question, but you okay?" I ask after a few minutes when I feel her body stop shaking. I practically surround her. I'm on the edge of my seat, my body facing her, my legs open wide around her seat, one hand resting on her back, and my other arm across the bar in front of her. To anyone looking at us, I'm sure we look like a couple having an intimate moment, but I don't really care what anyone else sees right now. My focus is entirely on her.

She shakes her head, her face still covered by her hands. After a moment she wipes her eyes and cheeks, one arm falling to the bar, the other propping her head up as she turns slightly to look at me.

"Honestly, no, I'm not okay." Her voice is hoarse and barely above a whisper, but I hear her all the same.

"Do you want to talk about it?" I study her. Her eyes are a little red, but I wouldn't know she just broke down if I hadn't seen it myself.

"Not really."

"Okay."

She sits up a little straighter, shock flashing in her eyes. "You're not going to push?"

"No, I'm not going to push." I let her study me for a moment, seeing whatever she needs to before I pull away from her, sitting back on the bar stool. I give her a minute, glancing away briefly. Whatever just happened was intense, and I can't keep looking at the pain in her eyes, but I'm not ready to walk away either.

I turn back to her, asking the first random question that comes to mind, trying to distract her from the heaviness of the moment. "Have you had a chance to explore much of the town?"

"What?" she asks in disbelief.

"Have you explored the town any since you got here?"

"No, I heard you, I just..." She shakes her head slightly, momentarily looking down at the bar before picking her head back up. "Not really. Tonight was the first night I made it into town. I've been catching up with Declan and the Marks family."

"I assume, with how much Declan talks about you, that you're close?"

She studies me again as if she doesn't know what to do

with me before answering. "Yeah, we're close. I don't get out here to see him that much, but we talk as often as we can."

"Do you live in Harborview or Boston? Boston's where the law firm you work at is located, right?" I get a little more comfortable in my seat, resting my elbow on the bar, my head in my hand.

It feels like I already know a lot about Ava thanks to the way Declan talks about her, but seeing her this evening reminds me that even a proud older brother doesn't know everything. I know if Olivia was in as much turmoil as Ava is, and I knew about it, I would be stuck to her side until I could fix whatever was wrong. From how Declan talks about Ava, I know he feels the same way about his sibling as I do all of mine. It might be overprotective, but it hurts seeing the people you care about hurt.

"Yeah, the firm's in Boston. I have a place in Harborview and Boston, but I end up spending most of my time closer to the firm. It's just easier."

"Oh, fancy pants has two places?" I tease, causing a small smile to form on Ava's lips.

"I'm not sure it makes it any better, but my parents own my apartment in Harborview, so it doesn't cost me much, and my place in Boston is a tiny studio apartment."

"Hey, don't sell yourself short. Being able to afford two places shows how hard you work—it's definitely something to be proud of. I know how prestigious that law firm you work for is. They don't let just anyone work for them."

While there's plenty in the news I try to avoid, I also like to stay up to date on current affairs. I've seen the Henry, Wellsley, & Ford name quite a few times. It's no exaggeration that they are one of the biggest firms in Boston, representing some of the biggest names in the country.

She laughs, but it's more self-deprecating than anything

else. "I'm not so sure about that. My parents are close friends with one of the founding partners."

My eyes narrow as I look at her. "Do you represent clients?"

"What kind of question is that?"

"I'm going to prove a point—just answer." I sit up straight, getting serious. "Do you have clients you represent?"

She rolls her eyes but answers. "Yes, I have clients I represent."

"How many?"

"I don't know. It's a fair amount. More than most at the practice, at least for family law."

"Do you win?"

"Gage—"

"No, come on, do you win?" I stop her from avoiding the question.

She looks at me as if I might back down from my question. But if one thing is true, the longer you stay quiet, the more likely you are to get an answer.

"Fine. Yes, I win," she says, a little exasperated.

"More often than not?"

Her eyes narrow. "Yes, more often than not."

"Then I think it's safe to say you kept the job because you're good at it." She opens her mouth to say something, but I keep going before she can. "Look, let's be real: more often than not, it's about *who* you know that gets you in the door. But it's *what* you know that keeps you there. Your parents' connection might have gotten you the job, but I bet you worked your butt off the second you got there, and that's what made them keep you."

Her eyes bounce between mine for a minute before she looks down at the bar, a light blush creeping onto her cheeks. "Thank you," she murmurs.

I wait for her to lift her eyes back to mine before answering. "Anytime."

We get caught in another trance, just staring at each other. Something I'm sure we would have continued doing, yet again, if it weren't for Walt coming up behind the bar and my dad coming up from behind us.

"Sorry about the wait. There was a food emergency or something back in the kitchen." Walt laughs as he sets Ava's burger down in front of her.

"No worries, Walt. Thank you," Ava addresses Walt, turning back in her seat to face the bar straight on, her body going taut yet again.

"I know I took longer than I said, but I just couldn't leave until I'd finished organizing the tack room," my dad says as he takes the seat on my other side.

"Forget it. I know exactly who you are, Dad." I offer him a smile so he knows I'm only giving him a hard time as I turn in my seat.

I don't want to stop talking to Ava, and, if I'm being honest with myself, I want more than just this conversation. But whatever is going on with her is weighing heavily on her shoulders, and I won't be the reason she has more hurdles to jump. So, for tonight, I'll be a sounding board—a guy at the bar who's just there to talk.

"Well, it doesn't seem like it was a hardship for you to wait for me. Who's your friend?" Dad's voice is light, and there's a smile on his face, but when he sees the look in my eye, his head tilts, giving me a questioning look.

I shake my head minutely, trying to tell him not to keep going, but when he opens his mouth I jump in before he can say anything else. "This is Ava Day, Declan's younger sister. She's in town to help Scott with Nicole." Turning to Ava, I see her eyes have gone a little round as she takes a deep gulp from her beer. "Ava, this is my dad, Nick Flynn."

Dad leans around me, finally getting a look at Ava, and I see the minute he figures out what I was trying to tell him silently. She's not in a place to be making jokes about anything more than a simple conversation happening between us. Dad knows I'm not a person for serious relationships, and he knows Murphy's is a place I like to frequent to meet the rare tourist in town. And while I normally might enjoy Dad's witty banter in those situations, I know he can sense this isn't one of them.

He straightens in his seat—glancing at me so quickly I would have missed it if I hadn't been studying him—before offering his hand to Ava.

"Nice to meet you, Ava. It's awfully kind of you to come out here to help Scott."

Ava doesn't hesitate to place her hand in his, straightening in her seat, a mask of professionalism falling across her face. "It's my job, and that man deserves a break." She smiles, but it doesn't reach her eyes. "Plus, he practically adopted my brother, so how can I say no?"

My dad laughs at the joke but glances at me out of the corner of his eye. He's always been good at reading people as well, always picking up on the smallest tells, and I have no doubt he can see the mask she's wearing. That tension in her shoulders, the shadow in her eyes.

"I know you just got your burger, but join us for dinner. My son and I could use some of your spirit to liven up the evening." He stands from his seat, getting ready to find a booth for us.

"Oh no, I don't want to intrude on your dinner."

"Nonsense. I see this kid all the time. You aren't intruding." This time, he doesn't give her a chance to say anything before walking away.

I watch him go and am honestly grateful for him in this moment. He's just given me an excuse to spend more time with Ava. "I'd like to say you can ignore him, but he's not one to take no for an answer." I give her an apologetic smile. "He'll probably come back here and steal your beer or burger to take them over to the table."

She looks at me, a little dumbfounded, before Walt jumps in. "Unfortunately, Gage is right. Nick is not the kind of man to take no for an answer. Best to just get on with it and follow him." His kind smile is back on his face, his dimple popping through. "I'll bring you a fresh beer—on the house." And just like my dad, he doesn't wait for Ava to respond before he walks away.

"I—I'm not going to be good company. You literally just saw me in tears. Please don't make me do this."

Her voice is pleading, and the look in her eye makes me want to wrap her in my arms, but I hold myself back. Instead, I place my hand on her forearm, squeezing it. "Ava, you can do whatever makes you most comfortable. But, I can tell something is weighing on you, and truth be told, my dad's likely going to tell you any number of embarrassing stories about me that will be sure to take your mind off everything, so if you want to be distracted a little longer, you're welcome to join us. Otherwise, I'll see you around town."

I squeeze her arm once more before standing from my seat and joining my father at the booth he found for us across the room.

"She not going to join us?" he asks as I take the seat across from him.

"I don't think so." I reach out to stop him when he starts to stand from his seat. "Normally, I'm all for your meddling ways as I find them quite entertaining, but I think we let her be this time."

He falls back into his seat, mock outrage on his face. "What do you mean 'meddling ways'? I don't meddle."

I laugh louder than I intend to, but Dad is oblivious if he thinks he doesn't meddle. "Dad, you're always getting in Asher and Leo's business, just like you did mine in high school. Leo just told me about the impromptu get-together you organized for him and his friends last weekend. I don't know how I've avoided it the last three years."

He stares at me with a serious expression on his face long enough that I think he might actually be hurt by what I said, but then he's laughing with me, and the conversation carries on like it normally does with us—easy and carefree.

When a beer and a basket of food are placed on the edge of the table, I'm honestly surprised it's Ava standing there and not Walt with our regular order.

"Is the offer to join you still open?" Her voice is strong, sure of herself, exactly like it was at the courthouse on Monday, but she shifts nervously, waiting for a response.

I feel my dad kick me under the table, knocking me from my trance.

"Of course." I slide over in the booth, giving her room to sit down.

Ava takes the open seat, pulling her food in front of her. She gives me a small smile before she turns to my dad. "So, tell me you have some embarrassing stories to help shrink a bit of Gage's ego."

Now it's my father's turn to burst out laughing—loud and boisterous.

And I can't help the smile that forms on my lips.

CHAPTER
nine

GAGE

WITHOUT ANY OF us realizing it, we close down Murphy's. It's not until Walt comes over telling us everyone else has left and he'd like to close up that there's a break in the conversation.

Once Dad started talking, he didn't stop. He had an endless supply of stories about my childhood, and even a few second-hand stories from my days in the army to help "shrink my ego" as Ava said.

I couldn't even be upset about it, not when I heard Ava's first real laugh since meeting her. I thought she was beautiful when I first saw her from a distance and even more gorgeous when I saw her up close, but when she laughs, free and unafraid of what people think, she's breathtaking.

The longer we talked and the lighter she became, the more open she was to sharing about herself.

"Has he mentioned that he graduated a year early yet? He likes to say he doesn't brag, but it amazes me how often he finds a way to tell everyone he meets about that little detail."

"I do not!" I'm defensive and I know it, but not really upset when I hear Ava's laugh.

"He did! But I don't think I've met anyone who's done that, and I did go to Harvard, so it might be something worth bragging about." Ava shrugs like it's nothing.

"You went to Harvard?" I ask, forgetting anything my dad said.

"You mean *Declan* hasn't bragged about that?"

"No, I don't think so."

She nods, taking a sip of her beer. "Yeah, I did both my undergrad and law school at Harvard. Both my parents went there, and Declan; it wasn't really an option for me to go anywhere else."

I'm about to ask her more when Walt appears behind her at the end of the table. "All right, I can appreciate the good time you three are having, but it's time to close up. I want to go home."

I see Dad lift his wrist, checking the time on his watch out of the corner of my eye. "Sorry, Walt. We lost track of time." He slides out of the booth, picking up the remaining empty glasses. "Let me close the tab and we'll get out of here."

"Oh, let me—" Ava tries to slide out of the booth to follow.

"Nope, my treat. I haven't had this much fun at my son's expense since he was in high school." Dad's still laughing at his joke as he walks away.

I'm shaking my head and chuckling when Ava turns back to me, the look on her face cutting my laugh short.

"You okay?" I ask, concern evident in my tone.

Ava shakes her head, her eyes watering. "It's silly." She reaches up, swiping at the tear that slips free. "You have a really good relationship with your dad."

I have a feeling Ava doesn't cry often, and the fact that I've seen it twice tonight does something to my insides I've never experienced before. It's like there's a shift inside me, everything rearranging itself to make room for something. What that something is, I don't know, but I'm pulled to her.

It's almost like I can't help myself from quietly saying the next words out of my mouth. "It wasn't always the way it is now. It took a lot of work to get where we are. There were a few years there that we barely spoke. I probably would have cut him out of my life entirely if it weren't for my brothers." I look over Ava's shoulder at my dad at the bar, watching him talk with Walt as he finishes cleaning up.

I don't talk about it often—the period after my parents divorced. But it wasn't a great time for me. And it's not that either one of them did anything wrong. If a kid had to have divorced parents, they were the best you could ask for. They didn't fight in front of me, put me in the middle, or use me as leverage against the other person. I never heard a negative word from either of them about the other. They never made me choose between them, and they were both part of every aspect of my life. Honestly, they were practically best friends, still getting together without me just to hang out. I could tell they still cared for one another, just not in the same way a husband and wife should love one another.

It wasn't their divorce that was the problem for me. It was my dad's two following marriages and the subsequent divorces that were my problem. At the time, it felt like he brought these women into my life without regard for the impact it would have on me. In the beginning, it was difficult to accept anyone but my mom. But I became close with them, only to have them disappear from my life after their divorce from my dad. As a teenager, still trying to figure out life and the world, the constant change was scary.

Of course, in hindsight, while my dad dated quite a few women, he only ever introduced me to the women he either married or seriously thought he would marry. And, when they ended, he always took the time to explain why things didn't work out, making me feel important—ensuring I always felt like a priority to him. Even with the new wives and the new children, he was always there, never missing a moment. Even the things I didn't want him to witness, he was around for.

I bring my eyes back to her. "But that says more about me than it does him. He isn't a perfect father, but he always tries his best."

"It's clear how much he loves you and your brothers. You can hear it in the way he talks about you and the glint in his eye when he looks at you." Ava looks down at the table, tucking a piece of hair behind her ear, a nervous habit I've seen from her a few times this evening. "I've only ever seen that from your dad and Scott." She says that last part so quietly I'm not sure she meant for me to hear it.

"Ava—"

"No, can we forget I said that last part?" Before I can say anything, she's sliding out of the booth and slipping into her coat. "I had a really good time this evening. Thank you for distracting me from everything else going on. Tell your dad thanks for dinner." She turns, offering a wave in Walt and my dad's direction before heading out the door.

I slide out of the booth, grabbing my coat and following her out the door. "I'll see you both later!" I say, throwing a quick wave over my shoulder as a goodbye.

I'm shoving my arms into my sleeves as I step outside, looking all around for Ava. It only takes me a second to find her across the street, making her way through the center of town.

I jog across the street to catch up to her. "Did you walk here?" I ask a few strides behind her, not wanting to scare her.

She glances over her shoulder at me, stopping when she sees me jogging to catch up. "Yeah, Declan picked me up from the airport so I don't have a car."

"Let me give you a ride home," I offer when I stop in front of her.

It's late, and the only places open are The Diner and

Murphy's, making the streets relatively dark and quiet. It's also late November and pretty cold this evening. Something inside me doesn't want Ava walking home in either of these conditions, even if it's only a short walk away.

As if reading my mind, she says, "No, it's okay. Declan's house isn't far."

"I know, but it's late and it's cold. Ashford Falls may be a small town, and you might be safer here than most places in the country, but you still shouldn't be walking alone." I can tell she's going to argue with me some more, so I continue before she can. "Declan's house is just a few houses down from mine. It's really not a problem for me to give you a ride."

Sometimes I wonder if living in a small town is a good thing or not, but it does mean you know where most people live. And right now, I'm feeling pretty lucky this knowledge is in my favor.

"Okay. Thank you."

"I thought you were going to make it harder than that." I place my hand on the small of her back, guiding her back toward Murphy's where my Jeep is parked.

"If it wasn't so cold, I might have."

We're quiet on the walk to my Jeep and the drive to Declan's. It's not uncomfortable. More contemplative than anything else. I don't know what Ava is thinking about, but I know I'm trying to figure out how to make sure I can see her again. This night went nothing like I thought it would, but it might have been one of the best nights I've had in a long time.

I pull up to Declan's, putting the car in park, expecting Ava to be out as fast as she can, but she doesn't move. Instead, she looks out the passenger window at the house. It's dark except for the porch light, and I notice Declan's truck is missing from the driveway.

She doesn't turn to me when she starts speaking. "Thank

you for this evening—not just the meal with your dad but everything before that, too."

I wait for her to look at me before saying anything. I study her for a minute when she does, deciding how to play this. I could pretend it's no big deal and that nothing of importance happened this evening. We could go on randomly running into each other around town, flirting a little before moving on like acquaintances, but that's not what I want. I'm not entirely sure what I want from this, but I know I want more of her.

Maybe it's as simple as needing to solve the mystery that is Ava Day, but I'm being drawn to her, and I don't know if I can ignore that.

"Obviously, I don't know what's going on—who's trying to get a hold of you or why—but it's clear you don't want to talk with them. And I get that you're trying to tackle it all by yourself, and maybe that works for you..." I pause, making sure she hears me. "But based on the weight on your shoulders tonight —I have a feeling you're about to run out of strength. So, just know, I've got some extra if you ever need to borrow it."

Her eyes narrow slightly as she watches me. "Why would you do that? You don't even know me."

"I'd like to know you," I tell her honestly.

"Gage." It's just my name, nothing else. I'm not sure if she doesn't know how to finish that sentence or if that's all she was aiming to say, but I see the soft smile in the corner of her lips.

I give her my most charming smile, the one that normally gets me out of trouble. "I have a feeling this might be an inappropriate time to ask you out on a date."

Ava laughs, shaking her head as she unbuckles her seatbelt. "Gage, I'm the last person you want to ask on a date. My life is a mess and I have no idea where I'll be a month from now, let alone a week from now." She opens the door, hoping out. "Trust me, you're better off finding someone else." She smiles, gently closing the door and turning up the walkway to the house.

I watch her as she unlocks the door, turning to wave before she disappears from view—a few lights clicking on in the front windows. I should drive away, I know that, but I'm stuck where I am, thinking about what she said.

She might think that little speech would deter me from asking her out again—and normally it would—but with Ava, it does the complete opposite. Now I'm even more determined to get her to go out with me. She intrigues me in a way no other woman has before, and there is something inside me that can't let go of getting to know her more.

CHAPTER
Ten

AVA

"AVA, this is getting ridiculous. It's time to come home." I stare at my phone sitting on the counter, my mother's voice coming out of the speaker. "We've spoken with your brother. We know you're with him and that you told him you were fired, but you haven't told him about Brian. So clearly, you're trying to protect someone here. I just don't know if it's yourself from your brother learning what a hussy you are or if it's to protect us from his wrath about the arranged marriage."

I produce a very unladylike snort as if I would ever protect *them* from anyone's wrath. Hearing what my mother thinks of me should elicit some stronger emotion, but as I listen to her unending diatribe, I've gone numb to all of it. Ever since that dinner with Gage and his father two weeks ago, I haven't been able to feel much of anything when it comes to my mother.

It's not like I haven't seen healthy parental relationships before. I have. Caleb, Quinn, and Max's relationship with Scott being a prime example. But something about sitting there that night with Gage and Nick flipped a switch.

There's no excuse for how my mother has spoken to me over the last month—for selling me off to the highest bidder.

I don't have any proof—and I can't figure out why—but financial gain is the only reason I can see for their drastic actions. Brian's family is extremely wealthy, and I can see my parents pushing hard for this marriage—or, more accurately, this merger of two families. They want the wealth and prestige that will come with their daughter being a Wellsley.

"Either way, you missed Thanksgiving, and we can't put off the Wellsleys any longer. You need to come home and take your place by Brian's side. I've had enough of this temper tantrum." I hear the disinterest in her voice, and I can picture her sitting at her desk, working with her assistant sitting across from her—not a care in the world for the pain she's causing. "Ava. It's time to come home," she repeats after a few moments of silence.

I have to wonder if she's right—about why I still haven't told Declan the truth. He's asked about it several times, and I've still pushed him off.

I know Declan's relationship with my parents isn't dependent on this news. He was done with them six years ago when he got divorced. At this point, the only reason he goes home is to see me and his best friend, Ryan.

No, Declan's relationship with my parents wouldn't change a bit if he knew about what they were trying to do.

Is there a part of me that thinks he won't believe me about what Brian did in his office that night? Am I afraid of what he'll think of me? *No, absolutely not.*

Declan's never done anything to make me think he'd look down on me. In our entire lives, hes never once responded in a way that leads me to believe he won't support me with everything he has. And yet, I haven't told him about that night.

"Ava." Her tone is sharp now, as if she's reached her limit.

"I'm not coming home. At least, not right now. I may not be working for the firm anymore, but I do have a case here. I'm going to see that through before I do anything else."

I look around the kitchen and realize I'm exactly where I was two weeks ago—on the phone with my mother and about to go insane from how stagnant my life has become. But then I realize I'm hundreds of miles from Boston. I don't have to put up with her crap.

"I have to go." Without waiting for a response, I hang up. Standing from my seat, I move to the front door and bundle myself up in my coat before grabbing my purse and walking out the door.

Without thinking about it, I find myself walking through the door at Murphy's, looking for what has become that familiar head of honey-brown hair and set of broad shoulders.

While I haven't spent any significant time with Gage over the last two weeks, I've seen him around town—our exchanges turning flirty, with him inevitably asking me out.

I've turned him down every time, but the man is relentless, and that charming smile is making it harder and harder to keep saying no.

It's funny—I mean, not really—how one moment in time can change everything about how you view the world. Maybe not when you're younger and still learning how the world works, but as an adult, you would think it takes more to shift your entire worldview.

And yet, that night with Brian changed everything.

I've heard the stories of those in high places feeling entitled and doling out grossly unwanted attention, but being the subject of that kind of attention from Brian was unexpected, and it broke something inside me.

Prior to that night, I would've said yes to a date with Gage in a heartbeat.

Even knowing he isn't the commitment type, I would've been up for a night of fun with Gage. I know that in my bones.

But between Brian's advances and my parents' reaction,

something is holding me back. I just can't explain exactly what that something is.

I'm pulled from my thoughts when Gage steps in front of me, that endearing smile stretched across his face. "Look, I know you find me attractive, but stalking might be taking it just a bit too far." He lifts his hand, his index finger and thumb held slightly apart.

"I don't know what you're talking about." I brush past him, moving toward a seat at the bar. Gage follows close behind. "The Diner and Murphy's are the only two places open that serve food at this time of night, and unless I want to crash my brother's date, Murphy's is the only choice on a Thursday night." I glance at him and see the teasing gleam in his eye, causing a small smile to grow on my lips.

"So, they've finally made it official, have they?" Gage asks, taking the seat next to me.

"Yeah, they have." And this time, I can't stop the smile from growing, content in the knowledge that my brother's found someone worthy of him.

Gage shifts in his seat, turning his body toward me and leaning against the bar. "They seem like a good fit."

"They do," I agree.

"Are we feeling another Guinness tonight, my girl?" Walt asks, walking up to us from behind the bar.

And that right there is one of the things I love most about small town living. If you take the time to have a conversation, you can come into a place once, and they'll remember your order.

"Yeah, that would be good."

"You want a menu?"

"Nope, I'll take a plain cheeseburger and fries."

He chuckles, taps the bar twice, and nods his head. "What about you, deputy? You ready to order?" he asks Gage.

"You know what, I'll do the same."

"Coming right up." He offers the two of us a smile before turning to leave.

"So, do you live at the bar or something?" I turn to look back at Gage. "I feel like this is where I find you more often than not."

"I could ask the same of you since this is also where I see you most often."

"If you must know—"

"I must," he says in mock seriousness, a smile quickly giving him away.

But that look causes me to smile again, something I find myself doing more and more in his presence. "I've been spending some time at the bookstore next door. I'm thinking about taking the open part-time position."

Gage sits up in his seat, his eyes widen slightly in surprise. "Oh yeah? You thinking about staying in town?"

I shrug. "I'm thinking about it."

That charming smile is back, aimed directly at me yet again. "I think it's a great idea."

"You do, do you?"

"Definitely." He turns in his seat, facing straight ahead as Walt places my drink in front of me, not sticking around to chat. "Gives me more time to get you to say yes to that date."

"You still haven't given up on that one?" I lift the pint, taking a large sip.

"I'm not one to give up on something so easily. Especially something I know could be amazing." He looks at me, and this time I don't see that teasing glint in his eye, and that makes me pause.

"You sound pretty sure of that." My voice is softer than I intend. It's not hesitance or fear coursing through me, but surprise. I don't know why. It's not a new experience, a man showing interest in me. But I guess I always held more confidence in myself than I've had as of late. The idea of someone being interested in me while my life is almost entirely in shambles is crazy. How can someone be interested in this mess?

Gage turns back to me, studying me. It's something I notice he does a lot, watching closely before responding. It's disconcerting in the moment, being observed so closely, but it's also comforting, knowing he's taking the time to really think about what he wants to say. I've learned that Gage is the kind of man who uses his words wisely and with great intent.

"Ava, your life might be a mess—and I have a feeling that's a result of something outside your control—but that doesn't mean you should put your life on hold until it's all neat and clean again. Life is all about the messy moments. It's about how you handle them. I'd just like a front-row seat to see you come out the other side—and maybe help, if you'll let me." He shrugs like he hasn't just offered me a life raft while I'm drowning out at sea.

"Why? You don't even know me."

"You're right. I've only scratched the surface of getting to know you. But I get the impression you haven't let your brother see what I've seen. I don't know why, and I won't push you to tell me, but everyone should have someone in their corner. Even if they aren't quite ready to let someone in."

Walt returns, placing our burgers in front of us. "Can I get you anything else?"

"No, thank you."

Gage gives Walt a small smile. "I'm good. Thanks, Walt."

Walt turns to leave, and Gage focuses his attention back on me. "When I got discharged from the army, it took me about a month to actually come home. My parents knew I was being discharged, but I lied to them about when it was happening. At the time I couldn't tell you why, but in my head I just couldn't deal with other people while I mourned the loss of not only the friends I fought alongside, but also the life I thought I was going to have."

"Gage, I don't—I'm not sure..." I stumble over my words, not sure what to say.

"All I'm trying to say is that I understand the drive to figure it out for yourself, but if I could do that month over again? I would've come home. Leaning on someone doesn't make you weak. We weren't built to go through this life alone. So don't force yourself to."

I swallow and tuck a piece of hair behind my ear. "I'm not working at that law firm anymore. I mean, I'm sure you figured that out with me looking at a part-time job at a bookstore in Ashford Falls when I'm supposedly living and working in Boston, but I was fired from the firm, and I'm not even mad about it," I rush to clarify. "Which is insane, because the reason for it is absolute bullshit, and I should be pissed about it." I exhale slowly, lowering my voice that I couldn't stop from rising the longer I spoke. "But I'm just not." Now it's my turn to shrug.

I fidget with the napkin in front of me, giving myself a second. Saying this out loud is scarier than I thought it would be, even if I've mentioned it to Declan.

"And if I'm being honest, I just don't know if I want to do it anymore. Practice law, I mean. I only got into it because my parents wanted me to—and I was good at it. But I hate the work I've been doing. I feel like a massive sellout, and it's not who I want to be."

Gage doesn't say anything. He just watches me—letting me get it all out.

"Declan knows I was fired, and he knows I'm thinking about doing something else with my life, but I haven't told him why. I think he's guessed that our parents pressured me into law, but I've never outright told him." I tuck another piece of hair behind my ear and glance down at the bar in front of me. "I don't want to disappoint him. He might have gone along with our parents' wishes initially, but he always did his thing on the side. He always went after what he wanted."

I feel the pressure in my nose and know if I keep going, I'm going to cry, which I've done more than enough in front of Gage. "There's more than that, but I'm not ready to talk about the rest yet."

"Ava." His voice is stern but gentle. He doesn't continue until I bring my eyes to his. "You don't have to tell me any of it. But I appreciate your trust in what you just gave me. And if you decide you want to give me more, I'll take it and keep it safe."

Now it's my turn to study him. The look in his eyes—the openness and sincerity—has me pausing. I don't know that I've ever had a man look at me like he's truly invested in me as a human—like he wants to know my inner thoughts and is willing to wait until I'm ready to share them.

"You're a good man, Gage Flynn."

"I have my moments, but you make it easy."

I want to say something, but I don't know what. Not that it matters. Before I can find the words, Gage smiles. "Plus, I know we'd be good together. I see a lot of fun for the two of us." He winks. "Now, eat your burger before it gets cold."

And just like that, the heaviness is lifted. We spend the rest of the night laughing and flirting, leaving when Walt tells us he's closing up for the night. Gage gives me a ride home, and when he asks me on a date, I almost say yes.

CHAPTER
Eleven

AVA

"GET OUT OF HERE, big brother. You've been trying to go on this date for weeks now. Go before something else comes up to make you push it again."

"Yeah, that's not happening." Declan shakes his head but doesn't get up from his seat at the kitchen island. He studies me as I make myself a sandwich for lunch.

"What?"

"We haven't really had time to talk, just the two of us since you got here. I guess I'm just wondering how you're doing."

I hear the concern in his voice, see it on his face, and I understand it. But ever since I let some of it go on Gage the other night, I've felt a little lighter. I know there's still plenty for me to figure out, and I still need to fill Declan in on all of it, but today isn't the day.

Today is Quinn and Declan's first real date, away from town and family, and I won't be the reason there's a cloud over it.

"I promise I'm okay. I'm exactly where I want to be. Honestly, I think I'm exactly where I *need* to be." I smile, and for the first time since I landed in Baltimore, I think it's a genuine smile. It's not the bright, cheery smile I used to give before everything happened with Brian and my parents, but it's a real one. And that feels like a good first step.

"Will you tell me what happened?"

"I will, but not today. Today is for you and Quinn." He opens his mouth to say something, but I don't give him the chance. "Declan, I'm not going to spoil your day by sharing anything that happened. I'm here, away from all of it. I'm safe, I'm not hurt, and there's nothing you can do about it right now. I promise it's okay to put this conversation on hold."

He stands from his seat, making his way around the counter to my side. "I just don't like seeing you in pain, and I can tell that you are."

"And that's why you're the best brother," I say as I pull him into a hug. "But the longer I'm here, the better I feel." I pull back from him, giving him another genuine smile. "I understand why you decided to stay here. There's something magical about this town and the people in it. Like it envelops you in a warm hug, creating a sense of peace and comfort."

"Yeah, there is." His smile is soft—happy and content—and I know he's thinking about Quinn.

"Get out of here." I push him lightly toward the door. "We can talk about everything later, I promise."

"Okay." He presses a quick kiss to my forehead before turning for the door and grabbing his coat from the hook. "I love you and I'll see you later."

"Have fun! Don't do anything I wouldn't do," I tease.

Declan shakes his head, a goofy smile on his face as he shuts the door behind him. A laugh escapes me, making me realize how much lighter I really do feel. I know it's Gage who helped me get here. Whether it's simply telling him that lifted the weight I've been carrying or his understanding nature and kind words that brought a new perspective, I'm glad I can laugh with my brother again.

A FEW HOURS LATER, I'm sitting on the couch continuing my rewatch of *Veronica Mars* when my phone rings. I look down and see an unknown number on the screen with a Boston area code.

And that lightness I found evaporates.

There's a moment when I think about ignoring it. There's a high probability that nothing good can come from answering this call. I've refused to speak with my father since the night they told me about the arranged marriage, and I've ignored every call from my mother since we last spoke. But something pushes me to pick up the phone.

"Hello?"

"I'm surprised you answered. Your parents were under the impression you would ignore my call." A chill races up my spine at the sound of his voice.

I've never spent much time with Brian, and even though we worked at the same firm and he's always been around, he's never sounded the way he does now—cold and unfeeling without an ounce of remorse.

I don't respond. I don't know how. I should hang up but I'm frozen in place, taken back to that night in his office.

"Good, it's better that you don't say anything. I just wanted to explain what's going to happen moving forward. I know what I expect from a wife, and your parents swore this arrangement would meet all my expectations, so this act of rebellion is unacceptable. You can rest assured that you're not who I would have chosen to marry either, but this was set in motion when we were young. You're who my parents picked, and I've sacrificed a lot for this, so we'll both play our part."

There's a clinking that comes through the phone—the sound of liquid being poured over ice. I hear him swallow before he continues.

"I'll give you one more week, and then you'll come home to Boston so we can officially announce our engagement. You'll begin planning the wedding with our mothers, and you *will* act happy about it. You'll move in with me and give up your apartment in Harborview, as there'll be no use for it."

Another drink is poured, another gulp.

"You'll begin your wifely duties immediately to give me an heir. The sooner you have a child, the better. From what your mother tells me, you have no problem whoring yourself, so doing what makes me happy shouldn't be an issue for you." He sighs like I'm boring him. "Truly, I'd rather take on a mistress, but I don't have the time or patience to ensure it's all kept under the table, so unfortunately, we'll have to make do with each other."

I feel the bile rise in the back of my throat, but I still can't speak.

I don't know what the hell my mother has been saying or what she could possibly know. I've never been shy about my sex life, but it's not something I blatantly flaunt, especially in front of my family. I've had multiple partners, but nothing out of the norm for someone my age. And I've always been discreet about my relationships. But what Brian is implying? That I've somehow been overt in my sexual preferences is so far from the truth I don't know what to say.

"If you don't come home within the week, know that every additional day that passes is a further step back your pleasure will take. You have a responsibility to your family and me. It's high time you saw to that responsibility."

One more pour. One more swallow.

"One week, babydoll." And then it's silent.

It takes me a second to realize he's hung up and even longer for me to finally pull the phone away from my ear. When I do, I notice I'm shaking.

I'm shocked and terrified. I know that. I feel that in my

bones. But unlike that night in his office, I feel this anger rising inside me.

I've met aggressive men before, ones who don't know how to take no for an answer, but none have treated me the way Brian has. Like I'm an object he has the right to take possession of.

I've seen egotistical men in the courtroom—defended their wives in custody battles—and even then, I still haven't heard one of them speak to their ex-wives the way Brian just spoke to me. Like I'm less than the dirt on the sole of his shoe.

The anger in me grows, overshadowing the fear and shock—and the shame I hate to admit exists. I've never let a man have this kind of power over me, and there is no way in hell I'm going to let this asshole change that. I won't let his repulsive actions alter how I live my life. I won't let what happened in his office make me feel any differently about myself and the decisions I've made up to this point.

I've let him bring me down for the last five weeks, and I'm not having it anymore.

I stand from the couch, the blanket on my lap falling to the floor without notice, and look around the living room. I want to take my life back into my hands starting now.

Looking at the clock on the mantel, I see it's just after eight in the evening.

What do I want to do? How can I take back my power? What's something I've wanted to do since getting to Ashford Falls that I've talked myself out of?

And then it hits me: I wanted to say yes to that date with Gage, but I held back because I feared Brian was right—that I was just a nice piece of ass, good for a quick lay and nothing else, nothing meaningful.

I move to the front door, stepping out onto the porch, trying to decide where I'm most likely to find Gage at this time of night. It's Saturday evening. For all I know, he's on a date with someone else.

I don't think he's the kind of man to pursue multiple women simultaneously. He may not be one for committed relationships, but I don't see him sleeping with multiple women. But that also doesn't mean he's waiting around for me. He may ask me out whenever we see each other, but what's to say he didn't take the last rejection to heart?

I walk down the porch stairs to the sidewalk, looking up and down the street. Gage said Declan's house was only a few houses down from his. If he's home, maybe I'll see his Jeep in his driveway.

This might be the most spontaneous thing I've done in years, but the further from Declan's house I get, the more right it feels. I need to find Gage. I can't wait until the next time I randomly run into him around town.

I turn right and head up the street, away from town. I don't know for sure but I think Gage's house is this way. I've never seen him turn around after he's dropped me off. He's always just continued up the street.

I only walk a few minutes before I see his Jeep parked in the driveway of a house across the street. Without paying attention, I cross and march up to his front door, knocking without hesitation. As I wait for him to answer the door what I'm doing starts to sink in.

Maybe this wasn't the most brilliant idea. I left my phone at Declan's. I didn't lock up the house behind me. And just as the door opens, I realize I'm not wearing shoes.

"Ava?" Gage opens the door, confusion clear on his face. His gaze travels down my body, quickly catching on to the thing I just noticed. "Ava, where are your shoes?" He grabs my arm, pulling me inside and out of the chilly fall air. "What's wrong? Did something happen?" He closes the door behind me and places both his hands on my arms, his gaze moving all over my body as if he's looking for injuries.

When his gaze comes back up to mine, I don't think. I just move. I reach forward, gripping the front of his shirt in both my hands, moving to the tips of my toes and press my lips against his. I know I've surprised Gage, but to his credit, it only takes him a moment to respond. His grip on my arms tightening. His lips pressing against mine with the same intensity.

There's an urgency to this kiss, a need that's difficult to ignore. I knew the chemistry between us was there long before now. I felt it that first day in the courthouse but ignored it like it was my job.

Casual relationships and one-night stands aren't new to me. They're not something I do often, but I've enjoyed a fling once or twice. The only rule I've set for myself is to never explore something sexual with someone I might encounter on a regular basis. Starting something with someone you'll see outside the bedroom is just asking for trouble.

But maybe one night with Gage is fine. We can scratch this itch, acknowledge the chemistry, and move on like nothing happened.

Like a bucket of ice is thrown on him, Gage's entire body goes tight. His lips stop responding to mine, and he pulls back, my arms still held in his hands.

"Ava, what are you doing?" He's not mad; I can see that clear as day in his eyes. It's concern that laces his voice—that's etched into every inch of his face.

"Make me forget." I know I'm begging, but I need this. In my soul, I know I need this. I need Gage's goodness, his empathy, his understanding.

I know Gage will take care of me.

His eyes bounce between mine, studying me, looking for the truth. "Ava."

I stop him before he can say anything else, my grip on his

shirt tightening even more. "This is me asking for that strength you offered. I can't do it anymore and I need help." I press my body against his, not an inch of space between us. "Make me forget," I whisper.

"Are you sure?" His voice is just as soft as mine. His grip on my arms loosens, but only so his can move around me, holding me close.

"I've never been more sure." And as the words leave my mouth, I realize how true they are.

I want this.

CHAPTER
Twelve

GAGE

I'D BEEN HOME from my shift at the station for about an hour when I heard the knock on my door. I honestly thought it was one of my siblings when I went to answer it. I never would have expected Ava to be on the other side. To find her standing there with her hair in a bun, glasses on her face, and in a pair of leggings, a sweatshirt, and no shoes was even more of a shock. When I finally registered that she was actually here, the look in her eyes was like a punch to the gut.

That first day in the courthouse I thought the look in her eyes was empty, but I see it for what it is now—devastation. And knowing her better, I know whatever caused it isn't something small. Ava Day is far too strong to let something small bring her down, and for her to reach out for help means this is something far greater than I imagined.

"This is me asking for that strength you offered. I can't do it anymore and I need help." Ava presses herself closer to me. "Make me forget." It's a plea, desperation clear in her voice and eyes.

"Are you sure?" I ask, my arms moving around her waist, holding her close.

"I've never been more sure."

I see the conviction in her eyes, but I need more than that. There's no doubt I want this, that I crave this. But I won't take advantage of her. I can't do this if she's going to regret it in the morning. I'd never forgive myself.

"We should talk about this."

"I don't want to talk about it." She leans forward, trying to kiss me again, and while I want to kiss her more than my next breath, I won't allow it.

"You don't have to tell me everything, but you have to give me more than this." I feel her body stiffen in my arms, and her grip on my shirt disappears. "Ava." My hold tightens, not giving her room to back away from me. "You're too important for me not to worry about the future. I'm not saying no. I'm saying talk to me. Tell me how we got here after so many nos."

She looks at me, disbelief clear across her face, and now I'm trying to figure out why she's so shocked that I care about how she went from saying "no" to saying "yes." Has she ever had a man concern himself with her wants and needs?

"Forget it." She tries to push away from me, but I won't let her.

"No, I don't want to forget it." She won't meet my eyes so I can't read what's going through her mind right now. "Just tell me this is about you and me, and not someone else." My voice is soft. I want to know so much more than that, but I know she's not ready to give all of it to me.

"This is all about me and no one else." She says it with such certainty it's hard not to believe her, but something in her eye tells me it's not the complete truth. "Yes, there are other factors, but this? Wanting you? That is all for me." Her hands come back to my pecs, resting there. "I'm not afraid of going after what I want. I may have forgotten that for a bit, but I know who I am. Help me forget about the rest of it. Please."

I'm not built to "*forget about the rest,*" but the please on her lips does me in. I see it in her eyes, the truth in what she's saying. Ava isn't a woman who shies away from what she wants, and watching her take that back is a privilege.

I pull her in, bending so my lips brush hers as I say, "Okay."

Our lips barely touch before she's pulling back. "Just one night. I still don't know where I'll be after the new year, and I'm not willing to start something with an end date. Especially with someone I'll see when I visit my brother."

I lift a brow and smirk. "You think one night will be enough?"

"We'll have to make it enough." She rises to her toes, brushing her lips over my cheek on a path to my ear. "Think you can make it worth my while?" Her voice is husky in my ear, causing a shiver to run up my spine.

"Oh, Rebel." I chuckle, my voice dropping an octave. "What a silly question."

I know one night with Ava Day won't be nearly enough to stifle the burning desire I feel between us, but I know I won't be able to convince her of that right now. And I sure as hell know I'm not ready to risk this one moment if it's all I'll get with her. I'll go along with her plan—for now—but this won't stop me from pursuing her beyond tonight. I won't give up easily on more time with Ava.

I contemplate being gentle for only a moment—Ava wouldn't want me to treat her like a piece of glass. Bending slightly, I place my hands on the backs of her thighs and lift her, pressing her back into the closed front door. She releases a small gasp, and I take full advantage, claiming her mouth in a heated kiss—a kiss I want her to feel in the morning.

Her legs wind around my waist, squeezing. Her arms move around my shoulders, holding me to her. And her kiss is just as greedy as mine.

My hips push into her, keeping her pinned against the

door as my hands travel up the sides of her body under her sweatshirt. The feel of her skin, soft and smooth, is in direct contrast to the roughness of my palms. My hands continue a path up, ghosting the sides of her breasts, finding she's not wearing a bra. I groan as my fingers slide over her pebbled nipples, pinching slightly.

"Gage," she moans against my lips, rolling her hips in search of the friction we both need. "I need you inside me."

My hips jerk unconsciously. A woman unafraid to ask for exactly what she wants is my undoing.

I lean back just enough to tear her sweatshirt over her head, letting it fall to the floor next to us. My gaze zeros in on her rosy nipples, and I can't hold myself back from taking one into my mouth, sucking hard.

"Gage." She tugs at my hair, pulling me away from her chest. "Please." Her hands fumble as she reaches between us, tugging at my shirt.

I bring my lips back to hers in a bruising kiss as I unwind her legs from around me and put her down to remove her pants and underwear in one swift move. On my way back up her body, I pause at the apex of her thighs. I want so badly to give this part of her all the attention it deserves, but I need to be inside her just as badly as she needs me.

I give myself a few moments, spreading her open and swiping my tongue over her wet center. Her hips rock forward, her hands diving back into my hair, and a whimper falls from her lips. The sound makes me groan, the vibrations traveling through her body as I slip a finger inside, pumping once, then twice, before adding a second.

A growl leaves her throat as she tugs at my hair again, pulling me away from her. "I'm not going to ask again."

I stand quickly, unbuttoning my pants and sliding the zipper down before reaching for my wallet lying on the table next to the door for the condom I keep there.

"I'm going to let you have all the control this time, but next time we're doing this my way," I tell her as I push my pants and boxers down just enough to release my aching cock.

I only get the condom out of the package before Ava takes control, sliding it over my length. "I thought we already established there won't be a next time?"

I lift her by the back of her thighs, pressing her back into the door, lining her center up with my hard length. "We said one night. I plan on doing this a few times tonight." And then I'm thrusting into her tight heat, groaning at the feel of her against me.

Ava's head falls back, bouncing against the door as I sink into her, her walls tightening around the intrusion. I give her only a moment to adjust, bringing my hand up to her neck and applying the barest hint of pressure. I don't want to scare Ava, but when she moans and I see the heat in her eyes as she brings them back to mine, I squeeze just a bit more, dropping my lips to hers in a frantic kiss.

I can't get enough, and based on the sounds coming from Ava, neither can she. I grind my hips into her, sinking further into her heat, our kiss sloppy. Ava's legs squeeze around my hips, her bare heels digging into my back as I thrust into her, her hips rocking in time with mine, our rhythm both in sync and wild.

My hand around her neck moves down her body, pausing briefly to pinch a nipple before reaching between us to find her clit.

As I draw small circles over her needy nub, her head falls back again, releasing my name on a long moan. "Gage. Don't stop." Almost immediately, she angles her head, bringing her eyes back to mine, and I see it: her untethered need for me.

"Does that feel good? Does your pussy like the feel of my cock buried inside you?" I press my thumb harder against her clit, and her walls clench around me as I drive my hips faster against her.

"God, yes. So fucking good." Her back arches off the door, and with one more hard swipe at her clit, her pussy squeezes in a tight grip around my cock, causing a chain reaction. Her thighs shake as she comes, and I follow right behind, pumping a few times as we ride out the waves of our orgasms together.

I fall against her, my head on her shoulder as we both catch our breath.

"We are definitely doing that again," Ava mumbles as she brushes her lips against my neck where it meets my shoulder. I nod against her, unable to form the actual words.

Her arms roam my back for a moment before she speaks again. "How the fuck am I completely naked while you're still wearing all your clothes?"

I chuckle as I slide out of her, gently removing her limbs from around me and making sure she's stable on her feet before ripping my shirt over my head. My pants and boxers quickly join them on the floor before I remove the condom, tying it off and letting it fall to the floor as well, a smirk on my face the entire time.

"Someone said they needed my cock inside them and complained I was taking too long." I surge forward, lifting Ava again and nipping at her lips. "I couldn't disappoint."

Ava wraps her legs around my waist, her arms going back around my neck as she rolls her hips, pressing her clit against my lower abdomen. "Well, I think it's safe to say you definitely didn't disappoint."

"Good." I turn, striding up the stairs to my bedroom, and gently tossing her on the bed. "But now it's my turn to take control."

Ava tries to scoot up the bed, but I grab her ankle, pulling her toward me. Her ass perches on the edge of the bed as I sink to my knees before her. I place her feet on my shoulders and cup her ass in my hands, angling her hips for better access.

"I need a real taste of this pussy. Then I'm going to fuck you until the only thing coming out of your bossy mouth is my name."

I see the shiver that runs up her body at my words, and the heat in her eyes has my dick growing hard far quicker than it should after the way I just came. But I'm right—one night with Ava is never going to be enough.

CHAPTER *Thirteen*

AVA

I FALL FORWARD, collapsing against Gage's chest, struggling to catch my breath. The man has unparalleled stamina, and although strong and uninhibited in bed, he's also unselfish—making sure I always finish first.

As I lie here on top of him, I don't regret showing up at Gage's door and asking him to help me forget, but I do regret telling him it was just for one night. One night will never be enough. Sex with Gage Flynn has ruined me.

But it doesn't matter how life-altering it felt—it can't be more than one night.

I haven't lied to him when I say my life is a mess. Gage is a good man and the sex is out of this world—making for a very dangerous combination. A girl could get used to leaning on a man like him. But I can't ask anyone to stand by my side while I deal with my parents and Brian.

Gage's arms tighten around me for just a moment, his heart beating rapidly against my ear. "I haven't done my job very well if you're thinking that hard right now." His voice rumbles through his chest.

"Au contraire, my friend. You've done your job very well."

I smile against him. I give myself another minute to catch my breath before pushing myself up, my thighs still straddling his hips, his softening cock pressed between us. "I'm going to be sore tomorrow. In all the best places." I lean forward, pressing a kiss to his lips.

Gage takes control quickly, rolling us so I'm under him. Something else I've learned during this sex marathon—giving up control to Gage Flynn is something I should've done the second he pulled me into his house. This man knows exactly what he's doing, and I've benefited from that multiple times this evening.

"Oh, Rebel. Friends is definitely not the right word for us."

"Hmm, probably not, but it will have to do for now."

I glance at the clock on his dresser. It's late, or I guess, technically, it's early—really early.

After Gage brought me to his room and made good on his promise of fucking me until I forgot everything but his name, we took a quick break to grab a snack from his kitchen. Where Gage bent me over the counter and made sure the only thing I would remember was the way he felt inside me.

Back in his room he pretended to give me back control by letting me ride him—only for him to remind me how good it feels to relinquish my control.

Four times in one night is a new record for me, and the amount of orgasms will likely go down as the most I'll ever have in one night.

Gage Flynn is very much a generous lover.

While I want to stay here and continue this night, the timer has run out. It's time to return to the real world and get home.

If Declan came home last night, I'm sure he's wondering where I am. Though, knowing him, if he came home to find the living room the way I left it—like I'd only run out for a minute—he would have called the police when I didn't come home. The fact that it's been silent likely means Declan didn't make it home—something I refuse to think about more.

"I should get home. I don't want Declan to worry."

"Hmm," Gage hums, his eyes bouncing around my face. He must find whatever he's looking for because he leans down, pressing a quick kiss to my lips before pushing himself up and rolling off the bed. "Let's grab a quick shower and then I'll drive you home."

"You don't have to drive me. It's just down the street." I watch Gage walk around his room, not a care in the world about his nakedness. And I have to admit, I don't blame him. The man is built like a Greek God—tall and lean, muscles rippling. Seriously drool-worthy.

He smirks over his shoulder at me still lying on the bed, the sheet pulled up to cover my chest. "Did you forget you weren't wearing shoes when you showed up at my door?"

"Right." I sit up, bringing my knees to my chest as I watch him move around, taking care of the condom and grabbing clean clothes from his dresser before throwing them on the foot of the bed. "Okay, a ride home would be much appreciated."

Gage stalks over to me, grabbing my arm and pulling me to the side of the bed. He leans over, placing his balled fists on the outsides of my legs, caging me in. "Let's maybe try to avoid walking in the cold December air without shoes again, all right?" There's a slight smile on his face, but I see the concern in his eyes. I know he wants to ask about what had me showing up at his door in that state. But I also know he won't press.

I push at his chest, giving myself room to stand from the bed, the sheet dropping from around me. "Well, that won't be an issue. This was a one-time thing, remember?"

"Mm-hmm," he hums, his gaze moving down my body, not an ounce of shame as he blatantly takes his fill. "One night," he says as his eyes land back on mine. He smirks again before bending and throwing me over his shoulder, slapping my ass. "Since you haven't left, it's still only one night if we have one more round in the shower."

"Gage!" I shout in surprise but laugh when he jogs to the bathroom, placing me on the counter as he moves to turn on the shower. "How do you still have the energy?" I mumble against his lips when he's back in front of me, standing between my legs.

He shrugs, his lips moving over my jaw and down my neck, nibbling at my skin along the way. "You've bewitched me. I can't seem to get enough."

Gage doesn't give me time to respond before lifting me and stepping into the shower, making me forget everything but his name yet again.

———

LUCKILY FOR ME, Declan didn't make it home last night. So when Gage pulls up in front of Declan's house, I turn and thank him. It's not just for the sex—though, that was amazing and something I won't be forgetting any time soon. No, I'm thanking him for helping me find myself again. For helping me take back the power I gave my parents and temporarily lost after the incident with Brian. Not that I explain any of that to him.

Gage laughs, leaning over the center console, kisses my lips and whispers, "Any time."

I smile at him before getting out and running up the front walk to Declan's house. Only turning around when I'm inside, giving Gage a quick wave when I see him watching me.

I close the door, fall against it, and smile—something I haven't done much of lately. Catching the time from the clock on the mantel, I shake myself from my thoughts and move to the couch where I left my mess from the night before.

It's only seven o'clock. I have a few hours before I'm supposed to be at Scott's for the weekly family breakfast. But with Declan not coming home and me not having a car in town, I quickly decide to text Emily to see if she and Caleb can pick me up on their way.

I could walk—Scott only lives a few blocks away—but it's cold outside and I don't really feel like freezing, not after my adventure last night.

> Hey! Do you think you and Caleb could pick me up on your way to Scott's?

I don't have to wait long for her response.

EMILY

Of course.

Where's Declan?

> ...he didn't make it home from his date with Quinn last night 😊

EMILY

Good for them!

But I won't be telling Caleb that 😄

I'm making breakfast at Scott's this morning, so we'll pick you up at 8.

> Sounds good. Thank you!

I giggle at the thought of Emily trying to explain why Declan isn't home to take me to Scott's as I head to my room to get myself ready for the day.

I tried to keep my hair from getting wet in the shower with Gage, but that plan went out the window pretty quickly. Gage has a way of making me forget all my plans.

I head to the bathroom in the hall across from my room, planning on quickly styling my hair, but get distracted by my reflection in the mirror—something I've been avoiding for weeks now.

In truth, I haven't recognized the person looking back at me since long before everything happened with Brian. But it's gotten much worse since being in Ashford Falls. Looking in the mirror now, I think I'm starting to see the real me again, and I'm not sure I'm ready to think about why I'm seeing that change *now*.

I shake myself from my thoughts and focus on getting ready. I switch my glasses for my contacts, quickly add a little product to my naturally wavy hair to stop the frizzing, and head to my room to switch out my leggings and sweatshirt for a pair of jeans and an oversized sweater. Comfy and cozy. Exactly how I always feel when spending time in the Marks' household.

I'm just coming down the stairs when there's a knock on the door, and I find Emily and Caleb standing on the other side.

"You could have just texted you were here. You didn't need to come up to the door."

"I thought the cool air might do Caleb some good." Emily chuckles.

I look at Caleb and notice the grimace on his face. While Emily might not have told him exactly why they were picking me up, I have no doubt he was able to figure it out for himself. I can't help but laugh along with Emily at his expense.

"Let me grab my phone and bag and we can go." I turn from them, leaving the door open while I grab my things before locking up and heading down the walk to their car.

Caleb looks at both of us once I get in. "Don't say a word," he grumbles as we pull away from the house, Emily and I laughing the entire time.

As we're walking up the driveway to the front door a few

minutes later, I link my arm with Emily's. "How are you feeling? I forgot to ask when you got to the house."

A big smile breaks out across Emily's face, her hand falling to her still relatively flat stomach. Last week at Thanksgiving dinner, Caleb and Emily shared the good news that they're expecting a baby in May. We spent the entire day so incredibly happy for them. But I know in the back of everyone's mind was the question of whether Scott would be around to meet the new addition to the family.

"I'm good. Really good." Emily looks over her shoulder, sharing a smile with Caleb whose scowl quickly disappears at the mention of their growing baby.

"I'm so happy for you both." My eyes bounce between the two of them. Seeing the smiles on their faces and the gleam in their eyes sparks a small prick of jealousy in my chest. I really am happy for them, but the look they share makes me realize how much I want that and question if I'll ever be able to find it.

I don't let myself think about it more and shift my focus to a smiling Max running out to greet us.

It's a mess of chaos for a few minutes as Max says a quick hello before dragging Caleb away to show him something in his room. Scott stands in the doorway to the kitchen, laughing softly at the look on my face.

"You get used to it." Emily chuckles as she pauses to press a quick kiss to Scott's cheek before continuing into the kitchen to start making breakfast.

"Do you want any help?" I ask as I stop next to Scott to do the same. He throws an arm over my shoulder, pulling me into a side hug, squeezing tight.

"No, I'm good for now. You can help set the table later, though."

"Come on, Shortcake. Sit with me for a bit." Scott guides me to the study at the front of the house—his favorite room.

We sit on the couch, each in a corner, angling our bodies to face each other, but neither of us says anything right away.

"I haven't really had a chance to talk to you one-on-one since you got here. I'm sorry for that," Scott says after a moment.

"There's been a lot going on."

"Maybe so, but that's not an excuse." Scott's eyes move over my face, studying me. "You know you can talk to me, right?"

"Of course." I smile at him. It's so incredibly fake, and we both know it.

"Ava." Scott doesn't have to say anything else.

I look down at the couch, tears pricking the corners of my eyes. If there's one person besides my brother I want to talk to, it's Scott. But talking to this amazing father about my parents' shortcomings feels ridiculous. I'm embarrassed by it, even though I know Scott wouldn't judge me for any of it.

He scoots closer to me, taking my hand in his. "If you're not ready to tell me or your brother, then just tell me I don't need to worry about you." He squeezes my hand, waiting for me to look at him. "You may not be mine by blood, but I love you as if you were and it breaks my heart seeing you hurt."

I hiccup, trying to keep the sob in, and while I succeed in that, the tears still fall down my cheeks.

Scott pulls me into a hug, holding me close. He doesn't say anything. He just holds me as I let the tears fall, soaking his shirt.

After a few moments—when the tears have finally stopped —I pull away, wiping my cheeks dry. "I'm not ready to talk about all of it. But it has to do with my parents and something that happened at work before I was fired." I shrug. "I haven't fought it, and I don't plan to, but I definitely could."

My mind is racing, and I know I'm not making sense. I take

a minute to gather my thoughts. When I look back at Scott I see the concern etched across his face.

"I've realized that I let my parents dictate my entire life, and I don't know who I am or what I want out of life. I mean, it's more than that, but that's where my brain and heart are currently focusing." Even sharing that little bit feels like another weight is lifted off my shoulders, and I can breathe a little easier.

"It's okay to be a little lost. We all get lost sometimes. All that really matters is how you go about finding your way again. Don't let other people's opinions on how they think you should live your life dictate what you do. I know that's easier said than done, but the people who really love you and care for you will support you in all your endeavors." Scott grips my hand, squeezing tightly. "Do what makes you happy. And if you don't know what that is right now, don't be afraid to try new things."

"I'm thinking about applying for the part-time job at the bookstore," I blurt.

Scott doesn't even hesitate. "Do it. If it's something you want and are interested in, then do it."

"It feels crazy to go from being a lawyer to working at a bookstore."

"So what? People have done much crazier things. This is your life. You have to be happy living it."

I fall into Scott, hugging him tightly. "Thank you."

"Anytime, Shortcake. Anytime."

CHAPTER *Fourteen*

GAGE

AN HOUR after dropping Ava off, I pull up in front of my dad's house to pick up Leo with a smile still on my face. I feel it in the ache of my cheeks, and yet, I'm not trying to stop it either.

Those ten hours with Ava were better than I ever imagined they could be. And boy had I imagined it—far more often than is probably appropriate.

I was intrigued by her that first day we met in the courthouse, and my interest has only increased with each additional encounter, but after last night—and this morning—I'm determined to help her break down some of those walls she's put up.

I have a feeling something significant happened before she came to Ashford Falls, and whatever it was broke her trust in people.

Ava doesn't seem like a woman who feels the same way I do about love, and from the little I know about her, I know she deserves to find someone who will love her with their whole heart. I might not be one for committed relationship, but that doesn't mean Ava agrees with me, or that she should miss out.

She's beautiful, inside and out. She's witty and quirky and

loyal and empathetic. She may have gotten knocked down by something, but she isn't afraid to go after what she wants. If given the chance, I know she'll be someone's biggest supporter and advocate.

There is someone out there who deserves her beauty and grace in their life. It would be a shame to see her give up on that because of whatever happened in Boston. She can get past that. The fact that she showed up on my front porch proves she can.

I'm pulled from my thoughts by the passenger door opening and my brother Asher climbing into the front seat. "Hey! I thought you were at school?" I say, shocked to see Asher instead of Leo.

Asher's in his second year at the University of Maryland College Park on a lacrosse scholarship. While the school isn't too far from Ashford Falls, he's normally too busy to come home all that often during the semester.

"I had a rare weekend open. Thought I would come home for a visit while I could."

"Why didn't you call when you knew you were coming home? I would have made time to hang out."

Asher smiles at me. It's a smile that tells me I'm being ridiculous. "I knew you would be here today for your normal hike with Leo. I figured I could just tag along."

Before I can say anything, the back door of the Jeep opens. "You suck," Leo says, glaring at Asher.

"Not my fault you weren't ready to go when I walked out the door." Asher laughs, turning in his seat to look at Leo.

"How is it fair that you get to sit up front when you're the one crashing my day with Gage?"

"You go on hikes with him regularly. I rarely get to spend time with him these days."

"It's not my fault you decided to go to college." Leo shrugs.

"All right. Come on." I know they're both giving each

other a hard time, but if I let it go on long enough, it'll turn into a real argument. While there's a thirteen-year age gap between Asher and me—often making me feel more like an uncle than a brother—there's only a three-year age gap between Asher and Leo. And even though they have different moms and spent half their time with them, Dad worked it out so he got all three of us at the same time, making sure we stayed close.

I shift in my seat so I can look at both of my brothers. Even though we're half-siblings, there's still a lot of similarities between the three of us.

At twenty, Asher is starting to look more like a grown adult every day. He's started letting the light stubble grow into a full beard—something he'll likely shave once the lacrosse season starts. Same with his darker brown hair that he's let grow into more of a shaggy look. His eyes are where we differ the most, though. Asher inherited our father's hazel eyes. Same with Leo, making them look less like half-brothers.

Leo turned seventeen a few months ago and is only recently starting to lose that baby-face look we always tease him about. And if I'm being honest, I'm not sure he'll ever look his age. Where Asher and I both started growing facial hair early, Leo only recently needed to start shaving on a regular basis. Though, I'm sure if he styled his dirty blond hair shorter all around, he would look a little closer to his age.

Leo falls back into his seat, buckling himself in. "Well, what are we waiting for?"

I chuckle as I turn in my seat, putting the Jeep in drive and heading back down the driveway and out of town toward Oaks Peak Trail.

It's not a hard trail—about six miles—but it's one of my favorites. It's got a great rest stop with beautiful views of mountains in the distance about halfway through. It's a trail Leo and I often find ourselves hiking on these shorter day trips.

"How's the semester going?" I ask Asher.

Asher turns to look out the passenger window, but I catch a glimpse of a smirk before his face is completely out of my view. "It's fine. Nothing all that interesting."

"What was that smirk?"

"What smirk?" He turns back to look at me, his face now totally void of any emotion—an indication he's hiding something.

I narrow my eyes and glance at him quickly before focusing back on the road in front of me. "You know what smirk I'm talking about. What's going on?"

Leo leans forward between the two front seats. "Come on, Ash. You know you can't hide anything from our deputy brother."

"Jerk," Asher grumbles, pushing Leo's face away from us and making Leo laugh.

I chuckle at their antics. "All right, now you've gotta tell me. What's going on?"

"Nothing." Asher turns back to the passenger window.

"He met a girl."

"Shut up." Asher glares at Leo.

"Oh yeah?" I ask, a smirk forming on my lips now.

"No, it's nothing," Asher mumbles.

The smile falls. Now I'm a little concerned. "Why is it a secret?"

"It's not, because it's nothing." Asher points another glare at Leo, clearly trying to communicate that he should keep his mouth shut.

It's quiet in the Jeep for a minute before Leo breaks the silence. "I only know because I caught him with a goofy grin on his face after dinner last night. But, apparently, it's pretty serious, and he's afraid you'll think he's stupid for falling in love with her, especially at his age."

"Leo!" Asher shouts, reaching for Leo between the seats.

"Whoa! Come on!" I grab one of Asher's arms. "What's

Leo talking about?" Asher falls back in his seat, his arms crossed over his chest, but he doesn't say anything. I catch Leo's eye in the rearview mirror and see him shrug slightly. "Ash. Talk to me. Why do you think I'd judge you over a girl?"

Asher shifts in his seat, and when I glance at him quickly I see the contemplative look in his eye. I don't say anything, giving him space, hoping he'll talk to me.

"You think relationships are stupid," he finally says. His tone implies that I should already know the answer. "You always make comments about Dad and his relationships. And about how stressful relationships are and how you have to give up parts of yourself to be in them."

"Ash—" I try to interrupt.

"No, Gage. You know it's the truth. You hate relationships, and that's fine for you, but I just don't want to hear the negatives about them. I really like Hannah. She's pretty, smart, and she supports me."

I glance in the rearview mirror, looking at Leo. I can see the pity on his face, and I quickly realize the pity is for me, not Asher.

"Ash." I sigh. "I'm sorry for ever making you feel like you couldn't talk to me about your relationships." I glance at him quickly, making sure he's hearing me. "You're right that I don't see them for me, and I do think Dad needs to take a break from them. But that's because I've never seen Dad *not* be in a relationship, and I think he could learn a lot about himself if he just took the time to be alone. Which I think would help him find someone who would last." I take a second to gather my thoughts before I continue down that train of thought—I have a lot of thoughts about our dad and how he handles relationships. But that is because of who Dad is and not my feelings on relationships—or at least that's what I've always thought.

"I don't think what works for me is right for everyone else. I know there are examples of good, healthy relationships out there. And you are definitely at an age where you should be exploring that." I glance at him. "You and I might be similar in a lot of ways, but I never for a second thought you would be like me when it comes to love. You've got too big of a heart not to find someone to share it with." I look in the rearview mirror at Leo. "The same goes for you."

Looking back at the road, I take another minute. I don't like that I've let my jaded views on love impact my relationship with my brothers and their willingness to talk to me.

"I never want either of you to feel like you can't talk to me about something. Regardless of what my views on the subject are, I'm always going to listen and support you."

It's quiet in the Jeep, and while I know there's so much more I can say, I leave it there. I don't want to influence their thoughts on the subject any more than I already have. I'm disappointed in myself for the stress I've already caused, and I refuse to cause more.

I feel more than see Leo lean forward between the front seats again. I'm prepared for there to be more conversation about Asher and his girlfriend, but I know better. Leo is far more like me when it comes to serious conversations than I would like to admit. We don't like them and will always find a way to change the subject.

"I heard a rumor you might be seeing that lawyer helping the Marks family."

My head whips to Leo's so quickly I'm surprised I don't drive the car off the road. "What?"

Leo smirks. "Yeah, something about the two of you getting awfully close at Murphy's?"

I look back at the road, having kept my eye on Leo for far too long. "I don't know what you're talking about."

Great, now I sound like Asher.

"Tell me more," Asher says, turning to look at Leo with a

completely different kind of smirk this time, the tension slowly leaving his body.

I want to be upset about the rumors and the fact that Leo has heard about them, but I can't. I'm all for lightening the heavy mood, and I like the feeling of Ava being linked to me around town. I'm almost giddy at the idea of it.

"Yeah. She's Mr. Day's sister, and she's hot. Like, crazy hot."

"Be nice," I tell him. Even though I agree with him, Ava is hot—and so much more.

"What? How is calling her hot not nice?"

"He means there's more to a woman than her hot factor," Asher says.

I nod. "Right. Just like you don't want to be judged solely on your looks, neither do women."

"I totally want to be judged on my looks. I *am* hot." Leo falls back into his seat, a cocky grin on his face.

Asher and I both laugh, catching each other's eyes. I love that my brother is so confident in himself. I know I felt the same way when I was his age. I even felt that way through my entire military career if I'm being honest with myself.

It wasn't until I got home after my discharge that my ego started to return to normal—and I remembered the importance of humility. I know I've got some good qualities about myself, but I also know there are plenty of things I can work on as well. The second we stop striving to be better is the moment we fail ourselves.

"So, you're seeing this lawyer?" Asher asks.

"No, I'm not seeing her. Though, I have had a couple of meals with her at Murphy's. Like Leo said, she's in town helping Scott Marks with a custody case. I'm just being neighborly."

"Yeah, all right."

I know by his tone he doesn't believe me. And honestly? I don't blame him. I wouldn't believe me either.

It's been a really long time since one night wasn't enough for me. Since I've even been *kind of* interested in knowing more about a woman. And while I've always wanted to fix the world's injustices, I've never been so invested in an individual person's problems the way I am with Ava.

I want to help her regain whatever she lost back in Boston. I want to leave her feeling better than when I met her.

"Dad says she's nice," I hear Leo say, pulling me from my thoughts.

"Dad's met her?" Asher asks, shocked, glancing between Leo and me.

"Yeah. He even had dinner with her."

"Okay, let's calm down here." I force a chuckle at the mischief I see in Leo's eyes. "I had plans to grab dinner with Dad at Murphy's, and while waiting for him, I happened to strike up a conversation with Ava. Dad walked in while we were talking and invited her to join us. That's all it was."

"Oh, he definitely likes her if he's getting defensive." Asher laughs.

"I'm not defensive," I mumble, causing both of them to laugh.

The conversation moves on to something else, but I'm not paying attention. I know I like Ava; I haven't denied that. But is it more than that? Asher's right. I've never felt the need to correct anyone's assumptions in the past, so why do I care what my brothers think now?

Not wanting to spend my day with Asher and Leo worrying about this, I decide that my feelings have to do with the conversation about Asher and his girlfriend. It's the only explanation I'm comfortable with. Because anything else goes against everything I've always claimed to want for my future— and my future has already been altered enough.

CHAPTER
Fifteen

AVA

I SET my alarm Sunday night for the morning even though I doubt I'll need it. I'm still not sleeping well after everything that happened, but I don't want to risk it.

That conversation with Brian might have given me a little push toward Gage, and that night with Gage might have made me feel like I had a little more control of my life, but it was the conversation with Scott that really got my butt in gear.

If I really want to take back all the power and control I inadvertently gave my parents, I need to get back into a routine. And I have to figure out what I want to do with my life, completely separate from the one they planned for me.

My first step is stopping by Falls Book Haven as soon as they open this morning to officially apply for the job.

Step two is to contact the landlord of my Boston apartment to give my notice. I still have six months on my lease, but I'll use my trust fund to pay the fees if I have to. I'll have to tell my parents at some point, but I'm giving myself a little bit more time on that front.

I may not know what I want to do or where I want to live,

but I know with 100 percent certainty that I don't want to live in Boston or Harborview.

Step three is finding a place to live here in Ashford Falls. I don't know if this is where I'll stay, but being close to my brother feels like a good call. At least for now.

I want to try new things to help me figure out what I actually like because I honestly don't know anymore. I didn't have much free time back in Massachusetts, but the little time I did have was taken over by my parents, and I'm done living my life that way.

I'm up and moving around before my alarm goes off, exactly like I thought I would be. But instead of lying in bed until I hear Declan leave for work, I'm already dressed and making coffee when he comes down the stairs.

"Hey! You're up early?" he questions when he sees me.

"Yeah, I've wallowed long enough. It's time to get back into a routine." I place a mug filled with coffee on the island counter for him.

His eyebrows draw in as he steps up to the opposite side of the counter and picks up the mug. "You're leaving before the hearing next week?"

I received notice late Friday afternoon they scheduled the hearing for Scott's custody case on the twentieth, the last day courts are open before the holiday break.

"No. I'm actually planning on staying indefinitely. If that's okay with you, that is." I stand across from him, my own cup of coffee cradled in my hands.

"Ava, you're more than welcome here as long as you want. Selfishly, I would love it if you were here permanently." He studies me for a minute before continuing. "I just want it to be because it's what you really want and not because you're running from something."

I take a deep breath, preparing to give Declan a little more of the truth. "It's probably a little bit of both." I shrug. "But I haven't been happy in Boston for a while now. The law firm was sucking the life out of me."

Declan sits at the counter, getting comfortable for a longer conversation. "You worked really hard to get your degree and prove yourself at that place. I'd hate to see you put all that to waste."

I move around the counter, taking a seat next to him, both of us facing each other. "Is it a waste if I learned something about myself?"

"No, but you seemed passionate about it in school. Was that real, or just for Mom and Dad's benefit?"

"I honestly don't know anymore. That's what I've realized since I got here. I don't know what was because I wanted it or because it's what Mom and Dad manipulated me into. It's all a jumble in my head, and I'm determined to figure it out." I look down at the mug on the counter and tuck a piece of hair behind my ear before looking back at him. "I'm not saying I'm done with law forever, but I am done with it for now."

"Okay." He lifts the mug to his mouth, taking a sip. "I'm all for taking the time to figure out what makes you happy, but you've got to do something." His voice is gentle, like he might be afraid of hurting me.

"I completely agree. That's part of why I'm up and ready so early. I want to get into a routine, and step one is getting a job." Declan opens his mouth to say something, but I don't give him a chance. "No. I was in town a couple of weeks ago and saw a help wanted sign at the bookstore. I haven't had the time to read in years, but I used to love it. I think it would be a perfect place to start. Plus, it's only part-time, so I'll have plenty of time to try other things."

"You've clearly put a lot of thought into it."

"I have."

We're both quiet again, Declan watching me closely. I'm sure he's trying to decide if I'm being honest about everything, and I understand. I've been holding a lot in and keeping him at arm's length, both things I don't normally do. But I haven't lied about a single thing this morning. I may not have given him the whole story, but I didn't lie.

Declan sets his mug down. "There's more, isn't there?"

I sigh, setting my mug next to his. "Yeah, but I'm still not ready to talk about that yet. But I promise, I'm okay." I reach for his arm, squeezing. "I might not be as happy-go-lucky as I was before, but I'm getting there. This is the closest I've felt to myself in a while."

Declan takes my hand in both of his, squeezing tight as he looks me in the eye. "I love you, Ava. I just want you to be happy and content in your life. I'll do whatever I can to help you achieve that. I hope you know that."

I give him a watery smile. "I've never doubted that." I stand from my seat, pulling him into a tight hug. "I love you, big brother."

Declan holds on for a few minutes, and when we pull away, both of us are a little teary-eyed.

"All right. Enough of that." I move around Declan toward the fridge. "What do you want for lunch? You'll be late if you don't get a move on."

A FEW HOURS LATER, I'm walking into Falls Book Haven, feeling lighter than I have in years. When I walk in the door and hear the bell ring, it's like a wave of peace washes over me—solidifying my decision to stay in Ashford Falls and apply for this job.

This is exactly where I'm supposed to be. I don't know how I know it, but I feel it in my bones.

"You're back," Abbey says from behind the counter, a small display case of sweets I didn't notice before at the end.

"I am." I step up to the other side of the counter without hesitation. "I'd like to apply for the open position." I gesture to the sign still in the window.

A large smile breaks out across Abbey's face. "Perfect. The job is yours."

"Really?" I ask, surprised. "I don't need to fill out an application?"

"Well, technically, yes, but that's only so there's a paper trail. The job is yours if you want it." Her smile softens slightly. "I have a good feeling about you. I think you'll be a perfect fit."

Abbey bends down and rifles around for a minute before standing back up and placing a couple of papers on the counter. "Here you go. Fill this out and sign the second page, which authorizes us to run a standard background check. Once that comes back clean, you're good to go." She grabs a pen from a cup next to the register and places it on the papers. "I don't think the background check will be an issue, considering where you worked before this." She winces. It's so small I would have missed it if I hadn't been looking. "Sorry. Small town living."

"It's fine." I shrug. "And you're right. As far as I know, my background is squeaky clean," I joke.

"Well, like I mentioned before, the owner doesn't want to bring on staff until after the new year, but if I can convince her to start you earlier, I'll let you know."

"That would be great." I smile, getting more excited about this opportunity the longer I'm here.

I'm just starting to fill out the application when the bell above the door rings. "Hey, deputy. What brings you in?" Abbey asks before I can turn to see who it is.

I know there's more than one deputy in this town, but the shift in the air gives me a good idea about which one is standing behind me.

And with the voice that responds, I no longer need to see to know my assumption is right. "Oh, just making the rounds and thought I'd stop by to see what kinds of treats you've got today."

I keep my back to him and try to focus on the application in front of me, but then I feel his heat at my back, and it becomes infinitely harder to focus.

I don't want to forget what happened Saturday night—and yesterday morning—but I'm also adamant that we don't repeat it. Especially now that I'm officially staying. Flings in small towns are just asking for trouble. Nothing ever stays secret for long.

The issue is that while my brain might recognize the logic of not starting a fling with Gage, my body doesn't. Just the sound of his voice and his heat at my back makes the memories of our night flash in my mind.

"Nothing special today, I'm afraid. Just a few different kinds of cookies," Abbey tells him.

"Does that mean you have gingerbread cookies?"

Abbey laughs as she moves to the case. "It does indeed. How many do you want today?"

"Just two." He pats his stomach. "I need to watch my sweets intake."

"Yeah, right," I mumble under my breath. Gage has nothing to worry about when it comes to his physique. Clearly, he takes care of himself, doing whatever he does to stay in shape.

I feel him step closer to me, his voice low in my ear. "What was that?"

"Nothing." I glance at him quickly, offering a small smile before turning back to the application.

"What's this? An application?" His lips brush my ear, and my thighs clench when his scent hits my nose. It's woodsy, like sandalwood and sage. It's just another thing that takes me right back to Saturday night.

I take a deep breath and release it, fortifying myself. I wanted that night with Gage—initiated it, was desperate for it. But I also set the boundaries, and now it's on me to keep things as normal as possible between us. I don't want to lose his presence in my life. We might not be friends exactly, but I'd like to be.

Without even knowing me, Gage offered me support when I've only ever gotten that from Declan and the Marks family. He's the kind of guy you want in your corner when the going gets tough, and I want that in my life—no, I *need* that in my life.

I put the pen down, turning to Gage, forcing him to step back a little bit. "Yeah. I've decided to stick around indefinitely."

Gage smirks, leaning against the counter next to me. "Is that so?"

I smile back, mirroring his position. "It is."

"And a job at the bookstore feels like the right fit?" There's no judgment in his question. It's pure curiosity.

"Yeah. I'm taking a step back from the lawyer thing. I'll finish with Scott's case, but after that...I don't know. I want to try something new."

Gage's smirk turns into a genuine smile, kind and affectionate. He doesn't say anything, but I see the understanding in his eyes. Maybe even a little admiration.

"On the house today, deputy," Abbey says, stepping back up to the counter where we're leaning.

"No, definitely not," Gage says, slowly turning to look at her. "I never let you give me these for free. I'm not starting now." He reaches into his back pocket, pulling out his wallet and handing her a ten-dollar bill.

"That's way too much."

"No, it's not. You don't charge nearly enough. You spend a lot of time on these, and they're fucking delicious."

"Gage—" Exasperation clouds her voice, but she doesn't have a chance to say more.

"Know your worth, Abbey." The words seem harsh, but the look on his face and the tone of his voice show the love he feels for her. It reminds me of the look I saw on Declan's face this morning.

Abbey doesn't hold his eyes long. She shifts her feet and looks down for a second before looking at me. Her eyes bounce between Gage and me, taking in how close we're standing and her brow lifts. "You two know each other?"

"Oh yeah, we go way back. Don't we, Rebel?" That smirk is back with a vengeance.

"Sure, if three weeks is way back." I turn to face Abbey, a smirk of my own forming. "We officially met at the courthouse my first full day in town, but it was next door at Murphy's where we had our first real conversation." I glance at Gage, a twinkle in my eye, before looking at Abbey again. "His dad invited me to join them for dinner. Seemed like this one might have been a little nervous to do it himself." I'm well aware I'm twisting things slightly, but if he's going to mess with me, I'm going to do the same.

Gage laughs a deep belly laugh. "Oh, I would have done it. He just beat me to it." He winks. "Besides, if I recall correctly, you were the one to show up at the same place two weeks later looking for me."

"I wasn't looking for you." I scoff. "I told you, Declan and Quinn have dinner at The Diner Thursday nights. If I want to eat out without awkwardly crashing their date, Murphy's is the only place for me."

"Sure. If that makes you feel better."

I laugh and lightly push at his shoulder. Without realizing it, we've both moved closer to each other, only inches of space left between us. It's the sound of Abbey cleaning her throat that has me realizing just how close we are. I step back, tucking a piece of hair behind my ear and glancing at the application I still need to finish filling out.

"Well"—Gage straightens next to me—"I better get back to work. Thanks for the cookies, Abbey." He grabs the bag Abbey placed on the counter earlier and turns to me. "Glad you're sticking around, Rebel." He reaches forward, untucking the piece of hair I just moved, tugging it lightly before leaving the bookstore.

I try to look away, but I can't help myself and end up tracking him as he walks past the front window and disappears from view.

"That was interesting." Abbey's voice has me jerking my head around to look at her.

"Sorry?" I play dumb, heat blooming in my cheeks.

Abbey gives me a break and doesn't say anything, but the look in her eye tells me she knows exactly what I'm trying to hide. And it's in that moment I realize I need to distance myself from Gage. Not forever, but at least until I can get my libido in check.

If I keep seeing him around town and spending time with him, there's no doubt we'll end up back in bed together. And no matter how good that would be, it can't happen.

CHAPTER
Sixteen

GAGE

HAVE I made it a point to be at Murphy's by the time the clock strikes six on Thursday nights in the hopes that a gorgeous brunette will walk in and I can have dinner with her? Yeah, I have.

Did that happen last week after our Monday morning run-in at the bookstore? No, it did not.

Is that stopping me from walking into Murphy's tonight? Ten days since I last saw Ava Day? No, it's not.

Have I been counting the days since I last saw Ava? Yes, I have.

"You doing all right there, kid?" Walt asks from behind the bar after the fifth time I've turned to see who's opened the door.

I know I'm acting a little pathetic and way out of character here, but that's not stopping me from watching that door like it's my salvation.

I turn back to Walt, forcing myself to continue looking at him even when I hear the door open for the sixth time in the hour since I've been here. "Yeah, of course." I pick up my beer and take a drink. "Did you talk to Jude today?"

Walt's face falls, but only for a moment before he forces a smile. "Yeah. Unfortunately, his trip to DC got pushed, so I won't see him for Christmas this year." He places the glass he was drying on the shelf behind him before turning back to pick up another. "Hopefully in the new year."

"Sorry, Walt. I know how much you miss him."

"This town had a way of bringing him down. I understand why he doesn't like coming back. I wish I were better at relinquishing control long enough to visit him more. But I'm an old man set in my ways, and you know what they say, you can't teach an old dog new tricks."

It's not the first time I've heard Walt mention the town being an issue for Jude, but I've never figured out what he means when he says it. From what I remember, when we were kids Jude never had any issues other than Abbey's dad. But my parents always said that had more to do with the history between Walt and Abbey's mom than anything else.

"You're not old, Walt," I say, ignoring the comment about Jude for now. "You're not even sixty yet. We've got years with you and plenty of time to teach you new tricks if you want."

Walt laughs as he puts the clean glass away and grabs another. "You definitely keep me feeling young, that's for sure."

"I have no idea what you mean," I say in mock outrage, sitting straighter in my seat. "I'm the epitome of acting my age and always have been."

"Not if the stories your dad told are to be believed," a feminine voice says from my side as they take the seat next to me.

I don't know if it was Walt's intention, but my conversation with him distracted me to the point that I hadn't even heard the door to the bar open. All night, I've struggled to fight my instinct to see who was entering each time the wind swept in. And no matter how much I fight it now, I can't stop the smirk from sliding across my lips as I turn to look at Ava.

I desperately want to know why she's been avoiding me—because I have no doubt she *has* been avoiding me. But I have a feeling if I call her out on it, she'll get spooked and run, avoiding me for who knows how long the next time.

I spin in my seat to face her. "I thought you figured it out that night. My dad loves to exaggerate. You have to look for context clues to determine which parts are true and which are inflated for dramatic effect."

"So you and your friends didn't toilet paper the principal's house when you were in high school? And your senior class prank didn't include moving the principal's office furniture to the roof?"

Walt laughs as he sets a pint of Guinness in front of Ava without her asking for it. She smiles in thanks before looking back at me.

"Well, if you knew anything about Dr. Killroy, you would understand why we did it. That man was a kill*joy*."

"What an unfortunate name," Walt mumbles. "But Gage is right. That man was principal when I was in school and was a complete grumpy ass back then. So that tells you how unpleasant he was by the time Gage graduated. Should have retired well before then."

"Hey, Walt!" Red Weaver, the town mayor, calls from the other end of the bar.

"Excuse me," Walt says before he walks away.

Ava and I are quiet—both of us nursing our beers.

"So..." she starts, taking another sip. I'm sure she wants me to say something, but I'm letting her take the lead on where this conversation goes. "I've been avoiding you."

I'm shocked she comes right out and says it. But I'm glad she does. "Yeah, I know."

Her brows pinch in, asking without words.

"It's a small town. Considering we've run into each other a few times outside of Thursday nights here, it was strange not running into you anywhere for the last two weeks," I answer the unspoken question, turning to face her.

"Okay." Ava turns in her seat, her legs sandwiching between mine. "I'm working on going after the things I want and not letting what I think other people will say or think dictate my actions."

"That's a good way to live life," I interject.

"Yeah, well, it's new for me..." Her voice trails off, and her eyes bounce between mine as she studies me.

I give her a minute, but when she doesn't say anything, I press. "What does that have to do with avoiding me?"

"Look, I've done the one-night stand thing before—though, I've never done it with someone I knew I would see again."

"Okay..." I hedge when she doesn't continue.

"So, it's not new to me. I know how it works, and I'm okay with it." She stops again.

"But?" I ask.

"But you and I didn't feel like a one-night stand."

"Agreed."

"I'm not looking for anything serious. As a matter of fact, I think I'm probably in the worst place I could possibly be to even consider a serious relationship."

I lean closer to her, whispering as if what I'm about to say is a secret, even though everyone in this town already knows it. "I'm not known for serious relationships."

She continues as if I didn't say anything. "I don't do casual with people I expect to see often outside the bedroom." She looks me straight in the eye, unafraid to speak her mind, and I find it extremely attractive. "But I think I want to make an exception. With the understanding that nobody knows."

"I like your honesty," I tell her.

"Look, it's no one's business. And I know asking to keep it a secret implies that I care what other people think—which I'm trying not to do anymore—but that's not why I want it to be a secret."

"All right."

Again, she plows right on through with her speech. "I don't care what other people think, but I already have enough noise in my head, and I just don't want anymore. I want to do something for myself, and I don't need to hear anyone else's opinions." The color in her cheeks rises, and so does her voice the longer she talks. It's clear this is something she's thought about for a while and feels passionate about.

"Ava." I reach for her arm, trying to calm her down. "As long as I can talk to you in public and we can have the occasional beer together like we are right now, I'm good with keeping it a secret."

"Okay." She collapses back into her seat, relaxing when she realizes I won't fight her on this.

"Just to be clear"—I lean closer, lowering my voice so only she can hear me—"you are asking for sex, right?" The blush on her cheeks deepens, and I imagine it travels down her neck to her chest the same way it did two weeks ago when I had her in my bed. "You're asking to use me for your pleasure?" I whisper in her ear.

Ava squirms, crossing and uncrossing her legs. She straightens in her seat, not backing down, and unafraid to go for what she wants. "Yes, that's exactly what I'm asking for."

"Good." I smirk. "Use me."

"GOD, YES!" Ava shouts as she grinds her hips against me, using me to bring herself right to the edge, exactly like I told her to.

"I'm no god, Rebel." I press my thumb against her clit,

rubbing in small circles, watching her head roll back as she arches her body. "Come on, baby."

Her head falls forward, looking down at me as her hands come to my pecs, nails digging in as she rolls her hips. "Don't stop," she breathes.

"Not a chance."

I keep my hand between us, playing with her clit as she rocks against me, my cock buried deep inside her. I reach behind her, pressing her back so her chest is in front of my face, sucking her nipple into my mouth.

She moans, her rocking becoming more erratic. "Let go, Rebel." I nip at her breast, thrust my hips once, and she falls over the edge, her walls clenching around me.

Without waiting for her to come down from her orgasm, I flip us, bringing her knees to her chest and driving my hips into her.

"Gage," she moans, her hips rolling in time with mine.

"One more." I move to my knees, watching where we're connected, where my cock disappears inside her.

"I can't."

"You can and you will." My eyes sear into hers. I release her knees, lifting her hips and angling them just right so on each thrust in, I hit her g-spot. Her walls tighten around me, her orgasm fast approaching. "That's it, Rebel. Let it happen. Let your pussy soak my cock." My hips move faster—harder, as I press my thumb against her sensitive nub, applying the lightest pressure before she detonates again.

"Gage!"

With her walls tightening around me, I thrust three more times before I follow right behind her. My thrusts slow as I draw out both her orgasm and mine.

I roll us so she's tucked into my side as we both work to catch our breath.

"Why is that so good?" Ava asks as I fall back into bed

after taking care of the condom and pulling her back into my side. Her voice is filled with disbelief. "I can't remember it ever being that good."

I don't think I was supposed to hear that last part, but I can't help the pride I feel move through my chest at the idea of being the best she's had.

"Maybe I am a god." I laugh when she swats at my chest.

"Shut up." There's no force behind her words, and it has me squeezing her closer to me.

"It's never been this electric for me either." I give her a truth I wasn't planning to. But if she's willing to be vulnerable with me, then it's only fair I do the same for her.

She lifts her head off my chest and looks at me with wide eyes. "Yeah?" It's cute the way she seems surprised by that.

"Probably why one night wasn't enough for us." My hand travels down her back, giving her ass a light squeeze. "If I'm being honest, I knew one night wouldn't be enough before it even started."

She rests her head back on my chest and is quiet long enough that I think that's the end of the discussion.

"I knew it that night but didn't believe it until you came into the bookstore," she says, so quietly I almost miss it. "My life is such a mess." She rolls onto her back, staring up at the ceiling.

I roll to my side, placing my head in my hand, my elbow digging into my pillow. "You keep saying that, but it doesn't look like it from the outside."

"That's because the mess is all back in Massachusetts."

"Do you want to talk about it?"

She rolls to face me, mirroring my position. "I haven't even told Declan about it."

"Sometimes it's harder to talk to the people you're closest to."

She's quiet for so long that I don't think she'll say anything, but she also doesn't move. Her eyes bouncing between mine, studying me, trying to decide something. I don't say anything, letting her see whatever she needs from me to feel comfortable in this moment.

I don't know what happened—or is still happening—but I know what it's like to feel like you're losing control of everything. I wish I had allowed someone to support me through that instead of trying to figure it all out myself.

"My parents aren't who I thought they were," she says finally.

"You alluded to something like that after dinner with my dad."

She takes a deep breath as if mentally preparing herself. Letting it out slowly, she starts, "I always knew our family was different than the typical family growing up, but I never would have said my parents didn't love me and Declan." She messes with a loose thread in the comforter beneath us.

Normally, I would be entirely focused on the fact that there's a naked woman in my bed, unashamed of her nudity and completely exposed to the air around us. But all I can focus on is the pain in her eyes.

"Now I wonder why they even had kids because there is no way they love either of us. Definitely not the way a parent should love their child."

"Ava," I say softly, waiting for her eyes to meet mine. "Did they hurt you?"

She shakes her head instantly, then stops. "Not physically."

"Rebel," I practically beg. For what? I'm not entirely sure.

I don't know what to say or do. I know what I want to do, but that would entail getting on a plane and flying to Boston, something I don't think Ava would appreciate.

"No." She shakes her head, rolling to her back again. "I don't want to think about it anymore tonight." She tilts her head to look at me. "Can we just have fun and not worry about anything else?"

I want to help her through this. I want to make all of it go away. I want to help her figure out the so-called "mess" of her life, but that feels more like a serious relationship than the casual fling we agreed to. And it scares me to think about how badly I want to do those things.

"Yeah." I smirk, trying to cover up my racing thoughts. "We can definitely have some fun."

I reach for her waist, pulling her to me and letting my lips trail across her skin, down her neck, and across her chest, following an imaginary trail toward the apex of her thighs.

I let the feel of her beneath my fingers, the warmth of her skin against my lips, and the sounds of her moans drown out all the other thoughts in my head. I focus entirely on playing the part she needs from me right now, giving her enough pleasure to block out the reality of a situation she's not ready to share while being thankful for the small pieces she was willing to give me tonight.

CHAPTER
Seventeen

GAGE

WHEN I WAKE up the next morning, I honestly expect to be alone. But Ava is curled up on the other side of the bed when I open my eyes five minutes before my alarm.

I surprised myself last night when I gave her a shirt after our shower and pulled her back into bed with me instead of letting her change into her clothes and leave like she tried to. But then again, maybe I shouldn't have been surprised with all the thoughts racing through my head. All the worst-case scenarios. All the ways I could help if she just told me everything.

I may not want a serious relationship, but that doesn't mean I can't be Ava's friend. That doesn't mean I can't support her.

I grab my phone from the nightstand, turning my alarm off so it won't wake her. Instead of getting out of bed, I roll to my side, giving myself these five minutes to study Ava.

She's on her side, facing me—her face perfectly at peace, not a single furrow in sight, no stress weighing her down.

She's breathtaking.

After she told me about her parents and I worshiped her

body, we ended up back in my kitchen looking for something sweet to eat. While I didn't have anything immediately on hand, Ava discovered I had the ingredients to make chocolate chip cookies—something I probably have my mother or sister to thank for. She pulled them out and immediately began mixing them together while I sat at the kitchen island and watched.

We didn't talk about her parents again, but we talked about practically everything else. We laughed and had fun, exactly like she wanted.

And while we waited for the cookies to bake, she decided it was her turn for a taste.

Sex with Ava is out of this world. More intense and vibrant than anything I've experienced before. But a blow job from Ava might surpass even that.

The feel of her lips wrapped around me, her hand at the base of my shaft, the sight of her on her knees, and her hand playing with her clit had me coming down her throat faster than I ever had.

Ava Day might just be my undoing.

She shifts in her sleep, bringing me back to the present, reminding me that I need to get ready for work. I climb out of bed quietly, grab my clothes from the closet, and head to the bathroom to get myself ready.

Ava is just starting to wake up as I step out of the bathroom.

"Hey," I say softly, coming around the bed and sitting on the edge by her.

"You have a shift?" Her voice is groggy and deep, still filled with sleep.

"Yeah, but you don't need to rush out. You're welcome to stay as long as you want."

She tried to fight me when I gave her a shirt to sleep in last night, claiming she needed to get home so Declan didn't find out about us. But she was quick to cave once she revealed that Declan rarely slept at home.

"No, I'll get up. I need to be in court later today for Scott's preliminary hearing."

Ava leans forward, pressing a quick kiss to my lips before getting out of bed and moving into the bathroom. She leaves the door cracked, and I see her washing her hands and face before brushing her teeth with the spare toothbrush I gave her last night.

I watch her from the foot of the bed, transfixed by how natural she looks there—how domestic it all seems. And I realize I like it.

"The hearing's today?" I ask, trying not to think about how much I like her in my space.

"Yeah, early this afternoon," she says as she comes back into the room. Shimmying into her panties and jeans before taking my borrowed shirt off. Her eyes bounce around the floor, a puzzled look crossing her face as she searches for her bra.

"Lampshade," I say, pointing to where it is in the corner, a smirk forming on my lips.

"I'm not going to ask." She plucks it from where it is and puts it on before doing the same with her sweater. "It should be a relatively easy day. It's just a preliminary hearing to determine next steps, which I expect to be mediation." Ava sits on the bed next to me, slipping her socks onto her feet then her boots. "Most judges want parents to agree to their own custody arrangements. It's less stressful for the kids, and really everyone involved." She tilts her head. "Most of the time."

"That makes sense." I stand from the bed, offering her a hand before we make our way to the kitchen. "Coffee before you go?" I ask, walking to the machine.

"You have time?" Ava pauses by the edge of the island counter.

"Yeah, I've got about forty-five minutes before I need to be at the station."

"Coffee would be great." She smiles as she takes a seat at the counter, watching me move around the kitchen.

I glance over and notice her eyebrows are pinched, a look of concentration on her face. "Is everything okay?"

"Yeah. I just—I forgot to mention that I'm going out of town on Sunday." She tucks a piece of hair behind her ear, studying the counter in front of her.

"Okay." I step to the island counter, standing across from her. "It seems like there's more you want to say."

She lifts her head, making eye contact with me. "I'm going to see my parents."

I'm shocked by that news, especially after what she shared with me last night, but I keep my face neutral, my eyes on hers, waiting for her to continue. I know she'll tell me more. She just needs to be ready to do it.

"I'll only be there for about a week." She shrugs. "My dad called me a few days ago." Her eyes go back to studying the counter. "I've been ignoring his calls since before I got here, and he finally left a voicemail. He sounded regretful, so when he called again I answered."

"Ava, you don't have to explain yourself to me." I move back to the coffee pot, trying to give her space to decide what she wants to share. I pour two cups, placing one in front of her before grabbing the sugar and creamer and placing them on the counter where she can reach.

"I know. But I feel like you deserve to know after what I told you last night." She grabs the creamer, pouring a small amount into her cup. "He apologized for how my mother has been speaking to me and for not speaking up sooner to stop her. I don't know if I believe him, but I need to go back to Boston regardless to pack my things." She lifts her eyes, looking back at me. "And while I might be furious with both of them, I don't need to stoop to their level, so they deserve to hear directly from me that I'm moving here."

"Okay." I offer her a small smile.

"That's it?" she asks a little incredulously.

I shrug. There's plenty I could say, most of which is arguing why Ava doesn't need to go home right now to talk to her parents. Christmas is next week, and she should be spending it here with people who care about her.

"Is Declan going with you?" I ask. If he were going with her, I might understand her decision better. Declan normally goes back to Harborview for the major holidays, but from my understanding, he does it because Ava is there. This year is different, though. Now he has Quinn, someone I know he feels very deeply for, and I can't imagine he'll want to spend the holiday away from her.

"No, he's staying here this year." She tucks that piece of hair behind her ear, glancing down at the counter, but when she lifts her eyes, they're filled with unshed tears. "It's unlikely Scott will be here next year. Declan wants to be here..." Her voice trails off, leaving the rest unsaid. And it doesn't need to be. No one in this town will be the same after Scott is gone, but the people closest to him will be devastated.

I move around the island counter, spinning her seat to face me. Her legs open, allowing me to step between them—and I do, without hesitation—pulling her into a hug.

With her arms around my waist and her head against my chest, I press a light kiss to the top of her head. I want to convince her that she should stay here for the same reason as Declan, but I have a feeling this decision was already a difficult one for her. I won't make it worse.

"I'll be here when you get home," I tell her softly.

I noticed when she spoke of going to see her parents she never once called it home, and part of me hopes that's because she's already starting to think of Ashford Falls as home.

Her arms around me tighten for a moment before she pulls back just enough that she can look up at me. "Thank you."

"For what?" I lift one hand, tucking that wayward piece of hair behind her ear.

"I know you want to convince me to stay here, but thank you for respecting my decision."

"You're a grown adult, Ava, and you don't owe me anything. I'm here to support you however I can. That's what I meant when I offered you some extra strength." I pause and study her. "I'll be here when you get home."

I hope, more than anything, this trip will be exactly what she wants and needs it to be. But based on the very little I know about her parents, I have a feeling it won't be. Maybe this will give her the clarity she needs to really move on from whatever happened before she got here.

As long as there's a lesson learned, then even the hard situations are worth moving through.

———

I'M SITTING at the counter at The Diner for lunch, just lifting the burger to my mouth for a bite, when my parents plop into the seats on either side of me. I freeze, looking between them. "Well"—I put the burger back on the plate and wipe my hands on my napkin—"this can't be good for me."

"Now why would you say that?" my mom asks, her tone filled with sarcasm.

"The last time you two looked at me like this was when I told you I was going to the police academy."

They'd been supportive but worried about me. They'd seen my mental state and were concerned I was trying to replace what I had in the military without actually addressing my feelings. They feared I would put myself in an unsafe situation—and they hadn't been entirely wrong. That conversation with them made me pause and think about my why. I needed that push, that reminder that I still had a life worth pursuing and finding my new purpose.

That knowledge didn't make me any less nervous about this conversation with them. And I had no idea what I'd done to warrant the looks on their faces.

"I want to know why you haven't introduced me to Ava, especially if you two are having dinner with your father. I thought you loved me." There's a twinkle in her eye, and she can't keep her face straight for long. The tension leaves my body and my shoulders fall at the realization this isn't serious.

I look at my dad, noting the smirk on his lips. He's done this on purpose. That dinner at Murphy's might have only been the second time Ava and I had seen each other, but my interest in her had already been piqued, and I know my dad noticed.

I look back at my mom. "Dad's just stirring the pot. There's nothing going on with Ava. We're friends." I make sure I don't look away from her. If my eyes shift even the smallest amount, she'll know I'm lying. Not that I like lying to her—or my dad. I tell them everything, but having this conversation at The Diner will surely result in someone overhearing, and I won't tempt fate.

"So you three didn't have dinner together over a month ago?" she asks.

"Yes, we did, but only because Dad invited her when he saw me talking to her. After he showed up late, I might add."

I hear Dad scoff, but Mom asks another question before he can say anything.

"And you haven't been seen having dinner together every Thursday night?"

"Don't you regularly have dinner with Dad?" I counter.

"Well, that's different." She waves me off, picking up a menu—something I've never seen her do in my entire life.

My eyes move to Dad, seeing him mess with the napkin holder in front of him, avoiding eye contact. They're hiding something, and in my gut, I know what it is.

"No," I say in disbelief, practically whispering. "You two are back together?"

"What? Of course not." This from my dad, who sits up straight in his seat, bringing his eyes to mine. But he's not able to hold it long. A sure sign he's lying.

My head whips to my mother, who's trying desperately—and failing—to hold in a smile.

"How long?" I ask.

"Gage—" Dad tries to cut in.

"No. We don't lie to each other."

"Right." Mom jumps on that, bringing the conversation back to Ava. "We don't, so why are you lying about Ava?"

"Nope, you first. How long has this been going on?" I turn back to my dad. "I thought you were seeing that vet a few towns over?"

"Uh, no." His eyes shift over my shoulder to my mom before coming back to me. "I only went on one date with her."

"But you let me think you've been dating her for what, six months now?"

He squints, thinking about how to respond to that and probably trying to decide if I'm unhappy about this new development.

Well, he can join the club because I have no idea how I feel about this. I know most kids would probably be ecstatic that their parents are back together, but I'm not a child, and I haven't been for a very long time. I've experienced a lot of life. Seen both of them in and out of different relationships. I watched them fight hard for the friendship they have today, and I guess if I'm honest with myself, I'm nervous about what happens when this one fails.

"Gage, what your father and I do isn't really any of your

business," Mom says gently, placing her hand on my forearm and bringing my focus back to her.

I lift an eyebrow. "Really? My parents getting back together doesn't impact me?" I keep my voice quiet. I don't know if I would say I'm angry, but I'm definitely hurt.

"That's not what she said," Dad interjects. "Look"—his eyes bounce to Mom and right back to me—"if we're being honest—"

"Nick," Mom interrupts.

"Laura." Dad looks at her over my shoulder, the two of them having a silent conversation. When his eyes come back to me, I see it—the love and devotion in his eyes. In that moment, I realize Dad has always had that glimmer in his eyes when he looks at her. It's never gone anywhere, even when he was dating or married to someone else.

"Wow." It comes out as more of a breath than anything else. I turn to look at my mom, trying to read her eyes. She's always been a little harder for me to read, but I see it in her eyes too—how serious and real her feelings are. "Okay." I push my plate away from me, my appetite now gone.

"Gage." Mom reaches for me, but I stand from my seat, stopping her in her tracks.

"No." I meet her eyes. "You have to give me time to digest this. This clearly isn't new and is quite serious, but I just found out, and I deserve to figure out what I'm feeling without input from you right now."

"You're right," Dad says, reaching for Mom's hand, offering her comfort as her eyes fill with tears. "But we also deserve a chance to explain."

"And I promise I'll let you, but not right now." I gesture around us. No one in The Diner is paying us any attention. It's not out of the norm for me to have lunch with both of my parents, but if we keep talking about this, I have a feeling we'll draw some attention.

I reach for my wallet but stop when Dad shakes his head. "We'll take care of it."

I look between them again, really studying them. I don't know what I'm feeling other than hurt, but they're my parents, and I love them.

So I lean forward, placing a kiss to my mom's cheek, and squeeze my dad's shoulder before turning to leave The Diner.

CHAPTER
Eighteen

AVA

"YOUR HONOR, based on the evidence we've provided, we feel it's only right Max's custody arrangements remain the same. Mr. Marks has done nothing to warrant the removal of Max from his home—"

"He's dying! How can that be good for Max?!" Nicole shouts from her side of the courtroom.

I shouldn't be surprised, based on everything I've been told about Nicole, but I am. I assumed her lawyer would have given her the same speech I gave Scott and everyone else. You don't speak in a courtroom unless the judge asks you a question directly. You always let your lawyer do the talking.

Honestly, things had probably been going too smoothly. I should have known an outburst was around the corner, but to say what she just did is uncalled for.

"Your Honor!" I call.

"Order! Counselor, get a hold of your client," the judge warns.

Joseph Henry, Nicole's lawyer, leans toward her, whispering something in her ear before turning back to the judge. "Sorry, Your Honor. It won't happen again."

"Ms. Day, you may proceed."

"Mr. Marks has always been present in Max's life. There's no evidence to show Mr. Marks as an unfit parent. What kind of precedent will it set to remove Max from his custody simply because his biological mother, who abandoned him when he was two, wants to be back in his life?" I pause, taking a breath.

I know I should be a little more impartial to this, but I can't. Scott Marks is the kind of father every man should strive to be. The way he loves those he cares for is something to be witnessed.

"That's all, Your Honor," I finish, retaking my seat next to Scott.

"All right. I've heard from both sides—"

"Your Honor—" Mr. Henry tries to interrupt.

"Mr. Henry, you had your chance," the judge stops him, speaking sternly. "This isn't a trial where you need to defend your client. This is a preliminary hearing to determine next steps. Which is what I'm about to go over with you." He pauses as if to ensure he won't be interrupted again.

The judge looks to me and back to Mr. Henry before he states, "I will be ordering the two of you to mediation. If an agreement has not been reached after two months, we'll schedule a hearing where I will make a decision."

He turns to Scott. "Mr. Marks, I do not envy your position, and while I'm sure you have prepared as much as possible for the future, I ask you to seriously consider what is in your son's best interest." Now he turns to Nicole. "Mrs. Williams, I know people change, and I hope you have. But I urge you to think about how the courts will view your absence from your son's life for the past ten years. Think hard about what you are asking of this court, and more importantly, your son. Know that all of this will influence any decision made." The judge looks down and shuffles some papers around in front of him before looking back up at Mr. Henry and me. "Thank you for your time today. Court is adjourned."

"All rise," the bailiff calls.

As soon as the judge has closed the door behind him, I turn to speak to everyone in the first row behind Scott and me.

"That's exactly what we expected and hoped for," I say, a comforting smile forming on my lips. "I'll—"

"Where is he? Why didn't you bring him today?" Nicole storms over, interrupting me.

Scott slowly turns, studying her. I don't know what he's thinking, but a flash of pain crosses his face. I can't imagine what this feels like. I don't know the full story, but I know he was madly in love with her. It would be so easy to assume, after everything she did, that one could simply forget those feelings and move on, but that crease in his brow and those shadows in his eyes prove that's not the case.

"We left the decision up to him. He chose to remain at school, rather than be here today," Scott says, his voice void of all emotion.

"What lies have you been telling him about me?"

"Mom, come on," Caleb interjects. "No one has told him any lies. What lies would we even have to say? You left him when he was two, and we haven't heard from you since." Caleb's hands clench at his sides, and Emily reaches for him.

"I think it would be best to wait to discuss this in mediation." I step forward. "Mr. Henry, you have my contact information. Let's schedule a time to discuss the mediation as soon as possible." I don't wait for a response before taking Scott's arm and ushering him from the courtroom.

It's not until I'm outside with him that I realize we're missing Declan and Quinn. We all look to the courthouse doors, expecting them to walk out momentarily. When they don't, I turn to the Scott, Caleb, and Emily.

"Look. I know it's not what we wanted, but it's what we

expected." I grab Scott's forearm, waiting for him to look at me. "I won't stop until you can rest easy knowing Max will never go anywhere. I'm going to do everything I can to make sure of that."

He takes my hand in his, squeezing and offering a small lift of his lips. "I know that."

"We should do something tonight," Emily says in the silence that takes over.

"What?" Caleb looks down at her, confused.

"Yeah, like, go out or something. Just forget about all of this for a night and have fun." She nods her head like she's really enjoying this idea the more she thinks about it.

"I don't—" Caleb starts.

"I think that's a great idea. You all should go out," Scott interrupts. "But I'm going to stay in, spend some time with Max. I know he's been nervous about everything. I think it'll be good for him."

"I'd like to join you, if that's all right?" Caleb asks, shifting his balance from foot to foot.

"Of course."

"Okay, then a ladies' night," I say.

"Yes!" Emily shouts.

It's then we hear the courthouse doors open, Declan and Quinn stepping out.

"Everything okay?" Caleb asks when they get closer to us.

"Not really," Declan offers after glancing at Quinn.

"What did she say?" Emily asks.

Quinn shakes her head, unable to form words.

Declan seems to catch on and answers, "Nothing meaningful."

"Emily and I were thinking we should have ladies' night out tonight. To...I don't know, decompress from this day?" I reach for Quinn's hand, trying to offer her comfort.

"I appreciate the offer, but I don't think I'm up for that tonight." She squeezes my hand before releasing it.

"Then breakfast tomorrow morning. I won't take no for an answer. I fly back to Boston on Sunday," I say definitively. I can see the tension in her body. It seems she needs a distraction more than anyone else.

"It's only for a week." Declan chuckles.

"I know, but you're leaving me to deal with Mom and Dad alone for Christmas this year. It's only fair I get to steal your girlfriend for a bit."

I know he doesn't agree with my decision to go see Mom and Dad, even not knowing everything that happened, but he begrudgingly agreed to support my decision. Besides, like I told Gage, I have to pack my things at some point. The sooner I do it, the better.

Declan chuckles softly before responding. "Hey, if Quinn wants to go to breakfast with you, I have no complaints. I'm just saying you'll only be gone for a week. It's not like you're leaving forever."

Quinn leans into Declan's side, looking at me. "Breakfast tomorrow sounds good."

"Great! Nine o'clock at The Diner?" At her nod, I turn to Emily. "Can you do breakfast?"

"Unfortunately, I can't. I've got a shift tomorrow. But both of you have fun. I'll see you at Sunday breakfast before your flight home."

"All right." Scott steps forward. "Let's get out of here. Who's riding with who?"

"Did you drive?" Quinn asks.

"I did. Picked up Ava on my way here," he confirms.

"Emily and I came together, but we can give anyone who needs one a ride," Caleb offers.

"I'll ride with you, Dad. I need to grab my stuff from Declan's truck."

"You sure? You and Dec don't have plans?" Scott asks, concern flashing over his face when he glances at Declan.

"Nope. I just want to go home, change into comfy clothes and loaf in front of the TV." She doesn't look at Declan even though he tries to catch her eye. "Besides, as Ava mentioned, she's going back to Boston. You should have some time together, just the two of you." She glances at Declan briefly before looking at me, an almost pleading look in her eye.

I hesitate, not wanting to get in the middle of whatever is happening here, but quickly decide to give her what she wants. "Yeah. She's right. We haven't had a night for just us since I got to town."

"Of course." Declan's voice is a little strained when he responds.

"Okay. Are we all parked in the lot at the side of the court-house?" Scott asks, reading the situation and trying to move it along.

"Yeah," Declan confirms.

We all begin moving toward the parking lot. Caleb and Emily leading us, with Scott and me behind them. Declan and Quinn bring up the rear, falling a little further behind while they talk in hushed voices.

"Don't stress about anything," Scott says, pulling me back to the moment. "Like you said, everything went exactly like we thought it would."

I breathe a sigh of relief. I don't know why I was holding such a weight on my shoulders, but hearing him say those words helps me release all of it.

"Thank you."

Scott throws his arm over my shoulder, pulling me into his side as we continue walking. "I'm sorry we'll miss you for Christmas this year, but I'm quite happy you'll be around indefinitely when you get back, so I'll accept the loss for now." He smiles at me, giving me a quick squeeze.

"I'm sad I'm missing Christmas with you all, too, but I'm excited for what the future has in store for me."

And I realize I really mean that. It's been a while since I've been excited, but even with all the uncertainty of my future, I can't wait to see where it takes me. And I won't lie; there's something even more exciting about this secret I'm sharing with Gage.

I'm already looking forward to seeing him again.

———————————

THE RIDE back to Declan's is tense. I can feel the energy pouring off of him from the driver's seat. And while I want to say something to make the situation better, I don't know what *to* say.

"Do you want to talk about it?" I finally ask as we walk through the front door.

He shrugs, opening the fridge and pulling a beer out. "There's nothing to talk about." He twists the cap off, tossing it to the island counter before taking a large gulp.

"Did she say anything before they left?" I follow his lead, grabbing a beer from the fridge and taking a seat at the kitchen island when he takes a position leaning against the counter.

"Not really. Just that she needed time to herself."

"Do you have any reason not to believe her?" I ask gently.

Declan and I haven't talked much about what's going on between him and Quinn. Heck, we haven't talked much, period. Part of that is my fault for avoiding talking about Brian and my parents, but part of it is on him, too. He hasn't been home much since he started seeing Quinn.

Declan sighs, setting his beer on the counter and shoving his hands into his pockets. "Quinn doesn't know what she'll do after Scott is gone." His eyes fall to the floor. "Living in

Ashford Falls was never part of her plan, and without Scott holding her here, she doesn't know if she wants to stay."

"It would probably be hard living here, seeing Scott around every corner. But he isn't the only one keeping her here. She's got her brothers. And you."

He nods his head almost absentmindedly. "That may be true, but I don't know if that's enough."

I don't know what else to say, so I don't say anything.

Declan visibly shakes himself from his thoughts before continuing. "I understand it. Her mom showing up stirred up a lot of emotion, and she was already in a weird place with everything going on with her dad. I don't blame her for needing a minute to figure out what all of it means for her."

"I know you don't," I tell him when he doesn't continue.

"I just want to support her—however I can."

"You're doing it." I lift my shoulders, letting them fall after a second. "You listen to her and trust that she'll tell you what she needs." I stand from my seat, moving around the counter and pulling him into a hug. "I've seen the way she looks at you. You're not alone in your feelings." I pull back, looking up at him. "You mean more to her than you give yourself credit for. You'll work it all out tomorrow. I have no doubt."

Declan leans down, pressing a kiss to my forehead. "Thanks, squirt." He pulls away from me, offering me a tight smile. "I'm going to shower and then probably veg on the couch. You're welcome to join me if you want."

"Yeah." I give him a closed-lip smile. "I'll change into comfy clothes and meet you back here. How do you feel about ordering some pizza for dinner?"

"Sounds perfect."

I watch him make his way up the stairs, wishing I could make all of this better for him. I didn't lie to him, though. I really do believe that everything will be sorted by the end of the day tomorrow. As it stands, Quinn and I are meeting for breakfast, and I don't see her agreeing to that if she plans to end things with my brother. That's just not who Quinn is.

Before following Declan upstairs, I grab my phone to text Gage.

> I'm not going to make it tonight. Declan's staying in.

GAGE

> All good. I'll see you when you get home.

This is the first text exchange I've had with Gage, having only gotten his phone number this morning, but something about the message has me worrying. I just can't pinpoint why.

CHAPTER
nineteen

GAGE

OVER TWENTY-FOUR HOURS later I find myself in the same spot, lifting a burger to my mouth when someone slides into the seat next to me.

"You have got to be kidding me," I mumble, dropping the burger onto my plate and giving myself a second to collect myself. But when I turn to my left, it's not who I thought. It's still my mother's eyes staring back at me, but this time from my sister's face.

"What's that supposed to mean?" she asks as she steals a fry from my plate.

"Nothing." I shake my head. "What are you up to?"

Olivia looks around the diner, shifting in her seat, and I'm instantly on edge. Olivia's not one to beat around the bush. For the most part, she lacks a filter when she's around me. If she's uncomfortable telling me whatever's on her mind...well, I guess I have a pretty good idea what it's about. Since Ava and I aren't exactly public knowledge, I can only assume she wants to talk about my parents.

"Olivia." My voice is stern, probably harsher than I mean

for it to be, but I don't appreciate being forced to talk about something I'm not ready to.

I've spent the majority of the last twenty-four hours thinking about my parents, and at the end of the day, I'm hurt and disappointed. I'm hurt they didn't tell me about it, and I'm disappointed in myself. This is now the second relationship someone in my family felt they couldn't talk to me about, and I hate that I've led any of them to believe I wouldn't support their decisions.

"Just hear me out." Olivia turns in her seat, her eyes pleading.

Releasing a heavy sigh, I turn to face her. "How long have you known?" I probably shouldn't ask. I'm sure it will only upset me more, but I need to know.

"I've known for a while now. Maybe three months?" There's pity in her eyes when she admits that.

"Wow. Okay then." I turn back to the counter, pushing the burger away from me yet again. *Maybe one of these days, I'll get to finish a burger.*

"Don't be mad. I only know because I came home from my dad's one weekend without telling Mom. They weren't expecting anyone to be at the house."

I glance at her out of the side of my eye. "That doesn't make it better, Pickle. You've still known for months."

"I know." She grimaces, turning in her seat to face the counter. "I wanted to tell you, but...well"—she shrugs—"they made a good argument. And it wasn't my place to share their news with you."

"I know you're not wrong, but it doesn't make me feel better." We're both quiet for a few minutes, both of us lost in thought. "How do you feel about it?" I ask, shifting to look at her.

"Honestly?"

"Of course. I only ever want the truth from you, no matter what."

"I'm really happy." The smile on her face proves just how true that statement is. "Don't get me wrong, I love my dad. He's a great dad," she says emphatically. "But Nick's always been really good to me—even before they started dating. I've always felt a little like I was his, too." She shrugs, her cheeks turning a little pink at the admission.

That doesn't surprise me. My dad may have his faults, but loving isn't one of them.

I lucked out with my parents being the way they were with each other. I never had to choose between them, things like holidays were done with both of them. And while my parents had decent relationships with their exes, it wasn't the same as the close friendship they maintained after their divorce. Maybe, in hindsight, that's part of what brought them back together.

"You have a really great dad, too," Olivia says softly.

"Yeah, I do." I reach over and squeeze her shoulder.

"Are you mad they got back together?" Olivia asks after a moment of silence.

"No, I'm not mad. Just hurt they didn't tell me sooner."

"They wanted to be sure before they told you. You're their son." She shrugs. "I think they were afraid of disappointing you or letting you down again. They didn't want to tell everyone if it wasn't going to last, especially you."

"Hmm," I hum. "Does that mean Asher and Leo know?"

"I think they told them last night." *At least I wasn't the last person to know.*

I look around The Diner, not looking for anything in particular, just thinking. "I'm surprised they could keep it quiet in this town. Maybe we're better at keeping secrets than I thought we were." I chuckle.

"When are you going to put them out of their misery?"

I huff out a laugh, glancing at her from the corner of my eye. "They're miserable, are they?"

"Okay, maybe not miserable, but they definitely aren't happy. I'd say they're sad, maybe a little disappointed in themselves."

I nod my head. "I can understand that."

"So?" she pushes when I don't say anything else.

"I don't know, Pickle. I hear what you're saying, but it's gonna take me a little bit to figure out where my head is at."

"You're still gonna come for Christmas, though, right?" she asks hopefully.

"I work this year, remember?" She nods her head but doesn't say anything. "You know I'll stop by at some point. I just don't know when exactly."

"Right," she mumbles, fidgeting with the paper placemat in front of her on the counter.

I pull her into a hug. "Me not being there has nothing to do with this news. If I weren't working, I would be there." Especially this year.

This is one of the rare years in which all my siblings will be under one roof with both my parents. Most years, it was just me, Mom, Dad, and one of my siblings. I hate that I'll be in town but working this year. When I was still serving overseas, it was easier to miss out on the big family events but to be this close—it sucks.

Before I can say anything else to try and make it up to her, my phone goes off with a text from the sheriff.

LYLE

I need you to head to the hospital. We need a
witness statement from Tyler Harrison.
Call me.

"Sorry, Pickle. I've gotta go. Duty calls." I reach over,

pulling her head to mine, and place a kiss to her temple. "I love you, and I'll talk to you soon." I grab a twenty from my wallet and toss it next to my still-full plate before lifting my phone to my ear and heading to my cruiser.

Lyle doesn't mince words and jumps right in when he answers the phone. "Sorry to interrupt your dinner. But I knew you'd want to be the one to take this statement."

"What happened?" I ask as I walk down the sidewalk.

"He was brought to the hospital this evening by two of his teachers. He was beaten pretty badly. He hasn't shared much, only told his teachers it was his mother." The sheriff is quiet for a moment, likely gathering his thoughts. No matter how long you're on the job, parts of it never get easier.

"The doctors think he was beaten with a bat." His voice is low when he says it, but I hear the anger clear as day. And I understand it because I feel the rage coursing through me, too.

"Is he going to be okay?" I ask once I'm able to control my voice.

"They're still checking him out, but he'll survive."

Survive. Because while he might be alive, he's definitely not okay. How could he if his mother beat him with a bat?

"I've already got Reid out checking the places she frequents. Just get the statement and come back to the station."

"Copy that." We don't waste time on goodbyes and hang up.

When I first decided to join the academy after being discharged, I seriously considered going to Baltimore or DC. After being in the service for so long, I thought the bigger cities were the only places I'd stay busy and feel like I was helping the most people. And while both of those cities meant I could easily visit Ashford Falls whenever I wanted, I ultimately decided I wanted to be as close to my family as I could—especially after being away from them for twelve years.

Ashford Falls might not have the major cases that Baltimore or DC does, but it wasn't entirely a sleepy little town either. But this call is the first involving someone I thought I had been keeping a close eye on. Someone I knew could potentially be in a dangerous situation. And right now I feel like I've let them down majorly.

NIGHT SHIFTS ARE THE WORST, especially when you pick up a case like the one I did. Instead of working a twelve-hour shift and getting home at six in the morning, I end up working an eighteen-hour shift.

I should go straight upstairs, shower, and pass out, but if I do that, I'll throw my entire week out of whack. At this point, it's better for me to just push through and go to sleep later this evening.

I don't think I could go to sleep right now if I tried. My mind is racing with thoughts of Tyler's horrible situation. He's just a kid, and seeing him in that hospital bed makes me furious a parent could do something like that. Even knowing we have his mother in custody, I can't help but want more justice for him.

I fall back onto my couch, checking my phone for the first time since I walked out of The Diner last night. I've got a few missed calls from my parents, a chain of texts from my brothers in our group chat, and a couple of texts from Olivia. But the one that catches my eye is the text from Ava.

She texted Friday night telling me she wouldn't be over, and I know I kind of snubbed her with my blasé response, but it was better that she wasn't here that night. I wasn't in the right mindset after finding out about my parents.

AVA

Declan and Quinn just told us about what
happened with Tyler. That's messed up on so
many levels. Hope you're doing all right…

I shouldn't be surprised by the message. Ava and I are friends—or at least I want us to be friends—but I *am* surprised. We've had a lot of conversations since we met, and in only one of them did we briefly talk about Tyler. It had been more about how her brother was worried about him than anything else, though I do remember expressing my concern and frustration with being unable to do more.

When I showed up at the hospital to take Tyler's statement, Quinn and Declan had been in the room with him. It didn't surprise me that Declan was the teacher Tyler went to, and I was honestly glad Tyler recognized he *could* go to Declan. But even knowing that Tyler had been beaten with a bat, I wasn't prepared for what I saw when I walked into that room.

He was more than just bruised and battered. His left eye was swollen shut, and it seemed his right eye wasn't far behind. His right arm was in a cast, with plenty of cuts that needed stitches and a few broken ribs to go along with the severe concussion. But it was how small he looked in that bed, as if he was folding in on himself—trying to make himself the smallest target for whatever would happen next—that really did me in.

It took allowing Declan and Quinn to stay in the room for him to tell me what happened. He'd been home when his mother came in ranting about everything going wrong in their lives being his fault. Continuing on a verbal abuse pattern of making sure he knew how worthless he was before turning violent.

It was a shit show. And while the case was cut and dry, finding his mother took more time than anyone thought it would. She was smarter than we all gave her credit for; though, not smart enough. She skipped town but didn't make it far before she decided to stop at a bar and get drunk, using her credit card in the process.

I could have left at the end of my shift, but I wasn't willing to go until that woman sat in a jail cell. Tyler deserves better, and I was determined to make sure he knew that, even if this was just a small step in making sure he feels safe.

> Sorry. I'm just getting home and caught up on everything.

> I'm sure I don't have to tell you what kind of night it was. I'm just glad it wasn't worse.

I wait a few minutes, waiting to see if she responds before I realize she's flying back to Boston today and could very well already be on the plane.

> Hope you had a safe flight.

My head falls back against the couch, and I let my eyes fall shut. *Maybe I* could *fall asleep.* I don't know how long it is, maybe five minutes, when I feel my phone vibrates in my hand.

AVA

> I just made it through security. I've got an hour to kill.

I don't get a chance to respond before I see the three little dots telling me she's typing.

AVA

> Do you want to talk about it?

> Not really. I'm sure Declan and Quinn filled you in.

AVA

When does your next shift start?

And even though it's only a slight subject change, Ava's response proves how well she already knows me. Something else I shouldn't be surprised by based on the time we've spent together and the conversations we've had, but it does. And what surprises me more is the realization that I don't think I mind Ava knowing me so well at all.

CHAPTER
Twenty

AVA

GETTING on the plane to fly back to Boston was harder than I thought it would be—not because of everything going on with Declan and Quinn. No, that worked itself out pretty quickly.

After my breakfast with Quinn at The Diner Quinn went home to talk with her dad before showing up at my brother's door, exactly like I said she would. I ended up staying the night at Caleb and Emily's so they could have their privacy, and by Sunday morning at Scott's it was like there had never been a hiccup between them.

Seeing the love in both of their eyes—even with all they went through with Tyler the night before—was a sight to see. Honestly, it made me a little jealous of the connection they had. I wanted that for myself, though I still wasn't confident I would get it. But going back to Harborview was step one in opening the door to that possibility.

No, getting on the plane was harder for a multitude of reasons: I wanted to be in Ashford Falls for Christmas with my brother and the Marks family. I definitely didn't want to see my parents. I still haven't spoken with my mother since our last conversation, and no matter how much my dad swears I won't have to see or talk about Brian, I don't completely trust his word.

Then there's the conversation with Gage.

I may have only known him for a little over a month, but I think it's safe to call us friends. I'm not willing to call us *lovers* —even if that title technically fits. And *acquaintances* feels too impersonal, which definitely doesn't fit. There isn't a lot more personal you could get with a person than sex.

And even though our text exchanges turned flirty and were filled with our normal banter, something felt off with Gage. It could have been the case with Tyler's mom—it's never easy dealing with child abuse—but I'd been concerned about his response to me before anything happened with Tyler. Something happened between me leaving his house Friday morning and Declan and me getting home from the courthouse. I just have no idea what.

I want to ask him about it but don't know if it's appropriate. He's quickly becoming the person I want to talk to about everything. Somehow, I trust he'll hold that information until I'm ready to share it with Declan. I trust that he'll give me that strength he talked about, supporting me in whatever way I need. And at the moment, I just need a sounding board, someone to truly hear me and listen without judgment.

While I might trust Gage, I'm not sure he feels the same way—though I think he might. And if I'm being honest with myself, I want to be close to offer my support if he does decide to trust me with whatever's bothering him.

Only three more days until I can go home.

And that thought has me stumbling over myself as I descend the stairs to the foyer at my parents' house.

Massachusetts isn't home anymore. Ashford Falls is.

"What's that smile for?" my father asks as he meets me at the bottom of the stairs.

It's their annual Christmas Eve party, where they invite

all their friends and colleagues to the house. I've never under-stood the purpose other than to show off their status. Why exactly they feel the need to show off to these people they call "friends" I'll never know. But I agreed to be here, so here I am.

"It's nothing," I say as he leans down to press a kiss to my cheek. I know it's only for appearances that he's being affec-tionate. Guests are already milling around, and it wouldn't look good if the Day family wasn't affectionate with each other. We wouldn't want anyone to think there's tension between us. That isn't a good look.

Neither of my parents have acknowledged me since I walked in their door a few hours ago to get ready for the party. For the last two days, I've been packing up my apartment in Boston and officially breaking my lease with the landlord. I still haven't told my parents about my plans, but tomorrow should be soon enough.

"You look beautiful," Dad says as he takes my hand and wraps it around his arm, guiding me into the formal sitting room where I'm sure my mother is greeting guests as they arrive.

"Thank you."

I decided on a simple vintage-style, velvet sheath dress in a deep forest green for this evening. The top has a faux wrap style, creating a low v-neckline and there's a slit going up the front center of the dress that allows my legs to peak out as we walk. It's simple but comfortable and elegant enough to make my parents happy.

"Gregory, there you are," my mother says, taking his hand and pulling him to her side once we're close enough.

Looking at the two of them together now, with their smiles and bright eyes, you would never know the hurt they've caused me and my brother. I can see the fakeness behind them, but their so-called friends eat it up.

Say what you will about my parents, but they make a fine-looking couple.

Even at sixty, my father still has a lean and athletic build. His hair, a distinguished grey color, is kept short and styled back to stay off his face. Most people would say he has a rugged appearance due to his high cheekbones and strong jawline, but most would also say he has an approachable manner.

A stranger would likely talk about my mother's striking beauty and poise. Like my father, she has high cheekbones and a defined jawline, though her eyes are bright blue whereas his are hazel. Most would say she's elegant, with a slender build giving her a graceful demeanor. And at fifty-eight, while she dyes her hair to cover the white, very few fine wrinkles scatter her face.

They're dressed like a couple walking the red carpet tonight—my father in a Tom Ford tux and my mother in an A-line, black Marc Jacobs dress. They look like the power couple they are.

"Ava, darling." My mother reaches for me, taking both my hands in hers, squeezing tight and pulling me in to kiss both my cheeks. The smile on her face as I pull away has never been more fake. "I'm glad you're home."

I offer her a polite smile but say nothing. Now is definitely not the time to tell them I'm moving to Ashford Falls. They hated when my brother did it and I wouldn't be surprised if they disown me when I tell them I'm doing it, too.

I stand with my parents as they greet their guests, smiling and saying all the right things but desperately counting down the seconds until I can slip away unnoticed.

While I've never been the biggest fan of these parties, I've never been as miserable as I am now. Maybe it's because this is the first one where Declan isn't standing by my side, but part of me knows it's more than that.

Until everything happened with Brian and my parents, I'd been content with my life. But since going to Ashford Falls and finally making decisions for me and no one else, I realize I was just going through the motions. I wasn't completely happy now, but I was much closer to it than I was before I left Massachusetts.

I was excited to go home and start this new adventure. I was going to take Scott's advice and try new things. I wasn't sure what I would try exactly, but there were so many options. I could go ice skating—something I hadn't done since I was a kid. Or maybe I could pick up crocheting or knitting. I could try painting like Declan, or maybe I could try a different art medium like pottery. Yoga, baking, rollerblading, gardening! There are so many things I could try, and I'm going to make a point of doing just that.

"Martha! Paul!" My mother's voice brings me back to the present.

My eyes immediately shift to my father, who swore the Wellsleys wouldn't be in attendance this evening. This might not be Brian, but it is his parents.

Before my father can say anything, my mother's voice breaks through my thoughts again. "Brian, I'm so glad you could make it back from Chicago in time." She presents her cheek for him to kiss.

"How could I miss my future mother-in-law's annual Christmas party?"

I glare at my father for a moment longer, realizing too late that this was yet another manipulation from him. "Excuse me," I say, pushing past everyone to get as far away from the Wellsleys and my parents as I possibly can.

"Ava." My father's voice is quiet but harsh as he reaches for my wrist before I make it far. "You will stay right here and do what is required of you," he says directly in my ear.

I suppress the shiver that wants to course through my body

at the feel of his breath on my skin and turn to look at him. I wanted so badly to believe that at least one of my parents would support me, that at least one of them believed me. Except, I don't think it's about them not believing me. I think they do believe me, they just don't care, which might be worse.

"No." I straighten my spine and pull my wrist from my father's grip. "I was going to wait until tomorrow to tell you, but now seems as good a time as any. I'm moving to Ashford Falls. Immediately."

I don't wait for their response. I turn and rush back up the stairs to grab the few things I brought here with me. There's no way I'm staying here for the rest of this party. My car is already packed with what I want from Boston. If I head to my apartment in town now and pack quickly, I could be in the car and on my way back to Ashford Falls tonight. I might have to stop for a quick nap, but it's only a seven-hour drive. If I push myself, I can be home in time to spend Christmas with the people that really matter.

I don't give myself time to think about any of it. I grab my coat and bag from my room and take the back stairs to the kitchen. I parked my car around back so I could leave whenever I wanted. I knew I didn't want to be trapped here, and in this moment, I'm so grateful I did.

I'm almost to my car when I see the shadow leaning against it, and the shiver I held back earlier runs up my spine. I start to turn back for the house, hoping he'll give up waiting for me and head back inside himself, but he sees me before I have a chance. No matter what I do, he'll find a way to corner me.

"What do you want?" My voice is firmer than I thought it would be. I never wanted to see Brian again after that night in his office, but to be alone with him? I can feel my body shaking at the thought of what he almost did and I'm terrified of what he might do now.

"We've already had this conversation, and you took longer

than one week to return." Brian pushes off my car, stalking toward me. "My patience is wearing thin. And it was thin before you started throwing this tantrum." His voice is harsh, anger slicing through every word.

I take a step back but stumble over the gravel beneath my heels. Brian reaches for me, his hands gripping my upper arms tightly, and I hiss in pain. I have no doubt I'll have bruises there in the morning.

"No wife of mine will disobey me," he growls.

"Good thing I'm not your wife." I try to pull out of his grasp, but his grip only tightens, making me gasp.

"Who do you think you are, speaking to me like that?" He shakes me, pulling me in tight to his chest. "Apparently, you're in need of a lesson," he whispers in my ear.

Brian spins me, pinning my front to the side of my car. My wrists bound in one of his hands, his grip tight and unyielding. I try with all my might to pull away from him, but with his body pressed against mine, his leverage is too strong.

"Brian, don't do this," I plead.

He grinds his hips against me, forcing me to feel his hardening length against my ass. "Please keep begging. It makes me so hard," he moans in my ear.

I struggle against him, his grip on my wrists getting harder. "Just let me go." I keep my voice steady even though that's the last thing I feel.

I can't believe this is happening to me again. I don't know how I'm going to get out of this. The likelihood of someone stumbling upon us is slim. The party is in the front of the house, and with the music playing, no one will hear me.

His hand not holding my wrists slides up the side of my body, ghosting the side of my breast before cutting across. It's just as his fingers are slipping under the v-neck of my dress to my bare nipple that the sound of voices stops him in his tracks.

His moment of distraction gives me exactly what I need—

space. Without thinking, I lift my heeled foot and stomp with all my might right on his, making him fall away from me in pain.

I don't wait. I grab my purse from the ground, jump into my car and lock the doors, speeding away from the house as quickly as I can, only stopping when I make it to my apartment in town.

It's not till I'm in my apartment that I register what I just escaped. It's at that realization the dam breaks, and I fall to the floor just inside the door.

I want out of this dress and a shower more than anything. I want his touch washed away from me. I want his words wiped away from my mind.

I don't know why I do it, but I dig through my purse and find my phone. Pulling it out, I find my texts and pull up my most recent exchange.

Tell me something good.

CHAPTER
Twenty-One

GAGE

IT'S NOT that I'm surprised to get a text from Ava—we've texted daily since she left for Boston. I'm just surprised at the timing and the request.

AVA

Tell me something good.

I know she had her family's Christmas Eve party this evening—something she was secretly hopeful would turn out better than she thought. But this text makes me think she was right to prepare for the worst with her parents. I still haven't gotten the full story from her, but I'm starting to realize that she'll tell me when she's ready.

I glance at the time and notice it's only eight. The party should still be going strong right now, and unless she was able to sneak her phone down to the party with her—she's not there. My concern rises at that thought, but I give her an answer anyway.

My parents are back together.

I look up from my spot in the family room to my parents in the kitchen, where they work together to finish loading the dishwasher. They're laughing, their love for each other shining through their eyes.

Since I'll be working tomorrow, we made plans to have dinner this evening, just the three of us. I thought about bailing on them as I still wasn't over being left in the dark about their relationship, but I realized it was their decision how they handled it. And honestly—with their track record—I can't blame them for wanting to keep it a secret while they figured out if it would last.

I wanted to stay angry with them, but watching them this evening? I think they might actually make it this time.

I don't think either of them stopped loving each other, but they got married and had a child young—before they really knew who they were as individuals. I think the time apart helped them realize who they are as people first. You have to know who you are before you can merge your life with someone else.

AVA

I'm going to assume if that was your response to "tell me something good" that you're happy about it.

I don't know how I feel about it, but they're happy, so I'm trying to be.

Shouldn't you be at a party right now?

The three little dots bounce for a solid minute before her response comes through.

AVA

I don't know.

I sit straighter in my seat, my gut telling me it's something more than just her parents. I contemplate texting her back but go with my instinct to call her.

"I'll be right back," I tell my parents as I stand from the couch and move to the stairs, taking them two at a time and booking it to my old bedroom.

Once I'm behind the closed door, I hit her contact, pacing the room while I wait for her to answer.

"You weren't supposed to call me." Her voice is quiet when she answers, almost inaudible.

"What happened?" I'm instantly on edge, hating that she's so far away and clearly upset.

"It's nothing." I hear the tears in her voice, even when she tries to hide them with a cough.

"Rebel. We haven't lied to each other yet. Let's not start now." I collapse to the foot of the bed, my body stiff as if waiting for impact. "Your honesty and ability to ask for what you want is one of the things I like most about you."

"You'll tell me to call the police," she whispers.

My body practically folds in half. My elbows rest on my knees, and my head hangs low. "I am the police." I keep my voice light but feel the fear coursing through me. There are very few good reasons a person needs the police.

"You can't help me all the way in Maryland."

"Rebel." It's a desperate plea. For what, I'm not entirely sure.

She's right, of course. Legally there's nothing I can do for her while I'm in Maryland and she's in Massachusetts, but I definitely can't help if I don't know what happened.

"Gage, please don't ask me." She takes a deep breath. "You're right. We've never lied to each other, and I don't want to start now, but I can't—" She hiccups, her words cutting off. I hear the panic rising in her voice, and I can't stand the thought of her being there alone.

"Just tell me you're okay," I beg.

It takes her a minute and a few deep breaths, but when she speaks, her voice sounds a little steadier. "Physically, I'm fine."

More than anything, I want to be by her side, making sure whoever hurt her can't do it again, but for some reason, she picked me as the person to talk to. I fight like hell and ignore the urge to push for more information.

"What do you need me to do?"

"Can you just talk to me?" Her voice is soft again as if she's afraid I'll deny her.

I don't think I could deny her anything. "Anything in particular you want me to talk about?"

"No. I just don't want to be alone with my thoughts right now."

"I found out about my parents getting back together because my mom wanted to give me a hard time about you." I don't know why, but it's the first thing that comes to mind, so I roll with it.

"What?" she gasps.

"Yeah. She found out we had dinner with my dad and decided it meant something much more than it did. She was jealous that he met you and she hadn't." I force a laugh, even though I don't feel it.

"How did that lead to your parents dating?"

"I told her we were just friends and she didn't believe me since we're seen having dinner at Murphy's once a week." I sink to the floor at the foot of the bed, my back resting against it and my knees pulled up. "I pointed out that she and my dad have dinner regularly, and that's when they both got fidgety."

She hums. "The telltale sign that someone is hiding something."

"Exactly. Turns out they've been seeing each other off and on since their divorce. Though, this is the longest stretch, coming in at six months. My sister's known for three."

"How does she feel about it?"

"She's actually quite happy about it. So are my brothers. I'm apparently the only one who didn't react well."

"No one would react well if they stumbled upon the information instead of being told directly about it. How are you supposed to react to finding out something before the person is ready to tell you? There was a reason they were keeping it a secret."

"Exactly!" I love that Ava gets it. "Granted, I didn't really let them explain anything, but in conjunction with Asher not telling me about his relationship, I just felt shitty and wasn't totally open to hearing what they had to say," I admit.

"Asher has a secret relationship, too?"

I hear movement on her side, and it sounds like she's turned the call on speakerphone.

"Yeah. I've apparently been very open about my views on relationships and love, leading my brother to believe I would think poorly of him if he told me he fell in love with someone."

"How do you feel about love and relationships?" Her voice is muffled as if she's moved away from the phone.

"I'm not sure I believe in love," I tell her honestly. "I don't have any examples of lasting love, and I struggle to believe you can just walk away from someone you claim to have loved. And that's all I've ever really seen—people saying they love each other but still walking away. That doesn't sound like love to me. That sounds like lust or infatuation."

There's more movement and rustling through the phone, but I hear her clearly. "And relationships?"

"My dad has been in a lot of them, like almost always in a relationship and never by himself. Or at least that's what it looked like to me. Turns out he wasn't in as many relationships as it seemed, but that's a conversation for another day." I release a heavy sigh. "I guess I talked about how I thought Dad needed to stop being in a relationship and just spend time with himself often enough that my brothers assumed I felt everyone should be alone."

"But you don't think everyone should be alone?"

"Of course not. Look, at the end of the day, I don't care what anyone does with their own life. As long as they aren't hurting anyone, you do you. When it comes to the people I love and care about? I'm going to support them in whatever makes them happy."

"I don't doubt that for a second." There's such conviction in her tone, and it startles me slightly that she can feel so strongly about anything regarding me.

We're both quiet for a moment, but I don't let it last long, remembering that she needs distraction from her thoughts. "I guess it just felt like everyone around me was keeping a secret, and it put me in a weird headspace."

"Who wouldn't be in a weird place?"

The rustling is back, and my curiosity wins out. "What are you doing?"

"I'm packing up my apartment in Harborview. Well, at least the things I care about. I can't stay here any longer than I need to. So I'm just going to throw what I care about in a bag, pack my car, and start driving. I don't know why I booked a flight for Friday. I should have always planned on driving. I know I can get around town without a car, but it's winter—a car will make my life so much easier."

I don't think I've ever heard Ava ramble. She's usually much more organized with her words. If I were anyone else, I might have been able to forget the reason I was on the phone with her in the first place, but the rambling would have reminded me instantly.

"Are you okay to drive?" I ask a little hesitantly. I don't want her to go back to wherever she was mentally when she called me, but her safety is far more important than that at the moment.

"I don't have a choice. I can't stay here." Silence takes over for a moment. "I'll be smart. If I get tired, I'll find somewhere safe to stop for a little bit before I keep going."

"Do you want me to stay on the phone with you?"

"Just for a little bit longer. Tell me more about your siblings."

And I do. I end up talking to her for another hour. I tell her about every facet I can think of, all the little details. How I felt when each of them came home, how protective I feel, how much I hated being in the army because it took me away from them, and how I loved it because it felt like my purpose.

I keep talking to her until she's packed up her car and is driving away from Harborview.

"Call me if you need to. It doesn't matter what time it is."

"I will," she promises.

"And let me know when you get home?"

"Of course."

"Be safe." I know I'm just dragging this out, but for some reason, I'm not ready to hang up—even though we've been on the phone for almost two hours.

"Thank you," she murmurs. "I don't know why, but you were the first person who came to mind."

"You don't have to thank me. It's what—" I cut myself off, not sure how to label us. Friends doesn't feel right when I'm realizing *friends* is the last thing I want to be with Ava Day. *Lovers* doesn't feel right when I'm realizing I want more than that. Somewhere along the way, this thing with Ava has started to feel like a real relationship, and I'm starting to realize I don't hate it. "Just be safe, and call me if you need me."

"I will."

We hang up, and I sit there for another minute before slowly getting up from the floor. Sitting on the floor was probably the worst idea. I'll be feeling it in my back for days, but I wouldn't take it back for anything.

When I make it downstairs, I find my parents cuddled up on the couch watching *It's a Wonderful Life*. At the sound of my steps, Mom reaches for the remote, pausing the movie while Dad looks over his shoulder, concern etched on his face.

"Is everything okay? Your mother and I were worried."

"Yeah." I stay where I am for a minute, thinking about how I want to play this. I'm not known for serious conversations. I play things off like they don't affect me. Though, I don't know how true that's been lately. I've had more serious conversations in the last month than usual.

I shuffle over to the armchair, slowly lowering myself to the seat. I don't know why I'm nervous to have this conversation, but I can't expect people to be open with me if I don't do the same in return.

"Ava was supposed to be at her parents' Christmas Eve party this evening, but she texted, and I was worried. I went upstairs, only expecting to talk to her for a few minutes."

I'm speaking more to the floor than to my parents, but I still hear the concern in my dad's voice when he answers. "Is she all right?"

"I don't know," I worry. "She said she was fine physically but didn't want to talk about what happened."

"You talked for nearly two hours," Mom points out.

"She wanted someone to talk to." I shrug.

I see the two of them share a look, communicating something, but I don't know what it is.

"Are you okay?" Dad asks, turning back to me.

"I don't know," I repeat. "I'm worried, but there's nothing I can do from here or without knowing what happened. She was in the car and on her way home when we got off the phone."

"Should she be driving?"

"Probably not, but what else is she supposed to do?" I ask. "She said she couldn't stay there, and if that was going to cause her more stress..." I let my words trail off. I hate the situation, but the options are limited.

"You're right," Mom says, placing a hand on Dad's forearm.

"I think I'm going to head home." I stand from my seat. "I'm sorry about the interruption."

"Don't apologize," Dad says as he stands from the couch, pulling me into a tight hug. "I'm proud of you."

"You'll stop by tomorrow before your shift?" Mom asks as she follows Dad's lead and pulls me into a hug of her own.

"Yeah." I give her a peck on the cheek and squeeze Dad's shoulder before moving toward the door.

When I get I home I take a quick shower and climb into bed, but I can't shut my brain off. I lie there, staring at the ceiling, worrying about Ava, and wondering what the fuck happened with her parents.

It's four in the morning when I give up and climb out of bed, heading to the basement—my at-home gym—where I fully intend to work out every pent-up emotion I'm feeling. My body will yell at me tomorrow, but I can't sit still, so this is the best option for me until Ava lets me know she made it home safely.

CHAPTER
Twenty-Two

AVA

EIGHT HOURS after leaving Harborview behind, I find myself in the same spot I was in two and a half weeks ago, except with shoes on this time.

I don't think about the fact that Gage's is the first place I go when I get back to Ashford Falls. I just knock.

He opens the door in a pair of low-slung sweatpants and nothing else. His hair is a little damp, like maybe he's just gotten out of the shower. There's worry in his eyes and exhaustion carved across his face, but it's like it all falls away when he registers it's me standing on his porch.

"Ava," he breathes.

"Sorry, I know it's early, but I just..." I shrug, my words trailing off.

He shakes his head as he reaches for me, pulling me to him in a tight hug. His hold is fierce but somehow gentle at the same time. The last bit of tension finally leaves my body as my arms go around his waist. Sandalwood and sage surround me, letting me take my first easy breath since I left my parents' house.

"You're safe." It's said so quietly that I don't think it's meant for me, but I still nod my head against him.

"I thought I would stop in Connecticut for a few hours to sleep, but once I started driving, I didn't want to stop. I just wanted to be home."

Gage's hold tightens for a second before he pulls away, his eyes moving over my entire being like he's checking to make sure I really am okay.

"Sorry, come in." He moves to the side, giving me space to enter, but his hand falls to my lower back the second I'm in front of him, guiding me into his house. "Let me grab a shirt real quick." His hand travels the entire expanse of my back and down my arm as he walks away. He only stops touching me when he's too far.

I barely have time to remove my coat and slip off my boots, and Gage is back within a minute, pulling a shirt over his head and guiding me to the couch.

He winces as he takes the seat next to me, but it's gone so quickly I think I might have imagined it.

"Will you tell me what happened?" Gage turns his body, lifting one leg onto the couch so his shin runs the length of my thigh. He places one arm along the back of the couch and reaches for my hand with his other, bringing our joined hands to his lap.

The movement causes the sleeve of my sweater to shift, exposing the bruises on my wrist from Brian's grip. I try to hide them, but I'm not fast enough.

Gage's grip on my hand tightens just enough that I can't pull away from him, but as he brings his arm from the back of the couch down to push up my sleeve, his touch is gentle.

"You told me you were okay." His eyes are entirely focused on my wrist, gently turning my hand to get a full view of the bruise. It's as he turns my hand over that the outline becomes recognizable. There's no denying the discoloration is from a hand. "Ava." His tone is pleading, almost pained. "Did your parents do this?"

I swallow. I don't want to talk about this, but there's also no hiding what happened. I know Gage well enough to know he's fiercely protective of those he cares for, and I have no doubt I somehow fall into that category. If I don't tell him, he'll talk to my brother, and I'm definitely not ready to tell Declan.

"Not directly."

"Ava, talk to me," he begs. "You have all my extra strength. Whatever you need, you have it. Just talk to me."

"I don't know where to start." My voice is quiet, almost meek, and I hate it. I'm not a meek person. I know what I want and I'm not afraid to go after it, but something happened in Brian's office, and it altered me. I thought I started getting that piece of me back, but returning to Massachusetts proved it's still missing.

Gage releases my hand and shifts even closer, his leg now pressed along my thigh. "Start wherever you want, whatever makes the most sense. There's no rush."

I study him for a moment, and all I see is understanding in his eyes. There's no judgment or pity. Gage has always told me I could borrow his strength, and in this moment, I'm truly trusting him to give me everything he has and to help me carry this. I shift in my seat, turning to face him directly. My legs criss-crossing on the couch but still pressed against his. My hands rest in my lap, but I mess with the cuffs of my sweater, pulling them down to cover the bruises.

"I was fired from Henry, Wellsley, & Ford. I know you already know that, but the reason I got fired wasn't because of anything I did." I glance down at my lap, taking a fortifying breath before continuing. "I was fired because I refused to sleep with one of the partners' sons."

Gage squeezes my leg lightly, telling me he's here and listening. It contrasts the tension I see coursing through the rest of his body and the anger I see flaring in his eyes. But I'm not afraid of it. I know it's not aimed at me, but at Brian.

"Paul Wellsley and my father went to college together. They were roommates their first year and ended up pledging the same fraternity. They've been best friends ever since. And luckily for them, Paul's wife and my mom get along famously." My voice takes on a mocking tone. It's a defense mechanism, trying to cover the tears I feel building.

I take a minute, my head tipping down to study my hands in my lap. "I guess somewhere along the way, they decided their son, Brian, and I would make the perfect pair. As if living in the Elizabethan era or something, my parents arranged my marriage to Brian."

"What?" It comes out as more of a breath than a word, and I get it—the disbelief.

"Yeah." I nod absently, still looking at my lap. "I don't know why they didn't tell me or why they waited so long to actually follow through on it. But I guess Brian got tired of waiting." I lift my eyes to look at Gage. "His parents told him about the arrangement as soon as it was decided, and being eight years older than me, he felt it was high time we were married so he could begin working on getting his heir to the Wellsley empire." That mocking tone is back, but this time I can't stop the tears from welling in my eyes. They don't fall, but I feel them there.

Gage doesn't move, though I see the anger flare again.

"Brian has been working for the firm since before he graduated from law school, but he's a criminal defense lawyer, and I worked in family law. Our paths rarely crossed while at work. And personally, while he might have attended the same events I did, we always stuck to our own crowd. When I say Brian and I rarely talked, I mean it."

"Ava, you don't have to defend yourself to me," he says gently.

"I know, but looking back on it, I should have known something was off." I lift a hand and wipe desperately at my right cheek where a tear slips free.

Gage reaches forward, wiping softly at my cheek. It's with such care that it almost takes my breath away. He takes hold of both my hands, holding them gently. "You can't judge yourself for actions made based on the information you have now. There's a reason they say hindsight is twenty-twenty. Nothing that happened was your fault, regardless of what you know now."

"He asked to see me in his office one evening. I didn't really think anything of it, so I went. It was late, but that was normal. I wasn't even in his office five minutes before he tried to force himself on me."

His hands squeeze mine, only for a moment, as if he didn't have control for a second.

"I fought him the best I could." Another tear slips free, and he wipes that one away, too. "I got lucky. His assistant came in before he could do more than tear my blouse. I didn't even wait for either of them to say anything before I got the hell out of there."

A few more tears spill, and Gage's fingers remain there to catch every one. I give myself a second this time before I continue speaking. When I do, my voice is a little steadier—calmer.

"I went to my parents' place instead of going home. I don't really know why. I've never considered my parents as all that caring, but I thought they would support me. Or at least bring me some level of comfort, but they didn't believe me." I shrug, trying to make myself believe it doesn't matter more than trying to convince Gage of that fact. "Brian called his parents as soon as I left his office, and his parents called mine before I got there. They spun some story about how I came onto him and was embarrassed that his assistant walked in on us." I nod, a rueful smile taking shape. "That's when they told me about the arranged marriage. They informed me that the announcement would be made in the paper after the new year, with the wedding happening in July."

Gage's head falls, his grip on my hands tightening a bit. He takes a deep breath, holding it for a second before releasing it. When he lifts his eyes back to mine, I continue.

"I left and went back to Boston, carrying on like nothing happened. Except I made sure I went nowhere near Brian and didn't talk to my parents. Two weeks later I was fired. Declan called about Nicole suing for custody the following evening, and I got on the next flight out." I shrug. "You know the rest."

Gage lifts one hand, pushing the sweater back to expose my bruise. "That's not all of it," he says quietly.

"No, I guess it isn't." I look back down at my lap, not sure I want to see his face for this next part. "About two weeks ago, Brian called me." I feel the tension in the air rise. Gage knows exactly what day I'm talking about. "He told me I had a week to come home and begin planning the wedding. He made it very clear the longer I took to return, the worse it would be for me."

"Ava." It's hurt I hear in his voice now, and I hate that I've caused it.

My grip on his hand tightens this time. "I've never lied to you." I lift my eyes to his, wanting to make sure he hears me. "I told you there were other factors, and there were, but all Brian's call did was push me to remember that I don't cower to anyone. I go after what I want, and that's exactly what I did that night."

"Ava—"

"No, Gage." I take his face in my hands, forcing him to look at me. "That night was about me taking control of my life and forgetting about everyone and everything else."

His eyes bounce between mine, searching for something. I

know he'll find it because I'm not lying to him. Brian might have triggered something in me that night, but Gage didn't take advantage of me. I wanted everything that happened between us.

"Okay," he whispers, gently bringing his hands to my wrists and moving them back to my lap. "Tell me the rest."

"When my dad called a week later, he swore the arrangement was off with the Wellsleys and that he talked to my mother about how she'd been speaking to me since everything first happened with Brian. He swore I wouldn't have to see or speak about the Wellsleys or the arrangement again. He just wanted me to come home and for us to have a nice Christmas together." I take a deep breath, feeling the tears building again.

"I figured I needed to pack my apartments anyway, so what was the harm? I could pack and tell my parents about my move in one fell swoop." I shrug.

"Everything was going fine. I landed in Boston on Sunday and spent all day Monday and most of the day yesterday packing what I wanted and organizing the rest for donation later in the week. When I got to my parents, they were already in their rooms getting ready for the party, so I headed to mine and did the same." My head falls, and I study our clasped hands in my lap.

"I was a little late coming down the stairs, but Dad greeted me and we joined Mom to greet guests as they arrived." I shake my head slightly. "About thirty minutes later, Brian's parents showed up with Brian in tow."

"Rebel." I hear it in Gage's voice, how he wants me to stop, but his eyes tell me to keep going. He's giving me that strength, just like he said he would.

"They mentioned the engagement, and I didn't wait around. I told them I was moving to Ashford Falls and left them standing there. I went to my room to grab my things and booked it for my car, but I wasn't fast enough."

"Brian was waiting for you," Gage offers.

"Yeah. I tried to go back inside, but he saw me. He came toward me so quickly—berating me for my behavior—and I knew he would corner me no matter where I was. He tried to force himself on me again, and—" I gulp, trying to control my emotions, but the tears slip free.

I don't think I realized how afraid I was when Brian had his hand in my dress until right now. "I don't think I would have been able to fight him off. Not if it hadn't been for a caterer coming out the back door and distracting him long enough for me to stomp on his foot and get away."

Gage doesn't wipe the tears this time. He shifts on the couch, pulling me across his lap and holding me to him in a tight embrace. He doesn't offer any empty promises or platitudes about everything being okay. He just holds me until the tears dry up.

CHAPTER
Twenty-Three

GAGE

I DON'T THINK I've ever wanted to cause harm to another human being more than I want to in this moment. Brian-Fucking-Wellsley is a dead man if I ever meet him. And honestly? Ava's parents might be, too.

I know Ava comes from a different world than me—her parents are wealthy and have status—but that doesn't mean you can treat your children like objects that can be traded for something else.

I've only known Ava for a little over a month, and even I know there's no way she could be lying about what happened to her. Her parents must know she's telling the truth—they just don't care. There's no way a person who's known her for her entire life thinks she's lying. Not if they're paying attention to her.

I don't know what to say. I want to ask why she hasn't told her brother or why she didn't call the police after the first attack, but right now I know that won't help anything. I want to promise her she'll never have to see Brian or her parents again, but that's not realistic. I hold her instead—providing whatever comfort I can.

"I'm sorry," she murmurs, her head still buried in my chest.

My arms tighten around her. "Don't apologize, Rebel. You have nothing to be sorry for."

Her tears dry, but her body starts to shake, and shivers rack her body. "I don't know why I'm shivering." Her teeth chatter.

"It's the shock. You haven't stopped moving or worrying since you left your parents. Your brain is starting to recognize that you're safe now."

I stand from the couch, Ava in my arms. My back protests at the movement but I ignore it. Ava is more important than a shot of pain telling me I'm doing too much—and have been for the last eight hours.

I don't stop moving until I reach my bathroom, where I set Ava on the counter. "Don't move." I turn to the tub and start filling it with warm water.

When I started my house hunt after joining the police force, I knew I needed a bathroom with a large tub—something I could soak in on days my back doesn't let me forget about my life-changing injury. This house didn't have a tub when I moved in, but the bathroom was the perfect foundation for the peaceful atmosphere I was able to create.

I've never been more grateful for what I did with this bathroom than I am now.

Once the water is hot enough, I lower the plug and turn back to the sink, grabbing the Epsom salts and dumping them in.

"What? No bubble bath?" Ava tries to joke, her teeth still chattering.

"Sorry, just the salts," I murmur in her ear as I step between her legs. "I'm gonna undress you. Is that okay?"

She nods, lifting her arms. Placing my hands at the hem of her sweater, I slowly lift it over her head and set it on the counter next to her. I move to unclasp her bra, and as the straps slip down her arms, I notice the bruises there. The sight of the handprints on her body makes me see red.

Taking a deep breath, I bend to place a light kiss to the bruise on one arm before copying the motion on the other side.

"I'm okay." Ava's voice is soft, but the chattering has stopped.

"I know," I tell her. "But I hate that you have these marks on your body."

I help her stand from the counter, bending to one knee to slide the leggings down her legs, her underwear pulled down with them.

There's nothing sexual about what's happening between us, and I find I'm more than content with that. I'm not happy about the circumstances, but there's a peace that comes over me with the knowledge that Ava trusts me to take care of her. After what she went through last night—even if it could have been so much worse—I wouldn't blame her for pushing me away.

With her leggings and underwear removed, I stand and guide Ava toward the bathtub. "I can add some body wash to create some bubbles if you want."

"No, this is perfect," she says as she steps into the water. "But will you sit with me?"

"Of course." I turn to grab a towel from below the sink, placing it on the floor next to the tub, and start to lower myself, my back screaming in protest again. I wince before I can cover it up.

"What's wrong?" Ava's brows pinch, concern lighting in her eyes.

"It's just an old injury flaring up." I shake my head, preparing to lower myself to the floor again.

"Get in with me."

"Rebel, that's not what this is."

"I know. You can sit across from me. The tub is plenty big

enough, and I'm thinking that injury is the exact reason you have the tub and the Epsom salts." She reaches a hand out to me. "Get in with me."

I study her face for a minute, seeing nothing but honesty in her eyes. "Okay."

I grab a couple more towels from below the sink before carefully removing my clothes and climbing into the bathtub across from Ava—my legs moving to the outside of hers. The hot water instantly has my muscles loosening. My head falls back against the lifted edge, and a moan falls from my lips.

"That sounds like a bad injury."

I lift my head and see her studying me, that concern still evident in her eyes.

"It's the injury that led to my discharge from the army." If Ava can share what she did with me this morning, I can share this with her. "I don't know if you've noticed it, but there's a scar on my back above my right hip. My unit and I got caught in a firefight." I lift one of her feet and begin massaging it. "It's funny—not in a ha-ha way, but..." My words trail off, and it's the feel of her hand on my shin that brings me back. "I got shot twice, technically. Once in the shoulder—which was more of a graze than anything—and once in the chest."

I feel Ava's body tighten, but she doesn't say anything. Giving her foot an extra squeeze, I continue. "My gear did exactly what it was supposed to, but the shot caught me off guard, and I fell back. Landed on a rock *just right*." My tone is a little mocking at the end.

It's no surprise I remember that mission like it happened yesterday. I knew I hurt myself the second I landed. After catching my breath, I got up and kept moving, exactly like we were trained. I felt the pinch in my back, but I ignored it, thinking it was just a nasty bruise and it would be gone in a few days.

"A week later, we were on patrol. I stepped off a curb, and pain went shooting up my back. All of a sudden, I could barely walk." I switch to Ava's other foot. "Turns out, when I landed on that rock, I ended up with a broken back. They called it a compression fracture. I spent a year in and out of doctor's offices and physical therapy. They tried surgery, but the pain never went away."

"But you still have a physically demanding job." It's not exactly a question, but it is at the same time.

"I couldn't pass the physical fitness test to continue as a green beret. It wasn't a medical discharge. The army was more than happy to keep me, but I didn't want to be stuck behind a desk for the rest of my career." I shrug and offer a half-hearted smile. "Desk duty isn't my strong suit."

"How'd you decide to become a police officer?" Ava asks in the silence.

"I got tired of moping around." I chuckle. "And I still wanted to help people. It felt like a good fit."

"The pain is still there?"

"I can ignore it most of the time, but if I push myself too hard, it becomes harder to ignore."

"What did you do this time?"

I lift my eyes slowly, finally meeting hers for the first time since I started sharing. *We've never lied to each other.* "I couldn't sleep last night worrying about you, so I spent about two hours in the gym instead."

"Gage," Ava whispers.

I shake my head before she can say anything else. "I'm glad you called me, Ava. I'm glad you trusted me enough to be your strength. I don't want you to regret that because I sure as fuck don't."

I don't look away from Ava. I need to make sure she knows how serious I am. I'll never be upset that I'm the person she felt safe enough to call. That I'm the person she came to first when she got home. That I'm the person she's letting take care of her.

Ava shifts in the water, resting her hands on my shins and squeezing gently. Her gaze shifts to the window at our side, staring out at the landscape beyond. It may be winter and barren outside, but it's still peaceful and beautiful.

When I remodeled the bathroom, I had this window installed so I could enjoy the picturesque views through the backyard. I lucked out with my house backing up to the dense tree line the way it does. It creates my own private oasis. Adding the large window gives me an unobscured view, making it feel like I'm in the beautiful outdoors.

Even in the winter, I love looking out this window. Without the leaves on the trees, you can see the mountains in the distance and all the farmland surrounding the town. I still feel like I'm in my own corner of the world.

"What are you thinking about?" I ask gently, my hands resting on her feet that are against my stomach in the water.

Her gaze slowly returns to mine. There's still a weariness to her eyes, but there's also a slight glimmer to them. She's coming back to herself, and the knowledge that I helped get her there has pride swelling in my chest.

"Trying new things. Really experience life—on my terms instead of someone else's."

"What do you mean?"

"Practically everything I've done in my life has been because my parents manipulated me into it. I didn't recognize it at the time, but now I see it in everything I've ever done." She releases a self-deprecating laugh, her gaze drifting back to the window. "I think the only thing I ever did for myself was read, and I had to hide that from my parents because I wasn't reading the 'right' things." A tear slips down her cheek, and she brushes it away before turning back to me. "I'm thirty years old, and I have no idea what I want to do with my life. I have no idea what brings me joy."

"Rebel, that's not entirely true." I reach for her hand, pulling her toward me. She turns in the water, placing herself between my legs, her back to my chest. "You know what brings you joy—you just haven't been able to go after it until now," I whisper in her ear.

She shakes her head. "I don't know. I have no idea what I like and don't like." Her voice is tearful, and my arms around her waist tighten.

I bring my lips down to place a soft kiss at the spot where her neck meets her shoulder. "Okay, then we'll try new things. What do you want to try?" I say into her skin.

"I don't know. How messed up is that? I know I want to try new things, but I have no idea where to start." She lets her head fall back against my chest. "What do you like to do?"

"I'm a physical person. I like to stay active, so I do a lot of hiking. In the spring and summer I also go kayaking. Nature is my safe space, so any chance I get to be out in it, I'm there."

"Hmm," she hums, her head falling to look back out the window. "I think I like the idea of the outdoors." Her voice is so quiet it's almost a whisper.

"Then let's go hiking."

"Right now?"

"No." I chuckle. "But I'm off this weekend, so let's go."

"I don't know," Ava mutters. "I'll have to see what Declan's up to. See if I can sneak away."

I didn't have a problem with us being a secret before—I didn't have a problem with us being casual before—but this doesn't feel casual anymore, and I don't think I want it to be. I don't want to be a secret.

I lower my head, placing my lips against the skin at her shoulder. "Or we could tell him," I murmur against her.

Her body stiffens slightly, but she doesn't pull away from me. "I thought we agreed."

"We did, but I'm open to changing that agreement if you are."

"Gage..." She doesn't have to say anything else. I hear it clear as day in her tone—she's not ready for more.

It stings more than I want it to, but I understand. "Okay." I place a kiss to her shoulder and squeeze her to me. "Let me know if you can sneak away for a hike after you talk to Declan."

Ava shifts in the water, rolling herself so we're chest to chest, her back arching in the water. She studies me, looking for something, but I don't think she'll find anything other than truth in my eyes. It's not that I don't care. It's just that I understand. She's been through a lot over the last twelve hours. She needs time to figure out how she feels about all of it.

I'm not backing down from having more with Ava Day. I'm just giving her time to accept that it *will* happen.

"Thank you," she whispers.

"Any time." I reach up and gently push a piece of hair back behind her ear, leaning down for a light kiss to her lips.

CHAPTER
Twenty-Four

GAGE

I'M LEANING against the bar when I feel the air shift. I'm not totally shocked by it—the fact that I sense her in the room before I see her. Just like when I first saw her on the courthouse steps, my attention was immediately drawn to her. The only difference from that first moment to this one is now I know her. Now I understand that haunted look in her eye, and now I want even more desperately to help erase it.

I haven't seen Ava since she left my place two days ago on Christmas morning. We didn't talk anymore about telling Declan or anyone else what was going on between us that morning, but we did make a list of things she's interested in trying.

Even after everything the two of us shared, it was easy and comfortable between us. There was no pressure to be someone else. There was no pressure to come up with something for us to do—we just existed in the same space. And I want to do it again and again.

I smile as I see Ava grimace at something Quinn says to Declan before there's a brief exchange and Ava turns for the bar, picking her way through the crowd.

Friday nights are always busy at Murphy's—definitely busier than she's used to seeing on our Thursday evenings—but she doesn't seem to care.

Ava finds an open spot at the bar and catches Walt's attention, placing her order before he turns away to take another. I should stay where I am and let her do her own thing, but I can't stay away from her.

Grabbing my beer, I force myself into the spot next to Ava before someone else can. And from the grunt behind me, someone was very close to taking this spot.

"Rebel," I croon in her ear.

Ava turns, a small smile on her lips. She doesn't seem surprised to see me or troubled that I've stepped up to her side. Taking a chance, I step even closer—her arm brushing my chest.

"Gage." There's a teasing lilt to her tone, and my smile grows. I can feel my dimples pop. "What are you doing here?"

"Is it bad if I say I wanted to see you? Even if I wasn't sure I'd actually get to talk to you?"

While I haven't seen Ava, we've talked over the last two days. For instance, I know she still came to Murphy's last night. And while she had intended to spend the evening sitting at the bar talking to Walt, she ended up having a meal with my parents.

Have I talked to them more about Ava since Christmas Eve? Only to tell them she made it home safe and that I have indeed seen and spoken to her. I didn't want to tell them more and break Ava's trust in me. It's easier to keep things simple while talking about Ava with them.

Were they the ones who told me they had dinner with her last night? No, they were not. That was Ava—when she also told me she would be at Murphy's this evening with her family.

They want to help introduce her to the town now that

she's officially moving to Ashford Falls. Of course, Ava's already well acquainted with this part of town—not that she shared that with her family.

I also know from our conversation last night that she's starting at the bookstore a week earlier than originally planned—something Ava's really happy about—and that we won't be going on our hike this weekend.

The news about the hike is why I decided to hang out at Murphy's, hoping to steal a couple minutes of her time.

"That's some serious honesty there," Ava jokes.

"Well, I like the knowledge that we haven't lied to each other. I'm not going to be the one to break that streak—even on something as small as this."

"Hmm," she hums, turning to lean against the bar, bringing her chest to chest with me. "If I'm being honest—"

"Which you definitely should be," I interrupt, brushing my hand against her arm resting on the bar.

"I like that we don't lie to each other as well—even on something as small as this."

"So, you're not mad that I'm stalking you?" I tease.

"So you're admitting to stalking me?" she counters, her eyebrows raising.

If I didn't see the spark in her eye or know her as well as I do, I might think she was really upset with me, but I do know her, and I know she's enjoying the banter.

Before I can say anything else, there's a commotion at the end of the bar, drawing everyone's attention. I feel Ava's hand fall to my arm, squeezing slightly.

"You okay?" I ask, turning back to her, concern etched across my face at the look on hers. I follow her line of sight to the table her brother sits at and see Quinn standing.

"That's Quinn's mother," Ava whispers. I bring my focus back to Ava. "It's such a complicated story for all of them," she mumbles.

"I can understand complicated family dynamics," I offer, glancing back at Quinn and Caleb before turning back to Ava. "But they've got a great support system around them, and you being here to help is going to make all the difference."

"Yeah." Her eyes come back to mine. "You're right. They do have a great support system." The corner of her mouth lifts in a small smile. "They remind me a little of your family."

"Oh, you mean they like embarrassing each other and forcing their way into other people's lives?" I roll my eyes, and Ava laughs.

"They love you."

"They can love me and not force their way into my—" I cut myself off, not entirely sure how to finish that statement. "Well, into your life," I finish lamely.

Ava's hand, still resting on my arm, squeezes again. "It definitely seemed a little like an ambush." She laughs.

"Oh, it was. Small town living, remember? Most people know we're here Thursday nights. My parents might have known I was working last night, but they obviously hoped you'd still show up. Perfect opportunity for my mother to meet you."

"Sorry for the wait, love. It's a little crazy here tonight." Walt drops her drinks on the bar, and before she can say anything, he's called away again.

Ava watches him walk away, concern crossing her face. "Doesn't he have another bartender or something?"

"Technically? Yes, but he doesn't schedule them very often. Normally only when he goes out of town to visit his son." Ava turns to look at me, shock evident in her eyes, and before she can say anything, I continue. "It's hard for him to trust other people with the bar. I don't know the full story, but his dad bought the place shortly after moving here from Ireland. He built it up from nothing and took a lot of pride in the place. Walt almost lost it a few months after his dad passed. He's barely left ever since."

"That's so sad," Ava mumbles.

"It's worse when you find out his son never visits."

Ava's head whips to mine. "What?" she gasps.

"If you want another complicated story, it's that one. It's also the only secret this town doesn't know."

"For such a small town, there sure is a lot of drama."

"We've gotta keep it interesting." I laugh.

We stand there, just staring at each other. My eyes drift to her lips and I desperately want to kiss them. I don't know for sure, but I think it's both of us that start to lean in.

Before our lips brush, something registers for Ava because she places her hand on my chest, pushing me away gently, regret pouring from her eyes.

"I should get these drinks over to the table."

I take a small step back, my eyes falling to the ground for a second before I manage a smirk in her direction. "Yeah."

"I'll talk to you later?" she asks as she picks up her drinks.

"Sure. I'm around." And for Ava, I probably always will be.

AVA and I might not go on a hike over the weekend, but I do convince all three of my siblings to join me on an easy hike through Whispering Pines Trail Saturday morning.

I got lucky and saw everyone together for an hour on Christmas before leaving for my shift at the station, and I talked them into the hike. I've wanted more time with my siblings, and with Asher heading back to school and the season starting soon, we'll be lucky to get any time with him over the next five months.

"So, when do the rest of us get to meet your girlfriend?" Leo snickers from the front of the group.

"You have a girlfriend?" Olivia practically shouts from beside me.

"No, I don't have a girlfriend. Leo is just being a twerp."

"What Gage means to say is that he doesn't have a girlfriend, but he wishes he did," Asher jumps in on the razzing.

"What?" Another shout from Olivia.

"Okay, that's enough of that. Ava and I are just friends. Mom and Dad just don't want to believe that and decided to ambush her at Murphy's one night. You'll meet her whenever you meet her." I shrug.

"But do you want her to be your girlfriend?" Olivia asks.

Do I want Ava to be my girlfriend? For the first time since high school, yes, I want to be in a serious relationship—but only if it's with Ava Day.

I thought it was just the mystery of Ava that had me so intrigued and invested in spending time with her. But I know the answer to the mystery now, and I still desperately want to spend time with her. While I love my siblings and am honestly glad we're getting this day together, I'd rather be doing something with Ava—even if it's just sitting at home watching TV or reading a book.

There's still so much for me to learn about her—and for her to learn about me—but I want to. I haven't experienced wanting to learn more about someone else for well over a decade.

So, yeah, I want Ava to be my girlfriend. But am I going to tell my sister that? Probably not. But I also don't want to lie to her. Honesty might be something Ava and I are known for with each other, but it's something I strive for with everyone in my life.

"It's not just about what I want. Being in a relationship is about both people." Olivia opens her mouth, but I continue before she can ask something else I might not be able to talk my way around. "And more importantly, it's a conversation that should be had between those two people before anyone else."

Leo spins and walks backward, a smirk on his face. "So, yes, he wants Ava to be his girlfriend."

"All that talk of relationships not being for you, and you're throwing it all out the window?" Asher tries to hold his laugh in but breaks quickly.

"All right." I roll my eyes but smile along with them. "I get it. We can move on."

Leo turns back to face the direction we're walking with Asher jogging to catch up and walk at his side. I notice Olivia periodically looking at me, but she doesn't say anything, and I don't push. Olivia will ask the question when she's ready.

"What changed your mind?" Olivia asks after a few minutes of walking in silence.

"Changed my mind?"

"About love and relationships."

"Who said anything about love?" I lift a brow.

"No one, but one would assume you would only enter a relationship if you were open to the idea of love. You wouldn't waste someone's time if you didn't think there was a future with them."

"You know I'm not in a relationship, right?"

"Yes, but..." She looks ahead of us, where Leo and Asher are goofing around, and gestures to them. "Like they said, you want to be."

I release a sigh and look up to the sky above us, trying to figure out how to answer my inquisitive sister. Olivia has always been an observer, and her observations always lead to questions. Good questions that always get you to think about something in a new light.

I let my eyes fall to the trail before us. "I wish I had a

better answer for you, but I don't." I gently grab her wrist, making her stop and look at me. "Ava changed my mind." I shrug. "I didn't realize it when I met her, but as I've gotten to know her..." I look back up the trail to my brothers, who haven't noticed we stopped. "I don't know." I shrug again and chuckle before looking back at Olivia. "I don't want to stop learning more about Ava. It's cliché, but it's true—I want to know everything I can about her. And it's that thought that has me open to the idea of more."

"You really like her."

It's not a question, but I smile and shrug anyway. "Yeah, I really like her."

"Why?"

I laugh and throw my arm over her shoulder, starting our walk again. "Shouldn't you have grown out of the why phase more than ten years ago?"

"Do we ever grow out of the why phase?" Now it's Olivia's turn to shrug. "I think we just stop asking it out loud, afraid of what people will say."

"You might be onto something there."

"You're avoiding the question. Why do you like Ava?"

"She's not afraid to go after what she wants. She's sarcastic and easy to talk to. She likes my sense of humor." I chuckle to myself at that. "She's not afraid to admit she doesn't know what her future holds. She's smart and ambitious. Supportive and hardworking." I think back to Christmas Day. "She's brave and sensitive. Loyal and loving."

A lightness comes over me as I think of all the things I like about Ava Day. She's all of those things and so much more. I knew I liked her—I realized that before she left for Boston—but something about listing all the amazing qualities of Ava has me realizing how serious my feelings for her have become.

I was planning on pursuing a future with her regardless,

but as I tell my sister about Ava, I realize I'll only stop my pursuit if she tells me this isn't what she wants.

"I thought you would just tell me she's hot or something." Olivia smiles, lightening the mood, likely realizing the serious direction my thoughts have taken.

"Well, she's definitely that, too." I offer a smirk.

"Do we get to meet her?" Olivia whispers after a few more minutes of contemplative silence.

I chuckle, pulling her to my side. "Yeah, you're going to meet her."

CHAPTER
Twenty-Five

AVA

IT'S my third day at the bookstore, and I'm already in love with this job and place. I felt it before I walked in the door the first time and knew it for sure when Abbey and I started talking—this place is made to make you feel at peace as soon as you step inside.

I couldn't have picked a better place to start again.

I've been working with Abbey in the mornings when the shop is busiest. Though, I've noticed the shop is busiest in the mornings because people come in for the treats Abbey makes, not because of the books.

"You know you could open a bakery with these, right?" I ask, waving a croissant around with one hand and covering my mouth—half full of the bite I'm chewing—with the other.

Abbey laughs, but doesn't say anything.

"I'm serious. You need help in the mornings because of the crowd you're bringing in with the mini bakery you've already created. You would kill at selling these things for real."

"I've thought about it, but there aren't any buildings available here on Main Street, and I don't know if it would do well somewhere else." She shrugs as she wipes down the counter from the morning rush.

I don't know Abbey well, but something in that statement doesn't ring true. "The people of this town would come to you no matter where you're selling, believe me."

We're interrupted by the sound of my phone ringing. "Crap. I'm sorry! I thought I silenced that." I reach into my back pocket, pulling my phone out and muting the call.

"It's fine. Take it." Abbey waves me off.

I look down to see who it is first and see it's Nicole's lawyer. I don't waste time and answer immediately. "This is Ava Day."

"Ms. Day, I've got some news I'm sure your client will be quite pleased with."

"I KNOW I should wait for everyone else to get here, but I don't want to," I tell Scott when he opens the door for me a couple of hours later.

After the phone call with Nicole's lawyer, I shot Scott a text asking if he's free this afternoon. Once I had confirmation he was, I texted Caleb and Emily to tell them to meet me here around four, when I knew Declan and Quinn would be dropping Max off from school.

It's quarter to four now, but I can't wait to share the news with Scott. I don't hold the smile back as he closes the door. "Nicole dropped the suit. Max is yours. Technically, she can refile, but a judge will never give it the time of day—not after this." I feel the tears in my eyes before I finish speaking, and I see them reflected back at me in Scott's.

"It's over? Just like that?" His voice wavers, clearly overcome with emotion.

I give him a watery smile. "Yeah, just like that. It's over."

Scott stumbles slightly, catching himself on the wall next to him, and the tears slip free. "I don't think I realized how scared I was about losing him until this moment." He turns so his back is to the wall, his head falling back. As his shoulders shake, he lifts his hands, covering his face.

I know it's mostly relief coursing through him, but there's grief there, too. I know because that's exactly what I'm feeling. Scott might not have to worry about losing Max to Nicole anymore, but he will lose all of us. He's going to miss out on so many moments we all just assumed we'd have together, and it sucks.

I move to Scott's side, wrapping my arms around his waist in a tight hug, and I let my own tears fall. The only saving grace is that we don't have to spend the precious time we have left fighting to stay together. Now, we can just focus on us.

It takes him a second, but Scott's hands fall from his face, and his arms wrap around me, hugging me as tight as I'm hugging him. Scott might not be my father, and I might have only known him for the past five years, but he has loved me and treated me more like a daughter these last five years than my own father has in my entire life.

"I want more time," I whisper against him.

"Me too, Shortcake. Me too."

Guess who's getting their own place as of this weekend?

GAGE

That was fast.

Where?

The guest house behind Scott's place. Quinn and my brother are moving in with each other.

I'M in the middle of typing more when my phone rings—Gage's name on the display.

"Impatient much?" I laugh as I answer, curling up on the porch swing at Declan's with a large fuzzy blanket to keep me warm.

It might be winter, but it's still early winter, so while the temperatures are definitely dropping, they aren't unbearable. Of course, this is Maryland we're talking about, and I've learned over the last five years that in Maryland, it could be the dead of winter, and you might end up with a day that hits the mid-sixties. They don't say Maryland has twelve seasons for nothing.

"This felt quicker. Explain, please." There's noise in the background, but it quickly fades away.

"Aren't you at work?" He's been on nights the last two weeks, but he's still made time to talk with me—something I'm choosing not to look too closely at for fear that I might let my heart feel what his persistent attention likely means. And I want to talk to him, too.

"Yeah, but it's slow, and I'm at the station, so quit stalling and tell me what's going on," he teases.

"There's really not much more to it." I shrug even though he can't see me. "I got a call from Nicole's lawyer at work this morning telling me she dropped the suit."

"That's great news," Gage interrupts, and I can tell he means it.

"Yeah," I say softly, almost to myself. "I was so excited to tell Scott about it. I couldn't wait for everyone to get to Scott's to share the news. Which was probably a good thing." I feel the tears building, thinking back to Scott's reaction. "It hit Scott harder than he was expecting."

"I bet. Scott's an amazing father—and man. To go through everything he's currently dealing with and then have to fight for custody of his kid on top of that? He didn't deserve it." A small smile grows at the confidence I hear in Gage's voice.

I love that people see how amazing Scott is, and that I get to say I live in a town where the people support their neighbors like everyone here has supported the Marks family. It's what I loved about Harborview—despite my parents living there—and it's why I kept my apartment in town. I love that Ashford Falls has it, too.

"So, how does this lead to you moving into the guest house?" Gage asks after a moment of silence.

"Well, after sharing the good news, we were all sitting around talking when Quinn announced that she was moving in with Declan."

"And with the guest house empty and you looking for a place to live...it's kismet," Gage finishes for me.

"Yeah, it kind of is." I laugh.

"I'm not gonna lie. Selfishly, I'm a little sad you won't be a few houses down the street anymore."

"Yeah, but now I'll have privacy, and we won't have to plan around what Declan is doing because it won't matter if he's home or not."

"You make a good point."

"I know. I'm a genius. You should know this already," I tease. And the lightness I seem to always find in these conversations with Gage washes over me.

"Oh, believe me, I'm well aware of how smart you are." He laughs. "It's one of the things I find most attractive about you."

"Is that so?" I question. I'm not saying it's that out there to be attracted to someone's intelligence—it's just not something I've heard from other guys before.

"Of course. That, your honesty, and your confidence." He says it so matter of fact it makes me pause.

"I don't know about that last one. My confidence is shot," I mumble.

"No, it's not. It might be a little bruised, but you've still got it. You wouldn't have shown up at my door that first night if you didn't."

"I don't know if that was confidence." It felt more like desperation to take back a little piece of myself from my parents and Brian.

"You telling me exactly what you wanted that night was, and you can't argue that." His voice takes on a husky sound like he's picturing that night in detail, and it has my thighs clenching at the thought.

"Okay," I say, sitting up in my seat. "I think it's time for a new conversation."

"Is that so?" he breathes, copying my words from earlier.

"Yes. You're at work, and we aren't having phone sex, so new topic, please."

Gage laughs but changes the subject. "So, this weekend, huh?"

"Yeah." I relax in my seat, a smile on my face. "Declan and Quinn are spending the next couple of evenings packing her stuff. We'll make the switch on Saturday.

"Hasn't she been here for like three months?"

"Yeah..." My voice trails off, curious at what he's getting at.

"And it will only take them two nights to pack all her stuff?"

"Oh, yeah." I chuckle quietly, realizing he wasn't commenting on how fast their relationship seems to be moving.

Everyone is different, and I'm a firm believer that you shouldn't put things off, especially if you know what you want. You don't know what the future holds so you've got to do what makes you happy.

"Quinn wasn't planning on staying forever, so she never really put her own touch on the place. It's mostly just clothes and camera equipment."

"And you? You only need two nights to pack your things?"

"I only unpacked that first suitcase I brought with me." I look out at the dark sky, studying the stars. "I knew I was staying when I got back on Christmas, but I also knew I wanted to find my own place, so I didn't unpack everything I brought back with me. It's all still in suitcases and boxes. Most of it in Declan's garage."

"I'm off this weekend if you need any help." I hear the smirk in his voice.

"Hmm," I hum. "I might not need help moving, but a good soak in that bath of yours would be nice when I'm done unpacking." Now it's my voice that turns husky.

"That can definitely be arranged."

I'm reluctant to get off the phone with Gage, a thought I'm pretty sure I should be more worried about than I am, but I like talking to him. There's a comfort in hearing his voice, knowing he's there if—and when—I need him.

It's the needing him that worries me. Because I'm pretty sure I do need him. And I'm not sure I've ever needed anyone the way I need Gage.

Needing Gage means something more serious than I thought I was looking for—than I thought I was ready for. Needing him means trusting him to be there for me—not that I have any reason to believe I can't trust him. Gage has shown up for me every time I've asked him—and plenty of times I haven't.

But it doesn't feel right bringing someone into my mess of life. I know that Gage knows about all of it—and is still here. But my parents and Brian haven't stopped calling since Christmas, and something in my gut says it'll only get worse.

It's better for both of us if things stay as they are. Moving into the cottage means it will be easier to keep things simple and just between us. And that's exactly what I need right now.

CHAPTER
Twenty-Six

AVA

I DON'T HEAR HIM—HE can be very quiet when he wants to be—but I feel him enter the room as I stand at the counter waiting for the coffee to brew. He's silent as he moves behind me. His hands come to my hips, and I feel his nose hit the back of my head before I hear his deep breath.

"There's something about finding you in my home first thing in the morning..." His voice trails off, and I don't know if it's that he doesn't *know* how to finish the sentence or if it's because he knows I might spook if he finishes that statement the way I think he wants to finish it.

This morning has already been intense. If I'm being honest, I'm already on edge and I have no doubt Gage feels it— he's too observant not to. He knows me better than most.

He turns me in his arms, lifting me to sit on the counter and stepping between my legs before I can do or say anything.

"I liked waking up to you in my bed this morning." He says it so softly, like he knows I'm not ready to hear those words, but he's not willing to keep them buried inside either.

The thing is, *I* liked waking up in his bed this morning.

I might have been teasing Thursday night when I made a

comment about using Gage's bath, but after spending all day Saturday moving and most of Sunday unpacking, I was sore. The idea of a bath was too good to pass up.

After dinner with the Marks family last night I came to Gage's, where he already had the bath waiting for me. And not just a hot bath with salts. No, he made it a whole experience with bubbles and candles to create a cozy atmosphere.

He planned on leaving me to my bath while he went and did his own thing, but I wasn't having it. Setting all that up might have been the sweetest thing anyone had done for me. He was taking care of me in a way no one else has before, which was hot. But also terrifying. I liked it and I didn't *want* to like it.

Leaving me to relax in his bath like I belonged there wasn't an option. I made him climb into the tub with me—sitting across from me exactly like he did the first time. Only this time, we relaxed in the bath for about five minutes before things got heated—and not just because of the hot water.

I couldn't keep my hands off him. And even though it was hard for him—what with me practically throwing myself at him—he took the time to make sure I was truly okay before he laid a hand on me.

Yes, Gage has touched me since everything happened on Christmas Eve, but it wasn't sexual. He's only been concerned with taking care of me and making sure I've been okay since my return. And it's meant the world to me, but once I made it very clear I wanted nothing more than for him to touch me, things escalated quickly.

He was gentle with me but also demanding. He was exactly what I wanted, giving me everything he knew I *needed* without me having to put it into words.

Sex with Gage Flynn is out of this world, and I'm not sure how I'll ever get over it—if I even want to get over it.

Staying overnight had been an accident—we both have

work this morning, and I didn't bring any clothes with me. But considering I'd been exhausted before I got to Gage's last night —and he made sure I came three times before he even came once—there was no hope of me getting out of that bed when we were done. I tried to get up to clean myself up in the bathroom but ended up passing out almost immediately.

His alarm had gone off this morning, waking both of us from a dead sleep—something that seemed to shock Gage more than I thought possible.

There'd been a brief moment of panic on my part when I realized I was wrapped in his arms, my back to his chest. But it turned to lust almost as quickly as the panic had appeared. The feel of Gage's hard body behind me—and I do mean all of his hard body—had me moaning as soon as his lips touched my shoulder. The man had barely touched me, and I was already soaked.

"You're ready for me already?" he whispers in my ear as his hips grind into my ass and his fingers slide over my clit.

"I'm always ready for you," I moan.

He rolls away from me, causing the panic to show itself again, but it quickly fades when I hear him tear the condom wrapper and his arms are back around me as his lips trail a path from the pulse point at my neck to my shoulder. He plays with my clit for only a moment before he's lifting my leg and sliding his hard length inside me. It's slow and gentle—almost torturously so.

"Yes," he moans. "You feel so good"

His fingers come back to my clit as his other hand snakes under me, coming up to play with my nipple. He pinches and then soothes—a perfect rhythm in time with his strokes against my clit and his thrusts in and out of me.

He's moving so slowly, but I feel my orgasm building. He's winding me tighter and tighter, my body molding to his, my fingers gripping the pillow so tightly they almost hurt. I've never felt anything like this—like my entire body is on fire and might explode if he doesn't move faster.

"Gage," I beg. "Move, baby."

"Trust me, Rebel." His voice is so throaty; I know he's on the verge of his own release. His pace picks up, the pressure on my clit and nipple increasing, but it's his breath in my ear and the nip to my shoulder that has my back arching.

"Oh god, yes, right there," I practically shout.

"That's it." He shifts behind me, pressing himself even closer, angling his hips to hit exactly where I need him most. "Let go, Ava." It's the sound of my name that pushes me over the edge. My orgasm so intense my entire body goes taught as the waves wash over me. I hear Gage's release more than I feel it, so overcome with my own, I can't focus on anything.

It's minutes later when I come back down to earth. Gage is still wrapped around me—still buried inside me. I feel his heart pounding inside his chest and the light kiss he places on the skin where my neck and shoulder meet.

"You okay?" he asks so quietly I almost miss it.

"I don't think I've ever come that hard in my life," I whisper back. "It's never been like that for me."

His arms around me tighten. "That was a first for me, too."

Gage squeezes my hips, bringing me back to the present. "Hey, stop worrying," he murmurs against my lips.

"I can't stop worrying. This feels way more than casual." I lean away from him slightly, wanting to see his face.

Proving he knows me well, he pulls back just enough to grant the unspoken request but not enough to give me room to run.

"Maybe it is." He shrugs. "Would that be a bad thing?"

"I don't know." I play with the drawstring of the sweatshirt he's wearing. "My life is still a mess."

"I don't mind the mess," he jokes lightly.

"Gage." I sigh.

"Look," he interrupts before I can say more. "Isn't it my decision if I'm willing to deal with the mess? It's not like I'm blind to why your life got flipped upside down. If I'm willing to be part of it, does the rest really matter?"

I let go of the drawstring and raise my palms to cup his face. The roughness of his stubble against my hands has a shiver running up my spine from the memories of what it felt like between my thighs. *Not what I want to be thinking about right now.*

"I haven't spoken to either of my parents since I left their house on Christmas Eve, but they've been calling. Practically non-stop," I murmur, the worry clear in my voice. "I don't know what they'll do when they realize I was serious about moving here. They're powerful people, Gage."

"Okay. Then it's even more of a reason to let me be in your corner. I'm not one to back down from a challenge. Unless this is something you really don't want, I'm not going anywhere. If you don't want to put a label on it or tell people, I'll follow your lead." He presses a kiss to my lips. "For now," he whispers against me. "Do you really not want this?"

My hands fall from his face and move around his shoulder, pulling him in for a tight hug. "It scares me how much I want this," I tell him honestly.

"It scares me, too. I've never had a serious relationship—I've never wanted one. But I want this with you." He squeezes me. "It feels right with you."

I stay where I am, pressed against him, my head buried in his neck. Gage has a point. It's not fair to either of us if I'm doing his thinking for him. As long as he has all the information—which he does—then it should be his decision if he wants to be in a serious relationship with me. I shouldn't be making that decision for him. All I should be focused on is what I want. And the truth of it is that I do want more with Gage, but I'm scared. I'm scared of what my parents will do when they find out. I'm scared because I don't know what my future holds.

I know I'm happy working at the bookstore, and I'm so excited to finally have time to do things for myself, but the bookstore is only part-time. It can't be what I do with the rest of my life. And I thought I was done practicing law, but working with Scott reminded me of what I like most about being a lawyer. I love helping people and want to keep doing that, but I don't know what that looks like here in Ashford Falls. My only experience so far has been with the firm in Boston, and I know that's not the type of law I want to practice.

I pull back from Gage, studying his face. I don't know what I expect to find, but all I see is hope and trust. He's trusting me not to hurt him and asking me to do the same.

"Can this stay between us for just a little longer? Let me find a way to tell Declan about everything going on with my parents and Brian first, then we can tell him about us."

It takes a second, but I see the second he registers my words. A smile breaks out across his face, and his eyes light with pure joy. I'm on the counter one minute and in his arms the next. His lips firm against mine as he kisses me senseless.

My mind goes blank except for the feel of him against me. His body is solid, his grip firm but gentle. He doesn't ask for permission—he just takes exactly what he wants and gives me exactly what I need. It's the ringing of his phone that has us pulling apart.

"Sorry," he mutters against my lips. "That's probably my sister calling. I normally run to the farm Monday mornings before work."

"You should answer it." I push him away, a smile on my face. He shakes his head, pulling me back to him by my hips.

"It's fine." His lips land on my cheek and trail toward the pulse point on my neck.

"They'll worry if you don't answer. Go." I laugh at his resulting growl.

He doesn't step back from me, but he does pull his phone from the pocket of his pants. "Hey, Pickle." His eyes stay on mine as he listens to whatever his sister says on the other end of the phone. His thumb gently stroking back and forth on the skin at my hip causes goosebumps to form.

I force myself to step away from him as he continues talking to Olivia, moving back to the coffee pot to finally pour myself a cup. I grab another mug and pour a second cup for Gage. He watches me move around the kitchen, adding milk and sugar to each cup. I smile at him as I set his cup down on the counter next to him and make my way around the kitchen island to take a seat, watching him watch me the entire time.

Olivia must be ranting to him about something because he doesn't say anything; just makes a sound of affirmation now and then, sipping his coffee and making faces at me as he listens.

I know he loves that his siblings feel comfortable talking to him about what's going on in their lives. The fact that Asher kept his relationship a secret really hurt him. He didn't have to spell that out for me—I heard it in his voice when he told me about it on Christmas Eve.

It's another five minutes before he manages to hang up the phone. "Sorry," he says as he places the phone face down on the counter.

"It's fine. I like that you're close to your siblings. That's definitely a massive green flag," I tease, a glint in my eye.

"Do I have any red flags?" he asks as he moves around the counter to my side.

"Well, the lack of committed relationships should probably be a red flag, but..." I end with a shrug.

"But you're willing to look past that?" He spins my seat and steps between my legs.

"Have you seen how attractive you are?" I slip my hands under his sweatshirt, sliding them up his hard chest.

"Oh, so you're only with me because of my looks?" he asks in mock outrage.

"Well, that and your cock." I try to maintain a serious expression, but it doesn't last long. Especially not when Gage lifts me from my seat and marches us back to his bedroom.

"Well, I don't want you to regret giving me a chance. I better remind you just how good I am with my cock."

Gage and I spend the next hour in bed, and I don't think I've ever laughed or had so much fun. But it wasn't just fun. The laughs soften and turn into sweeter moments, pouring the vulnerability we confessed with our words into our actions. Gage makes me feel safe enough to trust that he has me no matter what comes my way.

I'm terrified of what that means, but the weight that's been lifted by finally being open with someone—with Gage—makes me think I'm exactly where I'm supposed to be. It feels right with Gage.

CHAPTER
Twenty-Seven

GAGE

WE END up needing another shower after I take Ava back to my room, and I might end up being a little late to the station, but it's worth it for this extra time with her.

There hasn't been a single time with Ava that wasn't amazing, but the sex this morning was more intimate than anything I've ever experienced before. And the fact that I got her to agree to give this a real shot has me practically bouncing with excitement.

I know she wants to keep it between us for a bit longer, but I understand her reasoning, and I support it. Her life has changed so much over the last month and a half, and starting a relationship with someone is another big thing to add to the list. I'm not surprised that it's a little overwhelming for her.

I'm just glad she's willing to give us a real shot, no matter how that looks right now.

"Let me give you a ride home," I offer as we make our way downstairs.

"I can walk, it's not far."

"I know, but it's cold, and you have wet hair. I'll feel better if you let me give you a ride." I grab her by the belt loops, pulling her into me and pressing a kiss to her neck, sucking gently.

"That's playing dirty," she moans, rocking against me.

I smirk and shrug. "I'll use whatever charms I need to get you to agree with me."

She laughs and shakes her head but agrees to let me take her home.

I pull up in front of Scott's and stop in front of the driveway. "You sure I can't take you to the front door?"

"Yes, you'll draw too much attention if you pull into the driveway. Besides, it's a myth about being outside in the winter with wet hair and that leading to a cold." She smirks at me.

Ava turns to get out of the Jeep, but I grab her wrist, pulling her back to me. "Thank you for giving this thing a real shot between us," I whisper as I lean over the center console, bringing her in for a kiss. She fights it for only a second before she leans into me, reciprocating the kiss.

"You know, you kind of suck at this whole secret relationship thing?" Ava laughs as we pull away from each other.

"Call it a relationship again." I feel the spark in my eye and the grin across my face.

"Shut up. You know what I mean." She pushes me slightly, but I pull her back, placing another kiss to her lips.

"No one's around, and I can't help myself. I need a proper goodbye." I can't stop myself from kissing her one more time before finally putting a little space between us.

"Gage—" A car honks before she can say anything else.

We both pull away and look behind us to find a black Mercedes-Benz pulling up. Right behind that is Declan's truck.

I glance at Ava but find her already climbing out of the Jeep and rush to unbuckle myself to meet her around back.

Declan makes it out of his truck first and moves toward Ava so quickly that I'm instantly on edge. The driver-side door of the Mercedes-Benz opens first; a tall man looking to be in his early sixties, dressed in a suit and wool coat, steps out of the car, turning to open the passenger door behind him.

From the rear of the car, a tall, slender woman, not much younger than the man, steps out in formal business attire of her own. The look on both their faces would make a lesser man run. I find myself taking a step closer to Ava. I don't touch her, but I want her to know I'm here.

"Ava." The woman's voice is harsh, and somehow, I just know this is her mother and father.

"Wh-what are you doing here?" Ava stumbles over her words.

Declan takes a few steps toward her, moving to her other side but angled so he can see everyone.

"We gave you some time to cool down after Christmas, but you've ignored our calls, so here we are."

"I ignored your calls because there's nothing for us to discuss. I said everything I needed to at Christmas."

"Ava." The man's tone is sharp, so sharp that Ava flinches.

I step even closer to her, my hand going to the small of her back, just under the sweater she's wearing. It's too cold for us to be out here like this.

"Maybe this conversation should wait." Declan steps in. "I told you to let me talk to Ava when you showed up at my place. There's a reason she hasn't been answering your calls. You need to respect that."

"Absolutely not. Your sister has been throwing this temper tantrum long enough. You may not care about this family, but your sister does. She always does what's right in the end." I can see how the look she shoots Ava might have made her fall in line in the past. But I know they've gone too far this time. Ava won't succumb to their manipulations anymore.

Ava glances at me over her shoulder, and I glide my thumb along her spine, trying to silently communicate I support her.

She swallows and glances at Declan before reaching for my hand, pulling me into her side.

"Mom, Dad, this is Gage," Ava says, and I squeeze her hand in return, offering her whatever strength she needs. "My boyfriend."

I'm stunned for only a moment. I know we talked about giving this a real shot this morning, but I also thought she didn't want to label it. Of course, that was before her parents showed up with the man now climbing out of the front passenger seat with a look of pure disgust on his face.

"Excuse me?" the man asks. I have no doubt this is Brian, and I feel the rage coursing through me. The need I feel to drive my fist into his smug face is something else I've never felt before.

He's tall, maybe six feet, and well-built—he clearly works out—but I have no doubt I could take him. He's too refined to know how to throw a punch—or take one, for that matter.

I squeeze Ava's hand once before stepping forward, putting my hand out toward the man I assume is her father. "Gage Flynn." I know the appropriate thing to say is that it's nice to meet them, but I've never been a liar, and I won't start now.

I don't know anything about these people personally, but after everything Ava's told me, I think it's safe to say I don't like them. Anyone who treats this woman the way they have doesn't deserve pleasantries from me.

"Gregory Day, Ava's father." He doesn't shake my hand. Instead, he places his hand on his wife's back. "Eleanor, Ava's mother, and Brian Wellsley..." He pauses. "Her fiancé."

I hear a choked sound behind me and know it came from Declan. When I turn, fury crosses Ava's face as she steps forward.

"That's not true! I am not engaged to that man, nor have I

ever been engaged to him." She stops in front of me, her eyes imploring. "I swear that's not true."

I reach to her, cupping her cheek in the palm of my hand, and lean forward to press a kiss to her forehead. "I know." As I pull back from her, I see her eyes slowly open, a sheen of tears in them.

"You need to leave." Ava turns back to her parents. "I don't want you here—and as we've already established—there's no engagement. I'm with Gage."

"You didn't tell us about him at Christmas, so it must be new and therefore can't be serious. Come. Let's go back to your brother's and get your things. The plane is waiting for us at the airport." Her mother reaches for her, but Declan steps in before anyone can do or say anything.

"I don't know what's going on here." Declan's voice is stern, firmer than I've ever heard him. "But I don't care. I know what you tried to do to my life, and I can only imagine what you're trying to do to Ava's. She's not going with you. So you need to leave."

"Declan—"

"No. Ava, do you want them here?" He looks over his shoulder at his sister.

"No." There's so much conviction in her voice I can't help but feel pride in my chest. I lean forward and place a quick kiss to the back of her head, my hands coming to rest on her shoulders.

"You heard her. You need to leave."

Brian steps forward, and in that moment I'm so glad I have my badge and gun hooked to my hip. I step in front of Ava, hand resting on my badge, drawing everyone's attention there.

"You've been asked to leave. If you don't, I'm more than happy to arrest you for harassment."

"You can't do that. That would be a lie." Her mother glares at me.

My eyes move to Brian and slowly back to Ava's mother. I see the moment she registers I know exactly what Brian has done. And I see she knows Ava hasn't been lying about any of it. It seems her parents just don't care how much of a monster Brian is. Whatever their reasons for wanting this marriage, it's more important than their daughter's safety and happiness.

"Are you sure about that?" I ask, my voice low and harsh.

"Eleanor. Let's go. We'll talk to Ava later." Gregory grasps her arm and pulls her toward the car.

Brian stands there glaring at me, but I don't back down. This man doesn't scare me in the slightest. "This isn't over," he growls before following her parents.

I don't move until their car has disappeared down the street. Once it has, I turn to Ava. There are tears in her eyes, and she fidgets with the cuffs of her sweater.

I step toward her, taking one of her hands in mine. "Boyfriend?" I ask, lifting a brow, trying to lighten the moment.

Ava shrugs. "I thought it would make them give up."

"Give up on what exactly. What's going on?" Declan asks.

"I'm not—I don't—" She swallows, eyes bouncing between me and Declan.

"Ava." Declan releases her name on a sigh, his eyes closing briefly. When he opens them, it's clear he's in pain. "Please." It's a desperate plea. One I know Ava can't ignore.

"They've planned for me to marry Brian. Like an arranged marriage. Apparently, it's been planned since I was a baby." Her voice is so quiet that I almost miss it.

"What?" It's more of a breath than an actual word from Declan.

I squeeze Ava's hand still clasped in mine. "Let's go inside and talk. You're not dressed for this weather." Without waiting for a response, I wrap my arm around Ava's shoulder and walk down the driveway. I don't check to make sure Declan is following us, but I hear his steps signaling he is.

"You have to get to work," Ava says, trying to pull away from my side.

"I can be late. This is more important." I press a kiss to her temple, lingering there for a second as we walk.

She doesn't argue more. She simply wraps her arms around my waist and squeezes, proving she wants my support while she tells Declan about everything that's been going on.

Ava unlocks the door and holds it for Declan and me to enter. It's not a large space—just a kitchen, living room, and a short hallway with three doors—likely the bedroom, bathroom, and laundry area—but it's plenty big enough for Ava. I haven't been here before, but a quick look shows it's well-decorated and cozy.

Ava toes off her shoes and moves to the couch in the living space to the right of the door, Declan follows close behind and sits in the chair to her right.

I take a second to text Lyle to let him know I'll be late before moving to sit next to her. I don't touch her, but I'm close enough that I can if she needs me.

Declan moves to the edge of his seat and takes hold of Ava's hand. His voice is gentle when he speaks, but I see the pain and anger lacing his features. "Talk to me. Tell me what's going on."

Ava stares at him silently for a minute before she falls forward, her forehead resting against their clasped hands, her shoulders shaking.

I place my hand on her back, rubbing soothing circles. When I look up, Declan stares at me with concern written clear across his features. I shake my head, trying to silently communicate that she's okay.

We sit here quietly, letting Ava feel whatever emotions are coursing through her. When she stills, I lean forward, circling my arms around her, and bring my mouth to her ear. "Rebel, what do you need?" I whisper.

She shakes her head and slowly sits up, wiping her face dry before looking at Declan again. And she starts her story. She tells Declan about that night in Brian's office, about running to her parents only for them to call her a whore and a liar. She tells him about getting fired from the firm and being happy about it. She tells him about her trip home at Christmas and what Brian did outside their parents' house. She tells him all of it.

And through it all, Declan holds steady. It's only because I'm good at reading people that I see the rage burning in his eyes and the tension in his shoulder. To anyone else, they would see a man silently supporting his sister through some of her worst moments. I see a man itching to hurt his parents the way they've hurt her. I see a man ready to break.

When Ava stops talking Declan takes a minute, his eyes moving to me before looking back at Ava. "What do you need from me?"

Ava's eyes fall shut, and her entire body slumps like she'd been holding the weight of the world on her shoulders and it's finally been lifted. When she opens them, she offers Declan a watery smile. "Nothing. You've already done it."

"I wish you had told me when you first got here," he whispers, almost hesitant.

"I know, but there was so much going on with Scott and Quinn, and I honestly needed to process all of it before talking about it." Ava squeezes Declan's hand. "I wasn't alone."

"I can see that." Declan tries to smile, his eyes bouncing to me quickly. "Boyfriend? It seems like you have another story to tell me."

Ava glances at me over her shoulder, reaching for my hand with her free one. I squeeze it and give a gentle smile in return.

"The boyfriend thing is new," she finally says, turning back to Declan. "But he's been a good friend."

"I have no doubt." I get a little uncomfortable at the sincerity in his voice. I'm not one for being the center of attention in serious moments.

"All right." I stand from my seat, needing to move. "Do you think your parents will leave that easily?" I ask, moving around the coffee table to stand facing the two of them.

"Definitely not," Declan says without hesitation, standing from his seat as well.

Ava sighs, pushing up from the couch and moving toward me. "It's not likely, but you two need to get to work, so now isn't the time to talk about this."

"You sure you're good?" Declan asks, begrudgingly moving toward the door.

"I'm all right." Ava offers him a smile.

"There's still a lot to talk about. Like why they're pushing this so hard and how to stop them."

"I know."

"Let's do dinner tonight. We can talk more and come up with a game plan." Declan glances at me over Ava's shoulder. "You're more than welcome."

"Oh, uh, yeah, of course," I stumble slightly. "Whatever Ava wants."

"It's probably a good idea," Ava agrees.

"Okay, I'll let Quinn know. Seven o'clock okay?" he asks, looking at me.

"Yeah, that should be fine."

"My place?" he asks Ava.

"Sure," she agrees, giving him a small smile.

Declan looks at her for another moment before he pulls her into a tight hug. "I love you so much, squirt."

"I love you, too, big brother," Ava says as they pull away.

Declan reaches to shake my hand before he heads out the door.

"You sure you're okay?" I ask as Ava turns to look at me.

"Not really, but I will be." She gives me a warm smile before stepping into me, her arms moving around my waist. "Thank you for being here."

I hug her tight, my head buried in the crook of her neck. "There's nowhere else I'd rather be." And I mean that more than anything.

Being by Ava's side has been a privilege. And while I wish there hadn't been a need for it, I'm so incredibly grateful I was able to bring her the comfort and support she needed.

"I'll see you after work, okay?" I ask softly as we pull away. "You don't have to go tonight if you don't want to."

"Where else would I want to be?" I ask as I cup her face in my hands. "This is out in the open now. I'm taking full advantage." I give her a charming smile as I bend to kiss her lips. "I'll see you later," I whisper against them, pressing one more quick kiss before heading out the door for work.

CHAPTER
Twenty-Eight

GAGE

"I KNOW I don't have the full story when it comes to you and Ava," Declan says as he pops the top on a beer and hands it to me where I stand in the living room looking at a painting of Scott on the wall. "But I'm grateful she's had you to lean on since she's been here."

I rub a hand against the back of my neck, glancing in Ava's direction to see her helping Quinn in the kitchen. I don't think I've seen Ava as relaxed as she is now, and I couldn't be happier she's finding her peace again.

"I don't think it's my place to tell you that story," I say, turning back to Declan.

He shakes his head. "No. And I'm not asking you. I'm just saying thank you for taking care of my sister."

"She's more than capable of taking care of herself."

"I know. But it's nice knowing she doesn't have to."

Like a scene out of a romance movie, we both turn to watch Quinn and Ava laughing in the kitchen, and neither of us can stop the smiles that grow across our faces.

My smile doesn't last, though. I turn back to Declan and

lower my voice, trying to make sure we aren't heard—not yet at least.

"You were right about your parents not leaving town. I saw them checking in at The Ashford Lodge this afternoon."

Declan continues staring at the woman in the kitchen, but his eyebrows draw in, telling me he heard me. It takes him a minute, but eventually he moves to sit on the couch, motioning for me to do the same.

He sits on the edge of his seat, his elbows resting against his knees, messing with the label on his beer bottle when he starts speaking. "I've never understood—especially with who my grandparents were and how they raised him—but for some reason, my father has this picture in his head of what our family must look like. It's like, because he's part of Harborview's founding family, we have to check these specific societal boxes, and if we don't we're a failure. A failure for what? I have no idea."

Declan takes a moment and looks back into the kitchen. "I had to fight tooth and nail for them to agree to let me pursue my art, and it was only after I sold my first piece that they started to listen." His eyes come back to mine. "When I told them about my divorce, they were so angry with me. The things they said are something a child should never hear from their parent—regardless of their age."

"I wish I could say that doesn't shock me, but from what Ava's told me..." I let my words trail off. It doesn't feel necessary to retell the story Ava did this morning.

"I know what they tried to pressure me into and why they did it, but this seems too far—even for them. If it were just about the perception of Ava being married to a successful man, they could find someone else. It has to be about Brian or the Wellsleys, specifically. I just don't know what."

"Ava said they're a pretty wealthy family. Could it be about the money?"

"I mean, anything's possible, but my parents aren't hurting for money either. They're pretty well off."

"As far as you know. But you haven't really been involved in their lives for the last five years."

"I'd be shocked if they could blow through all their money. But..." His words trail off.

Before either of us can say anything else, Ava and Quinn move into the living room, Quinn falling into the seat next to Declan. "What are you two talking about in here?" she asks as she grabs Declan's beer and steals a quick sip.

I sit back in my seat, placing my hand on Ava's thigh as she takes the space next to me. "I saw your parents and Brian checking in at The Ashford Lodge this afternoon," I tell her softly.

"Why didn't you say anything earlier?" she questions quietly.

"I knew we would talk about it now, and I didn't want to worry you twice."

Ava studies me for a minute before pressing a quick peck to my cheek and turning to her brother. "What do you think?"

"I don't know. That's what I was just telling Gage. If it were just about looks, they could find someone else with the same societal standing. Add in the fact that it was decided when you were a baby..." He shakes his head, leaving the sentence unfinished.

"What I don't understand is why they waited until now," Quinn says. "I mean, Brian's thirty-eight, right? And he's made a big deal about needing a son?" She looks between all of us. "Again, if it were about perception, isn't it strange for Brian to have waited so long to have kids?"

"Maybe," Declan admits. "But, you could argue that he compromised and agreed to let Ava establish herself in her career before getting married and having kids."

"But would the picture of a working mom be appropriate

for your parents? Not just a working mom, but a successful lawyer?" I ask

"Ugh," Ava grunts in frustration. She stands from her seat and begins pacing the room. "It doesn't really matter why. All that matters is making them realize I'm done doing what they want. I'm done being manipulated."

I stand from my seat, gently pulling her into my arms when I see the tears welling in her eyes. "Figuring out why they're pushing can help us figure out how to make them stop."

"I just want to live my own life. However I see fit," she mumbles into my chest.

"I know," I whisper in her ear.

"We're going to figure this out," Declan offers as he stands from his seat. "I won't let them force you into something you don't want."

Ava doesn't pull away from me, but she turns her head to see her brother. "I know you won't."

"Come on. Dinner's ready. Let's go eat," Quinn says a few minutes later when the silence becomes too loud.

Ava pulls out of my embrace but doesn't immediately follow Quinn and Declan into the kitchen.

I lift my hand to cup her cheek, my thumb wiping under her eye. "What do you need?" I ask quietly.

Her eyes shut, and she sighs. "I just want them to go away."

"I know, Rebel." I press a kiss to her forehead, resting there until she pulls away. She gives me a small smile before joining Quinn and Declan at the table.

I watch Ava as she takes the seat across from her brother, and I can't help but hate her parents for what they're putting their children through.

My gut tells me it has to be about money. Most people's motivations in life are love or money. If love were driving her parents, they would be listening to her about the kind of man

Brian is. The fact that they aren't...well, it could be something else, but my gut tells me it's not.

I wanted so badly to hurt that man this morning, but, somehow, I kept myself in check. Next time, though? I don't think I'll be able to do it. The idea of him being in the same state as Ava makes me sick to my stomach. In the same town as her? I don't want to take my eyes off her.

I'm not sure I'm ready to face what that means. I can see myself falling for Ava Day, and the thought terrifies me.

Shaking myself from my thoughts, I join everyone at the table, sitting next to Ava and across from Quinn. They've already moved onto brighter topics, and I try to join them. I try like hell to stop thinking about all the reasons her parents and Brian won't take no for an answer.

A FEW HOURS LATER, I'm lying in bed staring at the ceiling with Ava curled into me. There's a peace in me at the feel of her pressed against my side, knowing she's safe where she is right now. But another part of me worries about what happens when she's no longer by my side. What happens tomorrow when we're both at work? Her parents and Brian are staying in town for a reason; they aren't done trying to talk to her. Will they ambush her at work? Will Brian try to hurt her again?

"Promise me you'll call if you need me," I say into the darkness.

I feel Ava shift against me as she lifts her head, but it's so dark in the room neither of us can see much of anything. "What do you mean?"

"Just, if something happens, if your parents or Brian show up at the bookstore or somewhere else, and you don't feel safe, promise you'll call me."

"Oh." Ava rests her head back on my chest, her arm around me squeezing lightly. "I called you all the way from Harborview when I needed you."

"I know." I bend my head, pressing my lips against the top of hers and taking a deep breath. Apple and vanilla fill my nose, bringing another wave of comfort over me. "I just...I don't want anything to happen to you."

"Nothing's going to happen to me. I won't stop living my life, but I'll be smart. I won't go anywhere alone, and I'll be mindful of my surroundings."

"And you'll call me if you need me."

"And I'll call you if I need you," she repeats, turning her head to place a kiss over my heart. "Thank you for worrying about me."

"Of course I worry about you." I squeeze her. "You're important to me."

"You're important to me, too. More than I thought possible." She shifts again, moving her body up my side slightly so she can press a kiss to my cheek. "Thanks for not giving up on me."

"Oh, you're more than worth it." I roll to my side, keeping her in my arms. I can't see her clearly in the dark, but I can see enough to know she's studying me.

"How did we end up here? When neither of us was open to something real?" she whispers as she brings her fingers up to trace the side of my face—starting at my forehead and working her way down to my chin.

"Hmm...my mother would say it's because we weren't looking for it that we found it."

"But neither of us has ever really looked for anything serious."

"I don't know, Rebel. All I know is that I don't want to give this up." I pause for a second, trying to decide if I should give it all to her. It's not a lie if I stop there, but at the same time, is it true honesty if I hold it in? I know I'm giving her the power to hurt me, but I trust she won't.

"I've never felt at peace the way I do when I'm with you." I roll again so she's beneath me, my hips cradled by her legs. "Have I told you that I haven't needed an alarm clock since before I got home from the army? I always set my alarm, but it hasn't actually gone off once in the last three years. Not until this morning."

"I've never been as comfortable with someone else as I am with you—not even Declan. I feel like I can tell you anything, and you won't judge me."

"I won't," I whisper.

"I don't know how we got here, but I'm thankful we did. I don't know if I believe in fate or a higher power, but being here in this town and with you might make me believe."

And in this moment, I fall in love with Ava Day. I won't tell her—not yet. There's no way she's ready to hear those words, but I'll show her every day for as long as she'll let me.

Starting right now.

I bring my lips to hers and kiss her like she's my salvation. Like I can't live without her. And I wonder: have I really been living, or have I simply been surviving? Just going through the motions up until she entered my life.

I don't know, but I won't waste time thinking about it. Not when she's here and not when she makes me feel like this—like my life just got a hundred times better with her in it.

Yeah, this might make me believe in something bigger than us, too.

CHAPTER
Twenty-nine

AVA

THE FEEL of Gage's arms around me in the morning might easily become one of my favorite things if I let it. And if I'm being honest, I want it to.

Gage and I might have an official title, but that hasn't changed anything about how we interact with each other. He's definitely more open with touching me out in public, but then again, I quite enjoy that it's no secret we belong to each other. I like belonging to someone.

He might be a little more attentive than he was before Brian and my parents showed up, but I know it comes from a place of fear that something might happen to me or that I'll be hurt by their actions. Gage is still just as present, if not more so, and just as supportive and caring as he's been from that first night at Murphy's.

There isn't a single doubt in my mind that I made the right decision in giving this thing with Gage a real shot. I've loved spending my time with him.

So when I wake up a few mornings after my parents showed up outside Scott's with Gage's arms around me and snow on the ground outside, I couldn't be happier.

They've been teasing the amount of snow we would be getting with the storm that rolled through overnight, but the fact that the snow is still falling means it's a good one—at least, if you enjoy snow the way I do.

It's realistically not that far into the winter season yet—almost three weeks—but today's snowfall seems pretty significant.

"Time to get up already?" Gage asks as his arms around me tighten.

"Almost," I whisper, rolling over to face him.

He hasn't opened his eyes yet, and I take the time to study him. I knew he was attractive the first moment I saw him. With his aqua eyes, tousled hair, high cheekbones, and chiseled jaw, he was hard to miss. Honestly, the man could have gone into acting and would be a massive hit with how attractive he is. But getting to know him on a deeper level over the last seven weeks means I get to see how beautiful he is down to his bones.

Outside of his family and the occasional person around town, most people see Gage as the comedic relief, like he's not to be taken seriously. But this man is so smart and caring that those people are doing themselves a disservice by not seeing him for who he is.

Yes, Gage is great at lightening the mood and lifting people's spirits, but it's because he's so observant that he can do that. It's because he pays attention and listens. He knows exactly what kind of humor to infuse into a conversation to bring levity to someone when needed. Someone only trying to make people laugh and be funny wouldn't care the way Gage does.

He proves it with all the little things he does. Asking Walt about his conversations with his son, running to his mom's every Monday morning before work to spend time with Olivia, his weekly hikes with Leo, and his daily texts with Asher.

There are very few decisions Gage makes solely about what he wants for himself. Almost everything he does is with someone else in mind.

"What are you thinking about so hard over there?"

"How do you know I'm thinking about something?" I ask when he still doesn't open his eyes.

"You released a heavy sigh." His eyes finally open, squinting at the light pouring through his open curtains. Something he prefers to close before going to sleep but left open for me to see the snow first thing this morning when we woke up.

"I'm just thinking about how lucky I am to have you in my life," I tell him honestly.

"That's quite deep for seven o'clock in the morning," he mumbles as he buries his head in the crook of my neck.

"No, just true." I run my fingers through his hair, relaxing into the warmth of his embrace for a few more minutes. "I need to get ready for work. Go back to sleep. It's your day off," I whisper, pressing a kiss to his cheek before moving to get out of bed.

"No. I'll clean off your car while you get ready." He squeezes me one more time before letting me go and sitting up on the edge of his bed. He takes a second to stretch, a wince playing across his features before slipping on sweatpants and an "ARMY" sweatshirt.

"You don't have to. I can take care of it."

"I know you can, but I don't mind. There's no way I'm going back to sleep anyway." He smiles as he skims his hand up my thigh to rest under the hem of his shirt at my hip. "I only sleep as well as I do when you're in the bed next to me."

"You slept just fine before I came along," I tease, a smile on my face.

"Fine being the optimal word. I sleep peacefully now that you're in my bed."

"You're spending way too much time with my brother if you're being that cheesy." I laugh, pushing at his chest.

"Are you saying you would rather your brother and I didn't get along?"

"Of course not."

He shrugs. "Well, it's your fault I've spent so much time with him. You're the one who keeps planning dinners over there with Quinn."

"I like her. She's perfect for my brother."

"Yeah, she is." Gage laughs softly, pulling me in tight and pressing a kiss to my lips.

I pull away before either of us can get too carried away. "Morning breath."

"I don't care," he says against the skin of my cheek.

"I know, but I do. Plus, I need to get ready for work." This time when I push at his chest, there's a bit more force behind it.

"All right." He sighs, releasing his hold on me. "My parents are hosting a family dinner at the farm this evening. Last one before Asher heads back to school for the semester," Gage tells me as he sits at the foot of the bed, pulling on a pair of socks.

"Okay, I'm sure Quinn and Declan wouldn't mind hanging out, or I can go to Murphy's anyway and keep Walt company," I tell him while digging through my bag for the outfit I packed for today.

"Actually, I was wondering if you wanted to join us."

I freeze, jeans in one hand and my sweater in the other. My back is turned to Gage, but I feel his heat come up behind me.

"You don't have to. I know it's kind of fast, but you've already met my parents, and I'd like you to meet my siblings."

I place my things on top of my bag and slowly turn to face him. There's nothing but sincerity in his eyes. I know how much he wants me to be there, but I also know he'll respect it if I tell him I'm not ready. The thing that shocks me is that I am ready. He's right. I've already met his parents, and I absolutely love them.

I can see why Gage is the way he is. His mother is caring and attentive while being so incredibly strong and independent. But she doesn't let that independence stop her from leaning on Nick. And Nick is funny and genuine and so freaking warm and observant. I could see his love for Laura clear as day every time he looked at her that night at Murphy's.

There wasn't a single second I felt uncomfortable with them. They made me feel like I was part of them from the moment they sat at the bar.

I reach up to cup his cheeks in my hands, pulling him down to me. "I'd love to go to dinner with you," I tell him before placing a chaste kiss to his lips.

"You sure?" His eyes search mine, looking for a hint of hesitation.

"I'm positive. Plus, after all this snow? I just know the farm will be beautiful."

He laughs and pulls me in for a tight hug. One hand cupping the back of my head and the other against my back while he buries his head in the crook of my neck, placing a kiss where my neck and shoulder meet.

This feeling right here—the happiness and contentment—is something I never thought I could feel in the abundance I do at this moment. I don't want to give it up or let anything or anyone ruin it—even my parents and Brian. I want to hold onto this feeling—to protect it.

***

"SO YOU JUST LEFT?" Abbey laughs as she wipes down the counter.

"Well, yeah." I laugh along with her. "Why sit through a date you know isn't going anywhere?"

The bell above the door sounds, cutting off Abbey's response. When I turn to greet the newcomer, the smile on my face falls instantly.

I spin back to Abbey, whispering, "Call Gage."

I'm honestly surprised it took him so long to find me. I thought he and my parents would show up the day after they checked in to The Ashford Lodge, but it's been three days since I saw his face.

I want to say I was able to forget about him over those three days, but unfortunately, that would be a lie. No matter how much Gage or I try, my parents and Brian are constantly on my mind. I can't stop trying to figure out why they're still here or what they could possibly want from me.

"What?" Abbey asks in confusion.

Grabbing her wrist from across the counter, I say more firmly, "Call Gage." I wish I had time to explain, but I don't.

"Ava," Brian says as he stops in front of me.

There's a charming smile on his face as he leans forward, trying to kiss my cheek. I don't step away from him—I won't give him the satisfaction of seeing me cower—but I turn my head so he kisses air instead.

"You shouldn't be here," I tell him. I'm surprised my voice is as even as it is, but I'm grateful. I refuse to let him see the fear I feel coursing through me.

"Darling, that's no way to speak to your fiancé." The smile is still plastered to his lips, but I see the anger in his eyes.

I hear Abbey shift behind me and can only hope she's doing what I asked. I should have told her about my parents and Brian. It's not safe for me to keep this secret—not with the three of them in town.

"You're not my fiancé. Why won't you recognize that?" I seethe.

"Ava," he grits, trying to keep his cool in front of Abbey. "Maybe we could go somewhere else to talk?"

"No, I want you to leave. I have nothing to say to you."

"Ava." His voice turns more forceful, the smile officially slipping from his face as he steps closer to me.

This time, I do take a step away, but it's only a couple of inches before I feel the counter at my back.

"Abbey's calling the police. You should go before they get here."

Another step forward. "I haven't done anything wrong."

"I can still press charges for everything that happened back in Boston," I warn.

His hand wraps around my wrist, out of sight from Abbey, but the tightness in his grip causes me to wince. "I don't know what you're talking about. Nothing happened in Boston."

I steel my spine and lean forward, my voice deathly quiet. "We both know what you did in Boston, Brian. Leave me the hell alone, or I'll press charges."

Brian's eyes bounce between mine, and the rage I see there makes me nervous. So far, Brian hasn't done anything with witnesses around, but at some point, he'll be pushed to a breaking point. I just don't know what that point will be.

"I've called the police. You need to leave," Abbey says from behind me. I can't see her, but her voice is strong. "I have no idea what happened in Boston, but you've been asked to leave, so at this point, you're trespassing, and I definitely don't have a problem pressing charges."

Brian's glare moves to Abbey. "This is public property."

"Wrong. This is a privately-owned business, and I have the right to refuse service to whomever I want. This is now the fourth time you've been asked to leave." Her voice is so eerily calm.

I know I've only just started to get to know Abbey, but she's always come across as the quiet one. I don't think she would have a problem standing up for herself, but I would never have expected her to be so straightforward.

Brian's eyes move back to mine, and his grip on my wrist tightens even more. "This isn't over," he snarls before he storms out the door.

I watch out the window until he's long gone. I don't hear or see anything. It's not until I feel Abbey's hand on my arm that everything comes back to focus.

"Are you all right?"

"I-I...yeah." I swallow, giving myself a second. "I'm okay."

The bell rings again.

"What happened?" Gage asks before either of us has even turned to see him there. "Are you okay?" he asks, pulling me into his arms.

I sink against him, wrapping my arms around his waist and holding tight. I don't say anything but simply nod my head against his chest.

"Tell me what happened," he says softly as he pulls away just enough to look me in the eye.

"Brian showed up. He didn't do anything," I rush to say. "Just tried to get me to talk to him."

Gage studies me for a second before his eyes move over my head to Abbey. "Thanks for calling me."

"The second he walked through the door, Ava told me to. I didn't understand. But the look in that man's eyes..." Her voice trails off, and I don't need to see her to know a shiver runs up her spine.

She's right. The rage and hatred in his eyes made *me* nervous.

Gage takes a step back, his eyes moving over my body, looking to make sure nothing happened.

"He grabbed my wrist, but other than that, he didn't do anything. I swear." My voice cracks and I swallow, trying to calm myself down. Brian is gone, and Gage is here; he won't let anything happen.

"I know. I just need to see it for myself." He cups the side of my face, his thumb gently grazing my cheek.

"Why don't you get out of here?" Abbey offers. "The morning rush is over. It'll be quiet the rest of the day."

"Are you sure?" I ask, turning to look at Abbey. "I don't really want to go home and stew over this. I'd rather stay busy."

"Well, go find something to do somewhere else. Go play in the snow. You've been staring at it all dreamy-eyed since you walked through the door."

I know she's trying to lighten the mood, to pull me out of my thoughts before they can fester. And before I can argue further, Abbey pulls me into a hug, holding me a little tighter and longer than she usually does.

"We could head over to the farm early. I'm sure Mom would love some help with the afternoon chores. Or it's early enough, we could go for a short hike."

"See." Abbey gestures to Gage as she pulls away from the hug. "You've got plenty of options. Get out of here."

"Thank you, Abbey."

"Of course. I'll see you tomorrow?"

"Yeah." I give her another quick hug before turning back to Gage. "I just need to grab my stuff from the back. I'll meet you at the cottage?"

"I'll wait and walk you to your car."

I don't bother arguing with him. Number one, it's not worth it because I won't win. And number two, I'd feel better having him walk me to my car.

"Thank you," I whisper.

He leans forward, pressing his lips to my forehead. "Of course, Rebel."

CHAPTER
Thirty

GAGE

I WATCH Ava as she nuzzles her nose against the horse's forehead, and I can't help but be amazed by her. Ava didn't let Brian's appearance at the bookstore hold her back. It might have taken her a minute to gather herself, but once she did, it was full force into the next activity.

I followed her back to the cottage, where she exchanged her things from last night for a new set of clothes for tomorrow. There wasn't a discussion on whether or not she would spend the night at my place again, but I wasn't complaining. I love that Ava likes spending time at my place. I love that it brings her comfort and makes her feel safe. And no matter how cheesy it is, I sleep better when she's with me.

The only discussion we had while at the cottage was whether or not she wanted to go on a hike, head to the farm early, or do something else. She decided on the farm. She wanted to enjoy the fresh snow in the open fields and help with the afternoon chores with the animals.

The horse is a new addition to the farm. Something I'm sure is my dad's doing. When my parents were married, there were always a few horses around, but they sold most of them after the divorce. Mom couldn't afford the extra burden of taking care of the horses.

"She's beautiful." Ava looks over her shoulder, a smile on her face. "Should I be calling you 'Cowboy'?" she teases.

"No, definitely not." I laugh as I step up behind her. "I may know how to ride, but that's as much of a cowboy as I am."

"Damn. I thought this might finally be my chance to live my cowboy romance fantasy."

"Well"—I slip my arms around her waist, pulling her back against me, her ass snug against my hardening length—"what's to say we still can't live out your fantasies?" I whisper in her ear.

"Hmm." She shivers against me. "You make a good point."

"Gage!"

I groan at the sound of my sister's voice behind us, my head falling to Ava's shoulder.

It's not that I'm not thrilled to see her and introduce her to Ava, but I would have liked a little longer with just the two of us.

Ava's soft laugh makes me squeeze her slightly. I love that sound, and I'm so glad it's a sound I hear often. Ava steps out of my embrace, turning to place a hand against my chest as she steps around me to greet my sister.

"Olivia. I'm so glad to finally meet you. I've heard a lot about you from Gage."

It doesn't surprise me that Ava immediately pulls Olivia into a hug. That's who Ava is. And I'm not surprised by the smile on Olivia's face either. She's always wanted a sister, and the fact that I'm bringing someone home to meet the family—something I've never done before—would imply that this is very serious.

"It's really good to meet you, too," Olivia offers shyly.

"Hey, Pickle. Have a good snow day?" I pull Liv into a

hug, giving her an extra squeeze. It's been a bit since I've seen her, and I've missed her.

"You know snow days around here mean I have to help with farm chores. It's not like it's a real day off."

"Good. It builds character." I laugh at the eye roll and throw an arm over her shoulder while reaching for Ava's hand.

The three of us make our way up to the house, where I see my mom standing on the back porch.

"Can't you come up with your own line? I know that's what Mom and Nick used to say to you when you were my age."

"Oh, she's good." Ava laughs, her left hand held firm in my grip as she steps up to my side, wrapping her right hand around my bicep.

"Ava, what a nice surprise." Mom reaches for Ava the second we reach the stairs. "Gage said you were coming for dinner, but I didn't expect you both so early."

"Oh, well, I..." Ava's voice trails off as she glances at me, unsure what to say.

I squeeze her hand before leaning in to kiss my mom's cheek. "I asked if she wanted to join me here or go for a hike after she got off work this morning, and she couldn't pass up seeing the farm covered in fresh snow. She loves the stuff."

Mom eyes me warily. I have no doubt she can tell I'm not being totally honest with her, but she won't push—not right now, anyway. She knows I don't hold anything back from her if there isn't a good reason.

"I'm glad you picked the farm. It really is beautiful in the snow." Mom pulls Ava into a hug, holding her a little longer than might be considered normal for people meeting for the second time. But I see Ava sink into the embrace, holding on just as long.

"It's so peaceful out here. I get why you didn't want to give it up," Ava says wistfully as she pulls away.

Mom studies Ava, concern pinching her brows. Her eyes bounce to mine before moving back to Ava. "Why don't you come help me with the pie I'm making for dessert? Gage and Liv can tackle the afternoon chores."

"Mom," Olivia whines.

I don't give Ava time to argue. "Come on, Pickle. Keep me company and fill me in on all the juicy gossip from school." I press a quick kiss to Ava's temple before tugging Olivia into my side and heading back down the stairs.

I think Ava could use a mother's ear right now. I wish more than anything Ava could turn to her mom at a moment like this, but I'm grateful my mother can step in for the time being.

I haven't told either of my parents what happened on Christmas Eve, nor have they asked. They know something bad happened that night to have Ava rush home so late in the evening, and they know I'd tell them if I needed to, but for now, it stays between me and Ava.

Mom won't push more than necessary, and she'll respect Ava's wish not to talk about it if that's what she really wants. But I've seen Ava since she spoke to Quinn and Declan. A weight has been lifted off her shoulder. She's freer with her laughs and the tension in her shoulders is practically gone. She's also started trying new things in the afternoons after she gets off work instead of heading back to her place and sitting around waiting for something to do.

Yesterday, she went to a yoga class with Emily. She didn't love it, but she also didn't hate it. She has plans to try a pottery class with Quinn over the weekend and rollerblading with Declan next week. She said she wants to try new things, and she's making it happen.

Spending a few hours with my mom means she's about to be introduced to another possible hobby. And hopefully she'll open up about what's going on. I'm doing everything I can to support her through all of this—and I'll continue to do so—but a mother's perspective couldn't hurt either.

"Is everything okay with Ava?" Olivia asks a few minutes later as we walk up to the goat pen.

"You're far too observant for your age." It's a diversion, and we both know it, but I'm not entirely sure how to answer that question.

Olivia doesn't say anything. She simply stares at me, waiting me out.

My hands land on my hips, and my head falls forward, a heavy sigh releasing from my chest before I look back at her and respond. "There's a lot going on in her life right now, and it's not my place to share. But in the grand scheme of things, she's okay."

Olivia absentmindedly nods her head as her attention drifts to look at the goats. "It's a good thing she's here then." She brings her focus back to me, a small smile forming on her lips. "There's no way she'll be able to think about whatever's going on in her life with all the craziness Asher and Leo will bring with them when they get here."

I don't even try to hold in the laugh that bursts out of me. Olivia has never been more right about anything.

CHAPTER
Thirty-One

AVA

"HOW'VE you been since Nick and I saw you at Murphy's?" Laura asks as she moves around the kitchen, gathering different ingredients.

"I've been good. I'm loving my job at the bookstore and that I actually have time for myself for the first time in years."

"Here." Laura hands me a peeler and gestures to the apples on the counter. "Peel those for me." She moves to the kitchen island and begins measuring ingredients for what looks like the pie crust. "We didn't really talk about it at Murphy's, but you were a lawyer back in Boston, right?"

"Yeah." I pick up the first apple and begin peeling. "I worked in family law at this big fancy law firm. I was fired the day before my brother called about Scott."

"Any particular reason you don't want to continue practicing law?" There's no judgment in her tone, just curiosity.

I set the first apple down and pick up the next, giving myself a minute to think about what I want to say. "I was raised by two very selfish people. People who probably never should have had children. But they did because that's what was expected."

I move on to the third apple, not looking at Laura. "I didn't realize it until recently, but almost everything I've done in my life was because of the manipulation of my parents. I joined the soccer team because that was an acceptable sport for someone like me. I joined the debate team because it would look good on college applications. I volunteered my time for the same reason. I was friends with only the wealthy kids in my class because that's what they wanted. I learned the piano because that's what ladies were supposed to do." I sigh, placing the peeler and final apple on the counter. "I went to law school because I was good on the debate team and was a logical thinker—or so I thought."

"If you feel comfortable doing it, those need to be cored and sliced." Laura gestures to the peeled apples. I appreciate her giving me a task and letting me word-vomit so much of what I've been holding in.

"I've never done that before."

"I can show you." She wipes her hands on the towel thrown over her shoulder and comes over to me. "This is a corer. It does exactly what it sounds like," she says, picking up the metal tool and piercing the apple. "Slowly twist the corer around the center of the apple, and then pull the core out." Her movements match her words, and the core pops up with little effort. "From there, it's simply slicing the apple into thin pieces." She cuts the apple in half and slices a few pieces to show me what she means.

"I can do that."

"Perfect." She wipes her hands again before squeezing my shoulder quickly and returning to the dough she was mixing.

Neither of us talk for a few minutes, my focus entirely on the apples in front of me.

"I recently discovered that my parents arranged a marriage for me. To the son of my father's closest friend." I glance at Laura, and while she pauses briefly in what she's doing, she doesn't say anything. "That same man tried to rape me two weeks before my brother called. It's why I was fired from the firm." That's the first time I've labeled that attack for what it really was. And surprisingly, it lifts the last remaining weight from my shoulders.

Laura slowly turns to me, her face filled with rage. "Excuse me? Did I hear you correctly? You were fired because a man tried to rape you?"

"I was fired because the man in question is the son of one of the founding partners, and at the end of the day, I insulted him when I said no."

"That doesn't make it any better." She twists the towel in her hands as if trying to strangle something.

"No, it doesn't. But when my boss called me in and told me I was being let go, I was relieved. And it wasn't only because I wouldn't have to see Brian around the office anymore." I pick up the corer and begin working on another apple.

"Being fired showed me just how unhappy I was in my life. I was living in a city I hated and working a job I found absolutely no fulfillment in. I didn't have friends and was so freaking lonely. I just didn't recognize any of that because my focus was that job."

Laura slowly turns back to the dough she's working, recognizing that doing something with my hands is helping me through talking about this.

"Then my brother called, and I jumped at the chance to escape all of it. To focus on something else. Something worthwhile. Something I could feel proud of."

"Exactly what you needed at exactly the right time."

"Yeah." I sigh. "I didn't have a plan when I got here, but somewhere along the way, this town started to feel more like home than anything in Massachusetts. When I saw the bookstore was hiring, I couldn't ignore it." I toss the last few apple slices into the bowl and move to rinse my hands in the sink.

I don't hear Laura move to my side, but she's there handing me a towel to dry my hands. "Sometimes not having a plan is the best thing for us. Not having a plan doesn't have to mean chaos. It just leaves the door open for unexpected possibilities."

"Unexpected possibilities," I whisper.

My eyes drift out the window above the sink, and in the distance I can see Gage and Olivia at the chicken coop. They're laughing about something when Gage throws an arm over Olivia's shoulders, pulling her into his side and giving her a noogie. The joy on his face sparks something bright in my chest.

My first instinct is to run from it. To fight this feeling growing inside me. It's too fast to feel this way for someone. We barely know each other. But then I think about it and realize that's not true.

I know Gage prefers the cold, especially when he sleeps. I know he likes classic rock and indie folk music but hates rap and pop. I know he prefers a comedy to an action-packed movie and hates reality TV. He takes his coffee with a little sugar and a decent amount of milk—though, he hates to admit it. He loves the outdoors and wishes he could spend more time hiking.

His favorite color is green, and his favorite food is spaghetti and meatballs. When he was a kid, he wanted to be a vet.

He loved his time in the military but is glad he's home and able to spend time with his family. He's glad his parents are back together and believes this might be the one that sticks. He worries about his siblings and whether he spends enough time with them or if he missed too much while he was in the army.

I know him better than I know anyone else. He's smart and funny. So incredibly caring and honorable. Adventurous and determined. He's everything I could want in a partner and so much more.

It might be fast, but it doesn't make it any less true. I am in love with that man.

"Unexpected possibilities indeed." Laura's voice tears me from my thoughts, and there's a knowing smirk on her face when I turn to look at her. She squeezes my hand before returning to the kitchen island, this time to the spices set next to the bowl of sliced apples. "Can I ask if it's practicing law you were unhappy with or if the law firm was the issue?"

I move to her side and watch as she measures the spices, pouring them over the apples. "The law firm was definitely an issue, but I don't know about the rest."

"Stir those for me." Laura pushes the bowl toward me before returning to the dough and rolling it out. "I know you said your parents manipulated you into being a lawyer. But if manipulation, and not force, got you there, then it implies you might have enjoyed it at some point." Her voice is gentle and genuine. I still don't hear an ounce of judgment.

"I loved it when I first started. I felt like I was really helping people and making a difference, which is what I wanted. But somewhere along the way, it became all about the money I could make for the firm, and it stopped being about helping people."

"I'm not trying to push you back into doing something you don't want, but that sounds like the atmosphere you were in was the issue. If you wanted to, you could easily create the environment you're craving and still use your degree. It wouldn't have to be here." There's a twinkle in her eye when she looks at me. "But Benny Meriwether is getting closer to retirement and has been looking to bring on someone else to take over his practice when he does." She gestures for me to bring the apples to her where she's got the bottom pie crust ready in the baking dish. "It's not just family law when you're talking about a small town firm, but it's also not about the money either."

We're quiet as I watch her lay the top crust across the apples, cutting off the excess before crimping the edges with a fork. She picks up a knife and gently cuts a few slits across the top for venting. When she's done, she puts the pie in the oven and sets a timer.

She studies me for a minute before she moves to me, taking both my hands in hers, offering me a comfort I didn't realize I was missing. "It's just something for you to think about. I heard what you did for Scott, and it sounds like you're an amazing lawyer. I'd hate to see you give it up because some bastard ruined it for you." Her grip on my hands tightens. "Don't let some man who means nothing ruin anything for you. He's not worth it."

I try to keep them in, but the tears fill my eyes and slip down my cheeks. Laura doesn't hesitate the second she sees them. She pulls me into a fierce hug, rocking me slightly. It's a mother's hug, something I can't remember ever feeling.

Without thinking, I wrap my arms around her and hold on just as tight, the tears falling even more freely now. I've known since early on in my childhood that I didn't have the kind of relationship many daughters had with their mothers, but I didn't realize how much I craved a mother's touch and under-standing until I got it.

It shouldn't shock me that Laura freely offers this to me. Her son has been nothing but understanding and caring since the first moment I met him. We may have flirted that first day in the courthouse, but I can see it for exactly what it was now. He saw I was hurting and he wanted to help me forget, even if it was only for a few minutes.

I hear the back door open and the deep timber of Gage's voice, but Laura doesn't loosen her grip on me, and neither do I. I know the moment Gage sees us because his voice cuts off, and I feel his heat at my back almost instantly. He doesn't try to pull me away from Laura or touch me, but his presence is enough, and he knows it because he knows me the same way I know him.

"Everything okay?" he asks softly a few minutes later when I pull away from Laura. He doesn't give me the opportunity to wipe my tears before he's reaching to do it himself.

I give him a shaky smile and nod, unable to form the words.

"Yeah, we're just having a moment." Laura smooths the hair at the back of my head—another touch I've never experienced from either of my parents—before moving to the island counter, where she starts cleaning up the mess. "Nick and the boys should be here shortly. Want to help me with dinner, Liv?"

"Sure." Olivia moves further into the kitchen and begins helping Laura, the two of them moving around each other and the kitchen as if in a choreographed dance.

"You sure you're okay?" Gage asks quietly, his hands still framing my face. It's a gentle touch, one I could easily move out of if I wanted to, but I can read the look in his eyes—he needs to see my eyes when I respond; he needs to see I'm telling the truth.

"I'm okay. Just realizing how much I've missed out on with my parents."

"Oh, Rebel." He pulls me into his chest, bending so his lips are at my ear. "They'll both love you fiercely if you let them."

"I know." Tears fill my eyes again, my gaze moving to where Laura and Olivia are at the kitchen island. "But why?" I lean back in his arms just enough to see his face, trying to process what it feels like to have parents who freely give their love, not just to their children, but to those their children hold close.

"Because that's just who they are."

When I don't say anything, his eyes bounce between mine, searching for something. He must find it because here, in his mom's kitchen, with her and his sister standing just a few feet from us, he says the three words I honestly wasn't sure I'd ever hear with such feeling. "And because I love you."

The tears fall, but this time, out of pure happiness. The brightness in my chest is back, and it pours from me in waves. I know I only just realized it, but I feel it down to my marrow. I love this man with everything I have and everything that I am.

I press myself closer to him, and our lips collide in a messy, tear-filled kiss. "I love you, too," I whisper against him.

His arms around me tighten, and his lips lock with mine in a heated kiss. Considering our audience, it's likely not the most appropriate kiss, but I don't care, as my entire being hums with happiness and relief at saying those words.

Before everything happened with my parents and Brian, I always wanted this—this joy and contentment. But since that night in the office and that conversation with my parents afterward, I just didn't know if it was real. I hoped it was, especially seeing Declan and Quinn together, but sometimes people see what they want, not what's actually in front of them.

But I guess that goes for everything. If I had been paying better attention from the start, I might have realized it sooner—the love I have for this man and the love he has for me.

"I really wish we weren't in my mother's kitchen," he whispers against my lips.

I smile, leaning back to see his face. "I get it, but I'm glad we're here. I didn't know how much I needed it until I got it." My eyes travel over to Laura, who tries to cover the smirk on her face as she focuses on the chicken in front of her.

"I know," Gage murmurs, smoothing hair from my face and cupping my cheek. "Now you're going to get it far more often than you want."

I shrug, a smile forming on my lips. "Maybe, but I won't take it for granted."

Gage leans forward, pressing a tender kiss to my lips just before a commotion at the front door and voices shout over each other.

"Liv said Gage brought his girlfriend home for dinner!" a raucous voice shouts.

"The girlfriend he swore he'd never have!" This one from a deeper voice.

"Boys! You saw his Jeep out front; you know he's already here." And that one is clearly Nick.

I laugh at Gage as he rolls his eyes, his grip around me tightening slightly. I lift to my toes and kiss his cheek, the smile never leaving my face. "I can't wait to meet your brothers. I think I'm going to really love them."

Gage laughs and swats at my ass as I scamper away, more than ready for the chaos I know is about to happen.

CHAPTER
Thirty-Two

GAGE

"NO, but you have to understand, I was ten, and Gage was only home for a few days!" Leo shouts from across the table.

"So you hid his underwear?" Ava laughs next to me.

"In my ten-year-old brain, if he didn't have his underwear, he couldn't leave, and I would get to spend more time with him." Leo's eyes jump between my dad and Asher before he looks back at Ava. "He spent all his time with Asher." He points at him like it's Asher's fault. "It was Gage's punishment to live without underwear for not spending time with me."

"If I remember correctly, didn't you spend the whole weekend at a friend's house, even though Dad tried to convince you to hang out with all of us?" I ask, my brow raised.

"That's beside the point!" Leo slams a hand on the table. This time, everyone—including Leo—laughs.

The warmth I've felt in my chest since telling Ava I love her hasn't dissipated in the slightest. If anything, I feel it more —especially when she glances at me over her shoulder, a twinkle in her eye. I never thought I could feel like this, filled with so much love for someone outside my family, but I do.

With how close her chair is to mine and the fact that my

arm is draped over the back of her seat when Ava sits back, she ends up leaning partially against me. Her body melts, and her hand falls to my leg. With just a tilt of my head, I place a kiss to her temple and relax even further into the moment. I'm surrounded by everyone I love most, and seeing the love and joy on everyone's faces is more than I could have ever dreamed of.

I understand the saying of floating on cloud nine because that's exactly what I feel.

"How's working at the bookstore going?" Dad asks after we all settle, lifting his beer bottle to his lips.

"I love it." Ava smiles, and her body melts even further into my side. "Abbey is such an amazing woman to work with. She's been so welcoming."

"She should be running her own bakery or something. That woman knows how to bake," Mom offers from the other end of the table.

"And how to make some amazing cider," Asher adds.

"I haven't had the chance to try her cider yet, but I swear I've already gained five pounds from all the sweets I've had. And this is only my second week!"

"Well, I hope that won't stop you from having a slice of pie. You did help make it after all."

"Oh! What pie did you make?" Leo's excited gaze bounces between Ava and Mom.

"Apple."

"Yes!" He pumps his fist in the air, causing everyone to chuckle.

"First, you and Asher need to clean the table. Then we can have pie," Dad tells him.

Asher doesn't argue and stands from his seat, picking up the dishes in front of him and Olivia before moving to the kitchen sink. Leo, on the other hand, gapes at Dad.

"I don't want to hear it. Go help." Dad isn't harsh, but his tone doesn't leave much room for argument.

"Thank you, Leo," Mom says, squeezing his hand when he reaches for her empty plate. He bends to kiss her cheek and nods slightly before moving to set the dishes on the counter by Asher before coming back for more.

"I'll help," Olivia says as she stands from the table, reaching for Dad's plate.

Dad reaches for her before she can pick up his plate. "No, Liv. You helped cook; you shouldn't have to help clean up, too."

She gives him a small smile. "I really don't mind. Besides, the pie needs to go back in the oven to warm anyway."

"Thanks, honey," Mom says as she lifts her wine glass to her lips.

Ava shifts in her seat, likely uncomfortable with not helping somehow. Before she can stand or say anything, I place my hand on her thigh, squeezing slightly. "They'll never let you help. Not this time," I murmur in her ear.

"You're our guest," Dad tells her, noticing her discomfort.

"At least for tonight you are," Mom continues for Dad.

Ava glances between the two of them for a second, but I see the moment it clicks—what all of us are saying. She's part of the family now.

She glances down at the table and tucks a piece of hair behind her ear before relaxing back into her seat.

"Thank you." It's said so softly, and with a slight wobble, I would have missed it if I weren't sitting right next to her.

Mom reaches for her hand, squeezing it lightly before she looks down the table at Dad. "How was everything at work today?"

"You okay?" I ask Ava quietly.

When she brings her eyes to mine, tears are welling in the

corners, but she smiles and nods before tucking herself into my side and turning back to my parents' conversation.

I try to pay attention to what they're talking about, but all I can focus on is the feel of Ava at my side. She fits so perfectly tucked against me, and this evening proves she fits perfectly in my family.

She gets along with my parents—something I already knew thanks to them ambushing her at Murphy's a couple of weeks ago and constantly asking about her. She also gets along with my siblings and always encourages me to spend time with them. She understands the importance of family and why I hold them so close. And even when she's hurting because she's never had this with her parents, she's still present and involved in everything going on around her.

Leaning in, I kiss her temple before dropping my mouth to her ear. "I love you," I whisper.

Her eyes close, and she takes a deep breath. Her exhale seems like one of utter contentment. "I love you, too," she whispers back, her eyes focused on mine.

"WHY DO YOU LOVE ME?"

I don't know how I manage to keep the car on the road when Ava's words actually register in my brain.

"What?" It comes out as more of a breath than an actual word.

"Why do you love me?" she repeats, her words quiet.

After enjoying the pie Mom and Ava made, we sat around the table and played a round of Monopoly.

Leo firmly believes you can't hide your true nature while playing Monopoly. It's his go-to game whenever anyone wants to introduce someone to the family.

If they don't want to play, they aren't fun, and, therefore, can't hang with the rest of us.

If they play but are afraid to win, they aren't tough enough to be part of the family. You can't be afraid to speak your mind in a family like ours.

But, if they play and aren't afraid to go for the win, then chances are, they're a good fit.

Ava wasn't afraid to go for the win, and she proved that in spades, taking all of us out one by one. And she didn't have a problem pointing that out to Leo a few times before we left, especially after he bragged about being the reigning champ three years running.

But we're on the way back to my place now, taking it easy with the snow coming down. We're only five minutes from the house, but I need to look her in the eye after that question.

Pulling off to the side of the road, I put the Jeep in park, unbuckle my seatbelt, and turn to face her. "Where's that coming from?"

"Sorry, it's nothing." She shakes her head, her eyes focused on her hands in her lap. "Forget I asked."

"Rebel." I reach across the center console, taking her hand in mine. "I don't want to forget you asked. I have a list of reasons a mile long, and I don't have a problem sharing them with you. I just want to understand where that question is coming from." My voice is soft, my tone gentle.

Ava releases a sigh before letting her head fall back against the headrest. She takes a few seconds before she turns to look at me, tears in her eyes.

"I don't know why I doubt it. I'm sure it has something to do with my parents, but it's not like others haven't shown me love." Her eyes may have tears, but her voice doesn't waiver. "I mean, Declan is the best big brother I could've asked for. I've never doubted his love for me. And Scott and the rest of the

Marks family. They've taken me in just like they did Declan." She reaches up and swipes at the tear that escapes.

"It's not the same, though," I say quietly.

She's quiet for a moment, but the next words out of her mouth break my heart. "I know I'm worthy of love."

"Yeah, you are." I cup her cheek in my hand, my thumb swiping at the tears that continue to fall. "I love you because of everything you are. Your strength and resilience. Your heart and your mind. I love you because of how you support me and everyone you care about." I untuck and retuck the piece of hair she's always messing with. "I love you because we fit together in a way that never felt possible. I love you because you gave me a life worth living instead of simply going through the motions. I love you because you give me peace."

"Okay." Ava places a delicate finger against my lips. The tears are still present in her eyes, but instead of anger and frustration at herself, I see love. "You can stop." Her finger slips from my lips as she moves her hand to cup my cheek. "You give me peace, too. I forget everything else when I'm with you and I can breathe easily again." She leans across the center console, bringing her lips to mine in a tender kiss. "Sorry—"

"No," I interrupt her, placing the thumb from the hand still cupping her cheek over her lips. "Don't apologize. I'll tell you every day why I love you if that's what you need."

"No," she whispers, shaking her head slightly. "I'd rather you show me like you have been for weeks." There's a twinkle in her eye now, and seeing it has the tightness in my chest dissipating.

"I can definitely do that." I smirk, touching my lips to hers in a soft kiss.

"Let's go home," she whispers against me, and I can't help but capture her lips in a demanding kiss. I know we're not there yet, but the fact that she could even think of my place as home has me desperate for more. She shifts in her seat, trying to get closer, but the pull of her seatbelt reminds us where we are.

Her moan—a mix of frustration and desire—has me tearing my lips from hers. "When we get home, your ass better be naked and in my bed within five minutes."

Without waiting for her answer, I turn back to the steering wheel, buckle my seatbelt, and drive the last few minutes home with a raging hard-on in my pants. I want fast and hard with Ava, but I also want soft and tender. I want it all with her.

CHAPTER
Thirty-Three

AVA

"GAGE." I laugh as he rushes around the front of the Jeep and lifts me from my seat. "I can walk, you know."

"Yes, but it's icy, and I don't want you to hurt yourself. I have plans for us." He nips at the skin of my neck as he kicks the door shut before carefully rushing up the porch stairs.

Without putting me down, he fumbles with the keys still in his hands, trying to unlock the door.

"Gage." I push at his chest lightly, trying to get him to put me down.

He stops trying to unlock the door and sets me down but doesn't let me go. His lips crash to mine in a searing kiss, and my mind goes blank. All I can focus on is the feel of him pressed against me—every solid inch of him. His chest, his thighs...his hard cock straining behind the zipper of his jeans. Everything about him sparks a fire inside me that I can't ignore.

Without realizing it, Gage unlocks the front door, and we stumble inside. Somehow, without breaking our kiss, we manage to toe off our shoes and shrug out of our coats, leaving everything in a pile on the floor. And then Gage is lifting me by the backs of my thighs, and my legs are wrapping around his waist while my arms wrap around his shoulders as he carries me up the stairs.

I can't get close enough to him. I need him in a way I've never needed anyone else. Not just sex—though I want that, too. But I need him in every aspect of my life. The good and the bad. The small moments and the big ones.

I know it's only been seven weeks, but I can't imagine my life without him.

Okay, that's not true. I can imagine my life without him, but I don't want to.

"I'm never going to get tired of this," Gage mumbles against my skin as he gently lays me on his bed. "The feel of you against me, the look of you sprawled across my bed. I want you in every way imaginable."

"Gage." It's more moan than an actual word. I can't focus on getting words out when I feel his hands slide against my skin as he pushes my sweater up, exposing my stomach. His lips trail a path up from the top of my jeans, over my stomach, and between the valley of my breasts. They aren't frantic kisses; they're soft and tender, almost like he's savoring every second his lips touch me.

"I don't know how I got lucky enough to find you," he whispers as he lifts my sweater over my head. "But I will do everything in my power to keep you." His lips mold to mine in a tender kiss, showing me how serious he is.

His hands slide beneath me, reaching for my bra clasp, and I arch my back to give him space to unclasp it. The second it pops free, he releases my lips and pulls away just enough to slide my bra off, his eyes darkening at the sight of my pebbled nipples.

"God. I'm a lucky man." His hands move to cup my breasts moments before he dips his head to pull one of my nipples into his mouth, biting gently.

I can't stop my moan, nor do I want to. One of my hands falls to his head, gripping his hair, while the other falls to his back, trying to pull at his shirt to feel his skin. I need the heat of his skin against me more than I need air.

"Please lose some clothes," I beg after he's had a chance to lavish my other breast with the same attention. "I need you."

He lifts his head, bringing his lips back up to mine. "You have me." He says it so confidently I don't have room to doubt he means it. And the truth of it is, I don't doubt him; I know he says exactly what he means.

Any doubt I feel is all about me and what I think I'm deserving of. But I'm starting to realize I'm worthy of all the good things Gage has brought into my life.

"I am madly in love with you, Gage Hunter Flynn." I hold his face in both hands, ensuring he can see the truth behind my words. "You don't have to do anything other than love me to keep me."

"Loving you won't be an issue," he whispers just before his lips land back on mine in a kiss so deep I feel it in my bones.

His lips leave mine and start a path down my neck and over my collarbone. And even though he's already paid close attention to my breasts, he still takes a moment to suck and nip at them before continuing down my torso, his hands working on the button and zipper of my jeans.

"I know you like it hard and fast, but I'm worshiping every inch of you tonight, so you're gonna have to deal with slow for a bit." And he proves just how slow he means as he sits up on his knees to remove my jeans and underwear, pulling them off inch by agonizing inch.

"Just know I'm going to get you back," I groan as he peppers feather-light kisses up the inside of my leg.

"I can't wait." I hear the smirk in his voice and then feel it press against my thigh, so fucking close to where I need his touch most.

My core clenches. I feel like I'm on the brink of orgasm, and Gage has barely even touched me. I've never felt this desperate for another person's touch, and I know no one else can ever make me feel this way again.

Gage is it for me.

I can't stop my hips from bucking at the barest hint of Gage's fingers sliding over my sex. "You're so fucking wet."

"Gage," I whimper, his fingers stroking light circles over my clit. "I-I..." My words trail off, unable to form a coherent thought as his tongue drags across my slit.

"Just let go, Rebel. Trust that I've got you." His heated breath puffs out against me, causing a shiver to run up my entire body.

I can't form the words, but I trust Gage more than anyone else. So I do exactly what he says, and I let go. Forgetting everything else but the feel of his touch as his tongue focuses entirely on my clit and his fingers slide in and out, crooking slightly to hit the perfect spot on every thrust in.

It's barely thirty seconds before I'm coming, my entire body trembling with my release. Gage doesn't let me come down from that high before he's working me back up again— his fingers and tongue never leaving my skin.

My second orgasm comes like the first, with a third arriving right on its heels and with a scream. "Gage! Please. I-I need a second." I push at his head, gasping for air.

He gives me the reprieve, but only so he can stand and remove his clothes. The look in his eyes—so dark with desire— proves my claims of needing a minute wrong if the clenching of my core is any indication. I can't take my eyes off him as he removes his shirt, his chiseled chest and abs coming into view. I want to run my tongue over every hard inch of him. Especially his cock once it pops free of his pants and briefs as he pushes them to the floor.

Gage moves to his nightstand, reaching for the drawer

where he keeps the condoms, but I reach for him before he can take more than one step. "Wait."

Concern floods his features. "What is it?"

"I'm on the pill, and I got tested a few weeks ago. After we...well, after we decided to keep sleeping together. I wanted to make sure I was clean in case we wanted to go without..." My words trail off as Gage leaps onto the bed, his body covering mine, every bare inch of skin touching, his hips cradled in mine.

"I had my annual physical a few weeks ago. I'm clean."

"Me too," I whisper.

His eyes bounce between mine. "Are you sure you want to?"

"Yes. I don't want anything between us."

"I've never had sex without a condom."

"Me neither."

His forehead falls against mine, and his hips shift, causing his cock to slide against my wet core, both of us moan at the feel.

Gage lifts his head, his eyes staring into mine. He supports his weight on one arm as he reaches between us and lines himself up with my center. "I am madly, deeply, irrevocably in love with you, Ava Margaret Day." He punctuates that statement with a thrust of his hips and a devouring kiss, swallowing my cry of pleasure.

Gage's deep and deliberate thrusts bring me right back to the edge faster than I want. I want this to be drawn out, but my entire body is on fire, and I can't hold out. My orgasm rips through me in waves, my body squeezing tight around Gage everywhere we touch.

I pulse around him, my hips matching his thrust for thrust. His grip on my hips tightens, and the muscles in his back contract. His head falls forward into the crook of my neck, and he lets out a loud groan as he comes, hot and wet inside me.

He collapses on top of me for only a second before he rolls us to our sides, holding me close as we catch our breath.

Sex with Gage has always been phenomenal, out of this world even. But this moment with Gage has been life-changing. I'll never be the same after tonight, and I'm perfectly content with that.

"Just so we're clear. You're stuck with me now. There's no going back after this," Gage mumbles against me, resting his lips on my forehead.

"Good. I don't want to go back from this. I'm exactly where I want to be."

THE FEEL of Gage stroking my back wakes me a few hours later.

"Hmm," I hum, nuzzling my head further into the crook of his neck as I lay across his chest. "Why are you awake?"

"Sorry, I didn't mean to wake you." He lifts his head to kiss my bare shoulder.

"It's fine." I lift my head to look at him. "Is everything okay?"

He studies me for a second before he flips us, his body blanketing mine. "Do you know how mind-blowing it is that we found each other? How mind-blowing it is that we fell in love with each other?" His eyes bounce between mine. "There are over 8.2 *billion* people in the world, and we found each other. How insane is that?"

I swallow, the love in his eyes shining through bright as the morning sun. "There's no guarantee this is it for us," I whisper. "This is still new. We're still learning about each other. We could wake up tomorrow and realize this isn't right."

He studies me, really thinking about his response before flipping us again. His arms move around me, gliding up my back and holding us chest to chest. I have to arch my back to maintain eye contact with how close he holds me. "I don't believe that for a second. I know you always planned on getting married and having babies, and I know before everything happened with that bastard, you were open to the idea of meeting someone you could spend your life with. But no one even sparked a hint of interest in you."

He removes one of his hands around me to tuck a piece of hair behind my ear before cupping my cheek. "And I honestly thought romantic love was something people forced themselves into because that's what they were supposed to do. But that is the farthest thing from the truth." He slides his hand from my cheek down my neck and shoulder before curving it around my body to hold me close again.

"You're Monday mornings and hikes with my brothers. You're family dinners and hanging out with Walt. You're spaghetti and meatballs and the color green. You are all my favorite things, and I can't believe I found you."

I let my head fall forward and rest against his chest, breathing in his sage and sandalwood scent. "If you don't stop talking like that, I'll become a blubbering mess." His chest muffles my voice, but I know he hears me when I feel it rumble.

I knew I loved him back in his mother's kitchen just a few hours ago, but if there was even an ounce of doubt before, it's gone now.

I lift my head and meet his eyes again. "I don't know how to follow up a speech like that. I don't know how you always have the right words, but I can't think of anything other than I love you."

"Oh, Rebel. Those are the only words I need." And then his lips are on mine in a hungry kiss.

CHAPTER
Thirty-Four

AVA

"ALL RIGHT! You guys are closing up, right?" Quinn asks as she marches through the doors of Falls Book Haven a week later. Emily right behind her, shaking her head in exasperation.

"I told her we should have given you a heads up, but she was adamant about doing it her way."

"What are you talking about?" I laugh as I grab the trash from behind the counter.

"We're having a ladies' night," Quinn declares. Since moving in with my brother, she's become more carefree and open with everyone in her life, and I couldn't love it more.

"You've been hiding out at Gage's and the Anderson Farm. Which is totally valid." She throws her hands up in the air to stop any arguments. "I know you're trying to avoid your parents and Brian, and Gage is being very protective of you, but I think it would be good for you to get out for a bit. And you"—she points at Abbey behind the register—"I know we were too far apart in school to hang out before, but these two don't shut up about you, and I feel like I'm missing out. So you have to join us as well."

I've been working the evening shift with Abbey for the last week. While I'm not likely to work this shift often, Abbey thought it would be a good idea for me to know the ropes in case they needed me to fill in. And while she's used to Gage coming in near the end of my shifts to hang out before heading home, this is out of the blue.

"Oh, um..."

"What if we already have plans?" I jump in, trying to give Abbey a second to catch up with Quinn.

"I already talked to Gage; you don't have any plans."

"Invasive much," I tease.

"Only because I love you," she returns instantly.

Abbey shifts behind the counter, pulling our attention to her. "Where were you thinking?"

"Oh, we figured we'd go to Murphy's. This one has a soft spot for Walt." Emily throws her thumb over her shoulder at me.

"How can you not like that man? He's so kind and warm-hearted."

"I'm not judging. He's the quintessential bar owner, and I love everything about it."

"So you'll join us?" Quinn asks Abbey.

"You know what"—Abbey closes the register drawer, avoiding eye contact with all of us—"I think I should just head home."

"What? No! Come! It'll be fun. I promise." Emily reaches across the counter, placing her hand on Abbey's arm. "Besides, we haven't hung out in a while, and I miss our book talks."

"I just—"

"We're not taking no for an answer," Quinn interrupts. "How can we help you guys close up?"

I see the tension coursing through Abbey's body and jump in to help the best I can. "We're almost done actually. Why don't you go over and get us a table? We'll join you in just a few minutes."

"Sounds like a plan. See you in a few." Emily turns and grabs Quinn's arm before heading out the door. I watch them walk past the window toward Murphy's next door before turning to Abbey.

"If you really don't want to go, I'll tell them something came up and you couldn't make it."

"It's not that I don't want to hang out with you all. I just..." Her words trail off as her eyes move to where we saw Emily and Quinn disappear from view. "I haven't seen Walt in sixteen years." She says it so softly I wonder if I'm supposed to hear her.

"I'm sorry. How do you live in this town, work next door to each other, and not see him for sixteen years?" I'm genuinely bewildered. "Better yet, why do you avoid Walt, of all people, for sixteen years?"

She offers me a gentle smile. "I think that's a story for another day." She reaches into her pocket, pulling out a set of keys to lock the register drawer. "Let's go."

"You sure?"

"Yeah." She steps around the counter, moves to the front door, locking it, and flipping the sign to *Closed*. "We can drop that out back and walk around to the front."

I don't know what changed her mind, but I see the determination in her eyes. So, without pushing more, I follow her as she shuts off the lights and heads out the back door, holding it open for me.

We drop the trash in the dumpster out back and make our way around the side of the bookstore, walking in front of the darkened windows on our way to Murphy's.

Abbey pauses outside the door, staring for a few minutes before she takes a deep breath and pulls the door open. A burst of noise hits us the second the door opens, and the feeling of home instantly overcomes me as we walk through the doors and my eyes catch Walt's.

Murphy's has become one of my favorite places, and I couldn't imagine walking through the doors and not seeing Walt behind the counter—a welcoming smile on his face. That smile I'm so used to falls the second he sees Abbey at my side.

It's like he sees a ghost.

I see his lips form a word, but I don't hear it from where we are by the door. It takes him a second, but he shakes himself from whatever stupor he's in and makes his way from behind the bar. Without stopping, he walks right up to Abbey and pulls her into a fierce hug.

"Mo stór." His voice is so soft I almost miss it. I have no idea what it means, but when Walt pulls away from Abbey, there are tears in both of their eyes.

"Hi, Walt."

He reaches to wipe a tear from her cheek, his eyes filled with so much pain. "It's been far too long."

"I know. I just...I couldn't be here."

"Neither can he," Walt whispers.

"If I could take it all back, I would," she chokes out.

"No. Never wish to take any of it back," he tells her sternly. He reaches to cup her cheek, offering comfort in the way a father might. "Just come in every once in a while. I miss your beautiful spirit just as much as I miss him."

More tears fall down her cheeks as she nods. "Okay. I can do that."

"Good." Walt glances at me briefly before wiping at Abbey's cheeks one more time. "I'll let you both enjoy your evening then." He quickly kisses her forehead before squeezing my shoulder and moving back behind the bar.

"Is that part of that story you mentioned earlier?" I ask a few moments later, trying to lighten the mood but failing miserably.

"Yeah." Her eyes follow Walt as he moves behind the bar, getting drinks and chatting with customers. "He looks different."

"Well, sixteen years will do that to a person."

"No." She studies him a few moments longer before she speaks again. "He looks sick."

I look at Walt, watching him for a bit, and realize that Abbey isn't wrong. I may have only known Walt for a little over two months, but he looks thinner than he did when I first met him. And the bags under his eyes are far more pronounced than I've ever seen them.

"It's probably stress." My brows draw in, concern for Walt running through me. "He was supposed to see his son around Christmas, but something happened, and they couldn't make it work."

Abbey makes a non-committal sound, her eyes never leaving Walt.

The sound of Quinn calling our names pulls our attention from the bar. Linking my arm with Abbey's, we go to the table for some quality girl time—something I didn't realize I was missing until taking my seat.

"I'LL BE RIGHT BACK." I laugh as I push myself from the booth we've been sitting in for the last few hours.

"Where are you going?" Emily asks, barely catching her breath from the story Quinn just told.

"Bathroom."

"You want someone to come with you?"

"No, I'm good. You stay and enjoy some more laughs at my brother's expense."

I make my way to the bathroom, a smile plastered on my

face. I may not have thought of the idea for a ladies' night, but it was exactly what I needed.

As I step out of the bathroom and into the back hallway of Murphy's, I pull my phone out of my back pocket. I'm surprised I haven't felt it go off more than a few times since Quinn and Emily showed up at the bookstore.

GAGE

Have fun tonight. I love you.

All right, I know it was supposed to be ladies' night, but Declan and Caleb have convinced me it's okay that we crash the last hour of your night.

Please don't be mad at me!

I can't stop the chuckle that falls from my lips. I check the time of his last text and see that he sent it ten minutes ago, meaning he's probably already here.

I'm slipping my phone into my back pocket when a body presses against my back. A hand comes up to cover my mouth and the other grabs one of my wrists as the person pushes me against the wall opposite the bathroom door.

It's such a cliché, the bathroom being at the end of a dark hallway, but it's a cliché because it's true—even at Murphy's, there's no one around.

"I told you this wasn't over." A shiver runs up my spine at the anger in Brian's voice.

My head falls forward against the wall in front of me in defeat for only a moment before my entire body stiffens. I won't make this easy for him, and I'll fight with everything I have.

"Scream, and I'll make this so much worse for you," he seethes in my ear. The grip he has on my wrist tightens to the point of searing pain as he roughly moves it to be sandwiched between my body and the wall, exactly where my other arm is.

"Let me make something very clear for you; if you don't come back to Boston with me and your parents tonight, I'll hurt everyone you care about." His body shifts just enough for him to fit his hand between me and the wall before he uses his weight to hold me in place again. "Your brother." His hand snakes down my stomach to the button on my jeans. "Your boyfriend." He slips the button free and roughly pulls at the zipper. "Everyone in the Marks family."

His hand is still over my mouth, but I manage to turn my head and look toward the end of the hallway. It's a Friday night, and the bar is plenty crowded. Someone will be coming this way; they have to.

Gage is here and has to be wondering where I am. There's no way he didn't ask where I was the second he saw me missing from the table. I just need to make it a few more minutes.

"You know how powerful my family is, how wealthy we are. I don't have an issue spending my wealth to make their lives more than miserable." His hand slips to the top of my panties.

"Please," I beg from behind his hand, tears welling in my eyes. I hate that he can see these tears, but I can't stop them.

"What was that?" he taunts, his hand on my mouth shifting slightly.

"I'll do whatever you want. Just please let me go," I plead. The words might be false, but the fear in my voice isn't.

"Oh, babydoll. If only it were that easy." His hand covers my mouth again, and he presses even closer, his breath fanning my cheek. "You've embarrassed me one too many times for it to be that easy now."

His hips press into my ass, shifting to make sure I feel his hard length against me. I try to hold in the whimper that slips free, but I can't, especially when I feel the tips of his fingers slip beneath the tops of my panties.

"Get your hands off her!" a voice booms seconds before Brian's heat at my back is ripped away.

A sob falls from my lips as I collapse against the wall, holding myself there as I try to regain just the slightest bit of composure. It takes me a second to register the sound of a flesh hitting flesh, but when it does, I turn to find Gage repeatedly slamming his fist into Brian's face.

"Gage!" I yell, trying to break whatever spell he's under. "Gage, stop!" I stumble forward, reaching for him, but I don't make it to him before Declan and Caleb pull him off Brian.

"He's out, man. You can stop." Declan struggles to hold Gage back but doesn't let him go until Gage's eyes come to me, and he instantly stops moving.

Gage raises his arms in surrender. "All right. I'm good. Let me go."

Declan releases him, and he's instantly in my space. He doesn't touch me, but his eyes roam over my entire body, and I see the devastation in his eyes.

"Rebel," he chokes.

"I'm okay," I whisper, reaching for him.

He shakes his head, pulling me into his arms. "No, you're not."

The second his arms are around me, I break. My body crashes into his, and the tears pour down my cheeks. I hold onto Gage so tightly my knuckles start to ache, but I can't let him go, and I can't stop crying.

"I've got you. You're safe now."

"Don't let me go."

"Never going to happen."

CHAPTER
Thirty-Five

GAGE

I CLOSE my eyes and try to focus solely on the fact that Ava is safe in my arms and not the fact that a man is bleeding profusely behind me or the fact he just had his hands all over the woman I love.

I don't think I'll ever be able to get the sight of Ava trapped against a wall with tears streaming down her face and terror in her eyes out of my head. All I saw was red.

I think I might have killed the man if Declan and Caleb hadn't shown up. Though, I might not be in the clear considering Caleb is still bent over that bastard's unmoving body.

I don't know how I missed the sirens when I see police officers and paramedics pour into the hallway. But considering my focus is entirely on the woman in my arms, I'm not surprised.

I see Reid out of the corner of my eye and prepare myself for the fact that I'm going to have to let Ava go. There's no way I won't get taken into the station after this.

I take one more deep breath, inhaling her apple and vanilla scent, before pulling away slightly, just enough to see her eyes. I cup her face in my hands and turn us so her back is to the scene in the hallway. She doesn't need to see that asshole ever again.

"I'm gonna have to go to the station with Reid."

"No!" she interrupts before I can say anything else, panic more than evident in her eyes and voice.

"Rebel," I say as softly as I can. "I don't have a choice."

"Then I'm going with you." Her grip on my shirt tightens

"We're going to need her statement as well," Reid offers quietly. The glare I send his way has him stepping back.

It's not fair, but right now, all I care about is keeping Ava safe and out of harm's way. I know Reid means absolutely no harm, but she shouldn't have to relive everything.

"Gage." Ava brings my focus back to her. She looks behind her to the piece of trash lying on the ground before bringing her eyes back to mine. Her eyes are clear and focused when they meet mine. "When he wakes up, he's going to press charges. They need my statement." She's gone into lawyer mode, and while I'm glad she's not shaking in my arms anymore, I'm worried about what happens when she doesn't have this to focus on.

I look over her shoulder to see the paramedics lifting him onto a stretcher, Caleb by their side, giving them orders. My focus comes back to Ava, trailing from her toes to her head. But I'm halted at the sight of her undone jeans.

Swallowing the urge to ram my fist into Brian's face again, I gently reach forward to button and zip her jeans, pulling her into another tight embrace.

"Okay. I don't think I can stand having you out of my sight anyway."

"You'll have to ride in the cruiser," Reid murmurs in my ear.

I nod, taking another minute to just hold Ava. Over her head, I see Declan step up behind her. Reluctantly, I pull away so he can have a moment with his sister.

Declan doesn't give her a chance to say anything before he pulls her into a fierce hug.

"I'm okay," she murmurs against him.

"I don't believe you." Declan's eyes find mine over her head, a look I can't quite decipher in his eyes. "What happens now?"

"I'm not technically getting arrested, but I have to go to the station." I might not be getting charged with anything right now, but that doesn't mean the charges won't come. No matter what, I don't regret a single thing.

"Arrested? Why would you be arrested?" Quinn demands from behind Declan.

Ava pushes from his embrace, stepping into my side and holding tight.

"Assault, excessive force, take your pick." I shrug, trying to play off the seriousness of the situation.

"Let's just start with a statement. From the both of you," Reid says.

"We'll meet you at the station then." Declan leans forward, pulling Ava's head toward him to kiss her forehead quickly before bending to meet her eyes directly. "I love you, squirt."

It takes her a second, but he holds steady until she responds. "I love you, too, big brother."

IT'S HOURS LATER, and I'm pacing the length of Lyle's office. I'm grateful they didn't put me in an interrogation room, but I haven't seen Ava since they separated us when we walked through the station doors, and I'm desperate to see her.

I know it's procedure to separate us to get our statements, but I still hate it more than anything in this moment. I want to be somewhere far away from here. Anywhere would be fine, as long as Ava's by my side.

The door to the sheriff's office opens as Lyle and Reid step through. "Well, I have good news and I have bad news." Lyle steps around his desk to take a seat, gesturing to the two seats in front of him.

I don't move from my position by the wall.

"All right." He leans forward, hands folded in front of him on the desk. "Brian Wellsley is going to be fine, but he's pressing charges."

My head falls forward. It's not a surprise, but it doesn't take the sting out of it. No matter what, if Brian presses charges, I'll lose my badge. I step up to the empty chair in front of his desk and fall into it.

"Ava corroborated your story. Brian assaulted her in the hall outside the bathroom, and you intervened. Unfortunately, it's the force you used that's the problem." Lyle studies me for a minute, looking for some kind of reaction, but I've been trained to keep my mouth shut in the worst situations. I know how to keep everything hidden.

He leans back in his seat, releasing a deep sigh. "Gage, you know I don't fault you for what happened this evening. And if it were my choice, you would walk out of the station right now, and things would carry on exactly like they always have."

"I know, sir."

He sighs again, his gaze flicking to Reid behind me for just a moment. "I don't want to do this, but I don't have a choice. The mayor will have my head if I don't follow the letter of the law. Especially with what Wellsley is threatening."

"I understand." I stand from my seat. "I don't regret it. I would do anything for that woman."

Lyle stands and moves around his desk, placing his hand out to shake mine. "You would have done it regardless of the person in that situation. It's what makes you a damn fine man."

Turning to Reid, I offer him a tight smile. I know he hates what he's about to do, but I don't blame him for a second.

"I'll talk to my dad, see if he can schedule an emergency hearing so you don't have to stay longer than a few hours."

"No. I know how much you hate asking your dad for favors. I can wait it out until Monday."

"Gage—"

"It's fine, man. I promise."

There's a reason Reid always gets uncomfortable when he has to go to court, and his father being a judge is just the tip of the iceberg. I know he wouldn't hesitate to ask his dad for a favor, but I won't put that pressure on him.

"Can I get a few minutes to talk to Ava?" I turn back to Lyle.

"Sure." He nods toward Reid, silently telling him to get her. "Keep your chin up." He squeezes my shoulder once before walking out the door.

I don't wait long before the door opens again, and Ava plows through, straight into my arms. "What's happening? I've been trying to get in here to see you for hours."

"Shh." I smooth her hair back and hold her face between my hands.

Her eyes are swollen and red-rimmed. I hate that she's been crying and I haven't been there to hold her, but I know Declan and Quinn haven't left her side, and I know she'll have the entire Marks family when she leaves here.

"How are you?" I can't stop my eyes from roaming her body yet again. I know I took inventory of every inch of her at Murphy's, but I need to see again that she's okay.

"Physically, I'm fine. He didn't have the chance to do anything other than pin me to the wall and undo my pants. You pulled him off before..." Her words trail off, and I can't blame her for not being able to say it. I can barely stand hearing it.

I slide one arm around her and cup the back of her head in my other hand, bringing her forehead against my lips. "You have to tell me what you need. I don't know what to do here," I whisper against her skin.

"I don't need you to do anything more than this. Just being here is enough."

My arms tighten around her. I hate what I'm about to tell her. I want nothing more than to be by her side until she's sick of me, but that's not in the cards for us, at least not right now.

Ava must feel the tension in my body. She pushes back, her eyes bouncing between mine. "What is it?"

"Brian's awake, and he's already told the police he wants to press charges." Ava's eyes fall shut. She's a lawyer; she knows what happens next. "It's late Friday, so they can't set a bail hearing until Monday."

"No." Her eyes fly open, and she shakes her head in denial.

"Rebel." I keep my voice firm, trying to instill a little bit of strength into this situation. "You know he's a powerful man with a lot of connections. He's already made threats that are making the mayor nervous."

"Gage." Her voice cracks, and my heart rips in two.

"It's just forty-eight hours. I'll be home by Monday, and I'll be stuck to your side like glue. You'll get so sick of me," I tease.

"I'll talk to him. I'll get him to drop the charges."

"No. Ava. Don't."

"Gage—"

"Ava, I'm serious. Just let everything run its course. If the charges stick—and that's a big if—I'll plead out and end up with community service. I don't have any priors, and I'm an upstanding citizen. I won't serve any time."

"But you'll lose your job over this." Her eyes fill with tears, and I hate the stress this is causing her.

"So I'll find a new one." I shrug. "It's just a job. It doesn't matter what I'm doing; as long as you're okay, nothing else matters."

"I hate this." Her head falls forward to rest against my chest as her arms snake around my waist, squeezing tight.

"I know."

We stay wrapped around each other for a few more minutes, neither wanting to pull away. "Maybe stay at your brother's this weekend. Or in the house with Scott and Max."

"I'll be okay." She pulls back to see my face.

"I know." I rest my hand against her neck, my thumb brushing her jaw gently. "I'll just feel better knowing you're not alone."

She doesn't answer; she simply moves to her toes to press a tender kiss to my lips. "I love you."

"I love you, too."

I kiss her one more time and wipe the lone tear that manages to fall down her cheek before we both move to exit Lyle's office.

I shouldn't be surprised by the crowd standing outside, but I am. I knew Declan and Quinn would be here, and I'm not surprised Caleb, Emily, and Abbey are here, considering they were at the bar. But to see my parents, Scott, and Walt has me momentarily stunned.

"What are you all doing here?" I ask, dumbfounded.

"Did you really think we wouldn't be here to support you?" Dad steps forward, pulling me into a hug.

"No. I just...who called you?"

"I did," Ava says. "I didn't want them to hear about it anywhere else. Plus, I wanted them to be able to prepare your siblings in case someone said something to them. I didn't tell them to come down here, though."

I pull her back into my side, kissing her temple to hide the bout of emotion I feel welling inside.

Swallowing, I turn back to everyone gathered. "Thank you, but you all didn't need to stick around."

"It's bullshit what's happening here," Declan growls. "I'll talk to my parents. Get them to—"

"No," I interrupt, reaching for his shoulder. "Just keep an eye on your sister for me. I know she can take care of herself," I say, releasing Declan and looking down at Ava. "But it doesn't hurt to have someone to lean on."

Declan steps forward, pulling me into a tight hug. "Thank you for loving her like you do," he whispers in my ear. The words are gruff and filled with so much emotion that I swallow back a lump in my throat.

Stepping back, I give everyone else a tight smile before turning to Ava, cupping her face in my hands. "I love you, and I know you've seen this before, but I don't want you to see me get arrested."

Ava opens her mouth to argue, but the pleading look in my eye stops her. "Okay."

"I'll see you Monday."

"I love you."

"I love you more than you know." I press a soft kiss to her lips and let her go.

Ava, being the strong woman she is, holds her head high as she walks out the door, Declan and Quinn right behind her.

"I need you all to go, too," I tell everyone else still standing around.

"We'll take care of her till you're able." Scott offers me a quick handshake before ushering Caleb and Emily out the door.

"If I knew who he was, I never would have let him in the bar."

"I know that, Walt. None of this is your fault, and no one blames you."

"Just...let me know if you need anything."

I nod and watch him and Abbey follow everyone else out the door—leaving my parents.

"I love you, Gage, and I respect that you don't want me to see this, but you're my son, and I'm damn proud of you." Mom's words get choked up, and she turns to look at my dad, swallowing thickly before she brings her eyes back to mine. "Like hell am I leaving you here."

"Mom, you can't stay here all weekend."

"Well, if that's how long you'll be here, then yes, I can."

My eyes shift to Dad, pleading with him silently to make her see reason.

"Sweetheart, he's right. You need to go home and be with Liv. She won't handle it well when she hears what happened."

Mom's eyes bounce between Dad and me a few times before her shoulders fall in acceptance. She pulls me into a fierce hug, holding on longer than necessary. But, I don't rush her, appreciating the love and support she's offering.

"We love you, son." Dad squeezes my shoulder before pulling Mom away from me.

"Love you, too. I'll see you in a couple of days." I offer a tight smile, watching Dad practically pull Mom out the door.

It's quiet; Lyle and Reid giving me a few more minutes to digest everything. It's a shitty situation, but I know I did the right thing, and that's all that matters.

AVA

"AVA! Wait! This isn't a good idea." Quinn rushes up behind me.

I may be four inches shorter than her, but when I'm on a mission it's as if I'm six feet tall. "No. This is a fantastic idea." I charge ahead, storming toward the hospital doors. "It's long overdue. I should have done it back in Boston before I came here."

"Ava, Gage doesn't want you to do this," Declan says from behind Quinn.

"Well, he isn't here right now, is he?"

"That's not fair."

"No, it's not. That's the point!" I stop so abruptly it causes a chain reaction. Quinn runs into me, grabbing my shoulders to keep us both steady, and Declan does the same to her.

"Squirt—"

"No," I interrupt, holding my palm out to stop him. "I know what you're trying to do using that nickname, and it won't work." I let my hand fall and swallow the lump forming in my throat before continuing. "If I had just done something about Brian after the first night in Boston, none of this would have happened."

"Ava." Quinn's voice is stern, more than I've ever heard it before. "None of this is your fault, so you need to get that idea out of your head."

"Quinn—"

"No." Tears well in her eyes, and I'm immediately on edge. "This isn't about me, and I don't want to make it about me, but when we make it through this, you and I are going to sit down and talk about how I know without a shadow of a doubt that this isn't your fault."

Declan's hands never left Quinn's shoulders after he ran into her, but I see them tighten a fraction as he steps further into her space, pressing a kiss to the back of her head.

"If you want to go in there and give Brian and your parents a piece of your mind, then we'll be right behind you. But you will not walk in there thinking this is your fault."

I don't know what happened to Quinn, but I can guess based on how she's talking to me—like she knows exactly what I'm thinking—and I hate that she gets it.

My eyes shift to Declan's. "She's right. We're behind you every step of the way."

"Thank you," I tell them, pulling them both in for a hug before turning away and marching to the desk in the main lobby.

"Good evening. Visiting hours are over for the night. Unless you're family, you'll need to come back tomorrow."

"My husband, Brian Wellsley. I believe my parents are already with him." The lie comes a little too easily, but all I care about is getting into that room—and I'll do whatever is needed to get there.

"Oh, yes, of course. He's been taken up for observation. Third floor, room 314." The look in the receptionist's eye tells me everything I need to know. Brian has already made his presence more than known in this hospital. The fact that he didn't even need to check the computer in front of him to tell me where Brian is proves it even more.

"Thanks." I offer a tight smile before turning for the elevators to our right.

We're quiet on the ride up to observation. I don't know what Quinn and Declan are thinking about, but all I can focus on is figuring out how to get Brian to drop the charges. I'll never forgive myself if Gage loses his job over this. I know Quinn doesn't want me to blame myself, but it's easier said than done.

There's a sick satisfaction seeing the bruises on Brian's face when we walk into his room. I've never wished harm on another human being, but there isn't a single ounce of me that feels bad for Brian.

"Oh, thank God. I knew you'd see reason." My mother stands from her seat beside the bed.

"I don't know why you think I'm here, but I can promise you it's not because I've finally agreed to whatever you have planned."

"Ava." My father pinches the bridge of his nose, exasperation clear in his voice.

"No. I'm done listening to all of you. Here's what's going to happen." I step to the foot of the bed, eyes zeroing in on Brian. "You're going to drop all charges against Gage, and then you'll go back to Boston where I'll never hear from or see you again."

"And why would I do that?" he sneers.

"Because if you don't, I'll press charges against you, both in Boston and here."

"They'll never stick."

"I'm not done," I seethe. "I'll also talk to every news outlet that will listen to me. You're right that the charges might not stick, but the media? They'll eat this story up, and you'll be ruined anyway."

I see the anger flare in his eyes, but I also see the moment he recognizes the truth in my statement. The press picking up this story will destroy him and the firm if I share that they fired me after Brian tried to rape me.

He growls but nods his head. "I'll drop the charges."

I turn to my parents. "I don't care what you do, but you will never contact me again. I knew you were selfish, but I never thought you'd intentionally put me in danger. I'm done with you, in every sense of the word."

"Ava." My mother steps forward, desperation clear in her voice. She reaches for me, but I step back, and her hand falls. "If you don't do this, your father and I will be ruined."

"And I should care why?"

"We're your parents."

"You might have given me life, but you haven't been parents since I was old enough to walk."

"If you don't do this, we'll lose everything." My father finally speaks, standing from his seat.

"Okay, I'm curious." Declan steps further into the room, his arms banded across his chest. "Why will you be ruined?"

"There are things you don't know about, things that your mother and I did before we ever had you, and those things are coming back to haunt us."

"Well, I guess you have to live with that now, don't you?" Maybe I should care more, but I can't find it in me. I turn back to Brian. "You'll call the sheriff tonight and you'll tell him you've reconsidered and are dropping the charges. If Gage isn't out of that jail cell in an hour, I'll call the Globe. Melissa might not be my sister-in-law anymore, but she'll print this story faster than you can say objection."

I don't wait for a response; I leave the room without a backward glance. I'm surprised that I'm not even a little curious about what "things" my father was alluding to, but I truly don't care. I just want all of them out of this town and far away from me.

"Damn, girl." Quinn laughs as she jogs up to my side, throwing her arm over my shoulder. "I'm so glad I got to see that."

"That felt way better than I thought it would."

"Of course it did."

"Where's Declan?" I ask, noticing he's not with us.

"You know he had to give them all a piece of his mind. He's a fixer, and someone he cares deeply about was hurt."

I lean my head against her shoulder, taking comfort in the knowledge that I have so many people in my corner. I've always known Declan would do anything for me, and for the last five years, I've known Scott and Caleb would do the same. But since showing up in Ashford Falls two months ago, I've gained so much more than I ever thought possible. It feels good fighting for it.

———

I'M PACING the length of Gage's living room when I hear his keys in the door and freeze. I know Gage will be happy that he's not getting charged and won't lose his job, but he's also going to be pissed I didn't listen to him.

Declan and Quinn wanted to wait with me, but I wouldn't let them. This is something Gage and I are going to have to talk about alone.

He steps through the door and sees me immediately. "What the hell did you do, Rebel?" He doesn't sound angry. If anything, he sounds like he's in pain.

"I couldn't let you sit in a jail cell all weekend. Not when I could do something about it."

"I told you not to go see him. I didn't want you to have to

look that bastard in the eye, not after everything he's already done." He toes off his shoes as he drops his keys on the side table by the door before moving around the couch to stand in front of me.

"I know, but it wasn't right, Gage. You didn't deserve to be there, and I could fix it." I want so badly to be in his arms right now, but I keep myself where I am. "You would have done the same thing for me," I whisper.

Without warning, he cups my cheeks in his hands, pulling me forward and into a searing kiss. My hands fall to his waist, holding his shirt in a grip so tight my knuckles hurt.

If I'm honest, I was terrified this evening, not just when I was pinned against that wall at Murphy's but standing in that police station waiting to find out what would happen to Gage. Afraid that he might blame me for everything he was going through. I know it was stupid of me to think for even a second that Gage would blame me, but in that moment, I was afraid of losing him, and I couldn't have that.

"I love you more than I ever thought possible." Gage pulls back. Still holding my face in his hands, his eyes bounce between mine. "And you're right. I would have done the same thing and more, so it's not fair for me to hold it against you."

"You're my favorite thing," I repeat the words he said a week ago, finally understanding what he meant when he said them.

Gage is everything I love about the world and my life, all wrapped up in one beautiful soul, and I'm so incredibly lucky to have found him. I know there's still so much for us to learn about each other, and if I'm being honest, I'm excited to learn everything I can about this man. He was made for me, just like I was made for him. I feel it all the way to my very bones.

CHAPTER
Thirty-Seven

GAGE

"YOU DOING OKAY?"

"What do you think? It's winter, and we're hiking a literal mountain!"

"Rebel." I can't help the chuckle that escapes.

"Don't laugh at me." Ava stops so quickly I almost run into her. She whirls around to face me, arms banded across her chest. "Valentine's Day is supposed to be about romance, not roughing it in the woods."

She looks adorable, bundled in her winter gear, the tip of her nose pink from the cold. I step into her space, resting my hands on her hips.

"You did see the cabin we're staying in, right? That bathroom and kitchen are not roughing it."

"Gage!" She stomps her foot like a toddler having a temper tantrum, and I can't help but laugh as I pull her in for a kiss.

"While we might be hiking a mountain, it's a very small one, and I promise we're almost there."

The glare she shoots at me doesn't have as much heat as she wants. I know it's winter and a little cold, even with the layers and the fact that we haven't stopped moving, but I know she's having fun.

I could have planned some romantic getaway for the two of us this weekend, but in the almost two months since we talked about going for a hike, we never found time for it. Ava's tried every other hobby that's been even mildly interesting to her and every hobby her friends and brother have suggested, but hiking with me just hasn't happened.

It might have been a little selfish of me to plan this particular weekend getaway, but I originally wanted to rent an RV.

Besides, the longer we've hiked, the more relaxed Ava has become. This last month, since everything happened with Brian and her parents—while not necessarily stressful—has been busy. There are only a handful of evenings I can recall that someone wasn't at my house or we weren't over at someone else's place for dinner. It's like everyone in our lives wanted to make sure we weren't alone.

It was ridiculous, but I loved them all the more for it.

This is the first three-day weekend I have off from the station since everything happened back in January, and I'm not taking it for granted. The second I knew my schedule for this month, I ran to Abbey to make sure Ava could take today off. While there are very few nights we don't spend together in one of our beds, I'm desperate for some alone time with Ava. Seventy-two hours of uninterrupted time seems like a dream. And introducing her to one of my favorite pastimes feels like the best way to spend Valentine's.

"Is it really that terrible?" I bend and kiss the tip of her nose.

Her body relaxes, and her arms fall from her chest, wrapping around my waist instead. "No, it's not. I just wish it were a little warmer."

"We'll stay in the cabin the rest of the weekend. I just really want to show you this view."

"You'll build me a fire and let me crochet on the couch while you make dinner?" The gleam in her eyes has me laughing again.

I've laughed—really laughed, not just something to help lighten the mood—more in the last month than I have in the last three years. And that's all thanks to this woman in front of me. The peace I feel with her is something I used to only find when I was outdoors. It's something I craved and searched for in every hike and camping trip, and it's something I never thought I could feel every minute of every day. But I do. Just the thought of her—doing whatever she might be at any given moment of the day—brings me peace.

"Yeah, Rebel. I'll build you a fire."

"Okay." She presses a kiss to my lips, lingering there for a few seconds before pulling away. "Show me this view."

"It's right around this bend." I take her gloved hand in mine, walking at her side the rest of the way.

Maryland doesn't seem like it has much to see, but the Appalachian Trail isn't anything to sneeze at. The views you can get from this place will take your breath away.

As we round the bend, I feel the moment Ava sees it. And it's the moment I know she falls in love with hiking. Winter might be the worst time for hiking due to the cold, but it's Ava's favorite season—especially when there's snow on the ground. And Maryland did me well this week. It made this hike a bit of a bear, but seeing this sight of trees and valleys covered in snow is beautiful. Almost as stunning as the glow emanating from Ava.

Stepping up behind her, I wind my arms around her, pulling her back to my chest, supporting her in every sense of the word.

"It's amazing." Ava closes her eyes, takes a deep breath, and holds it. As she releases it, she opens her eyes, and I feel her entire body melt into mine. Any stress she was carrying is officially gone. "Thank you," she whispers, her words a little choked.

"Anytime, Rebel." I kiss her cheek and absorb everything I possibly can from this moment. Every feeling, every touch, every smell, all of it. I never want to forget this moment.

We stand here quietly, taking in everything around us longer than I thought we would. But I'll stand here as long as Ava wants to.

"Can we come here again next year?" Her words are so soft I almost miss them.

"We can come here whenever you want."

Ava turns in my arms, wrapping hers around my neck and pulling me in for a tight hug. "I know I acted like a child during the hike, and I'm sorry. This was more than worth a little discomfort."

"I love you, Rebel."

"I love you, too, Gage. More than I ever imagined."

I let my eyes roam over her face for a moment, taking in every facet possible. "I never thought I would have this, and I'm grateful every day that I found you." I press a soft kiss against her lips, pulling back just enough to look her in the eye. "You are the most unexpected love, but I wouldn't change any of it for anything."

Something sparks in Ava's eyes, but it's gone before I can identify what it means. "Unexpected love, indeed."

She smiles as she presses her lips to mine, and I feel her happiness soaking into every part of me.

Epilogue

GAGE

Four Years Later

"AVA! WE'RE GONNA BE LATE!" I yell from the bottom of the stairs, hoping to leave soon to get to Quinn and Declan's on time.

"I know, I know, I know," she grumbles as she races toward me.

I grab her hand before she can rush past me. "Are you sure you're good? I don't want you to stress," I tell her gently.

Her shoulders sag and she falls into me, her forehead resting against my chest. I wrap my arms around her, holding on tight. I know how hard this day is for her, and I wish more than anything I could take away her pain. Every year we gather on this day to celebrate Scott, and every year it hits Ava just as hard.

After Ava cut her parents out of her life for good, Scott became more of a father to her than Gregory Day ever was. That was one of the most remarkable things about Scott; he loved those he cared for as if they were his blood, no matter what. He loved her for who she was with no expectations, exactly like any parent should.

It was with his help and guidance that Ava truly accepted that it was okay to still be a lawyer, even if her parents pushed her into the career originally. I think it was his custody case that first sparked the thought that she could help people who really needed it like she first hoped to do when she got her degree. Of course, everything that happened with the bookstore and Murphy's definitely gave her an extra push.

"I'm okay." Ava lifts her head to look me in the eye. "I want to go; I just wish it got easier with time."

I look at her, eyes filled with empathy and love. "Scott gave you the fatherly love you deserve. He made you feel encouraged, cherished, supported, and so much more. There's no limit on grief. No expectation on how, when, or even if it'll ever be easier." I smooth her hair back from her face, cupping her cheek. "Let yourself feel that without judgment or expectation. He loved you, Ava. It's okay to feel that loss."

Her voice is quiet when she responds. "But it's not like he was the only one. Your dad has loved me just as fiercely as Scott did. It's not like I've lost that fatherly love completely."

"We still lost someone we cared for deeply. Maybe we hold on a little tighter to those we still have, but we get to grieve our loss all the same."

Ava takes a breath, as if stealing herself for all the emotions of the day to come, and pulls away slightly.

"I just don't want you to stress about your feelings; they're completely natural, and the stress isn't good for you." I drop my hands to her small bump.

Four years together, two years married, and all we've been through, we both know I'm protective of Ava. But these last five months have been worse than ever before. Two miscarriages will do that to a person.

I have no reason to believe anything will happen with this pregnancy. We're well past the point when we lost the first two.

We didn't even know Ava was pregnant with the first when she miscarried. But it was that miscarriage that told us we were both more than ready to grow our family.

Even with being five months in, and everyone constantly reminding me that everything looks perfect with this baby, I can't stop the little voice in my head from convincing me otherwise.

Luckily, my wife is an understanding woman who never judges me when those voices get too loud.

She lifts her hand to cup my cheek, a gentle smile on her face. "We're doing good, honey. I promise." And as if the little pea can hear us, I feel a light push under my hand.

My eyes immediately bounce down to her stomach and back to her eyes. "Was that..."

Ava's beaming smile is the only answer I need, but she nods anyway, tears welling in her eyes. "Yeah, that was a kick."

"I haven't felt that before." I fall to my knees right there at the bottom of the stairs and place both hands on her stomach.

"I know." Ava laughs through her tears. "I think he's trying to tell you we're fine."

"Stop calling our little pea a boy. We don't know." I press my lips to Ava's stomach. "She doesn't mean it," I whisper.

I don't have to see it to know Ava rolls her eyes. "You know, we could solve all our problems by letting the doctor tell us what we're having."

"We could, but where's the fun in that?" I grin up at her from the floor.

"Oh my gosh! Get up! We're gonna be late." The smile on her lips and the sparkle in her eyes tell me exactly what she's really feeling in this moment—pure and utter happiness.

It's a feeling I know I mirror right back at her.

"I love you, little pea," I mumble against her stomach before standing. "And I love you more than I ever thought possible," I murmur against her lips.

"I love you, too."

NOT
Done Yet?

Neither was I.

Scan the QR code below to get your copy of an exclusive bonus scene.

If you'd like to stay up to date on all things Erin Graves, including new releases, bonus content, behind the scenes, give-aways, and more, be sure to sign up for my newsletter.

ENJOYED
Unexpected Love?

Or even if you didn't, please consider leaving a review on Amazon, Goodreads, Storygraph, and/or anywhere you review books.

Reviews are one of the easiest ways to help indie authors. Even a simple sentence and star rating can go a long way.

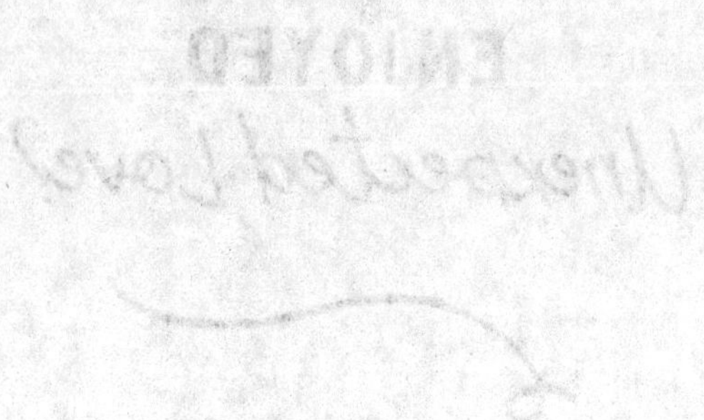

Acknowledgments

They say the sophomore slump is the worst, and I think I might have to agree. Writing this book was a challenge for me. To the point that there were a few instances I thought about no longer writing the book. So, there are quite a few people to thank this time around.

It should be no surprise that I'm going to start by thanking Kelly. She was with me from the very start of this project, letting me bounce idea after idea off her before I even started writing this one. She was my sounding board when I wanted to bang my head against the wall, and she was my motivation when I thought about throwing the entire thing out the door. I couldn't have done it without you.

Emily, I am so glad you filled out that alpha/beta reader interest form and I am so glad you jumped into my DMs to talk about this book. You were, without a doubt, a massive motivator for me while I was writing this book. You're stuck with me now!

My beta readers: Annelise, Courtney, Katie, Laura, Mary, Michelle, Paige, and Sarah. The love you had for Gage and Ava truly reignited my love for this story. I was finally starting to come around to these characters and this story when I did my read through before sending it to you all, but your comments really made me see the beauty in this story. Thank you for helping me fall in love with these characters all over again.

My editor. Caroline, I'm so very thankful for you and all you do to make this story presentable to the public. Me and grammar are not friends and some of the mistakes you catch have me cringing!

My sibling. I love you terribly and your support will always be something I cherish. Thank you for helping me bring my characters to life and thank you for always being there for me when I need you.

You. It's cliché but also so very true. I wouldn't be doing this author thing if it weren't for you sitting there reading these words. So, from the bottom of my heart, I thank you.

And of course, I can't forget to mention my husband. He still might not have read more than a line here or there, but he's been my biggest supporter in every way that matters. There are silly things I gave Gage that are from my husband, but the biggest one of all is the feeling of peace Ava finds in Gage. That aspect of this story was the easiest thing for me to write because I feel that every day with you. Thank you for always being that place for me.

CONTENT
Warning

Please note that some of these trigger warnings are discussed in detail and on page, though none of the scenes they are discussed in are long. That being said, please take care of yourself first and foremost.

- Sexual Assault (both on page and off)
- Emotional manipulation by a parent (both on page and off)
- Physical abuse of a parent (side character, brief description on page)
- Violence (both on page and off)
- Cancer (side character, briefly mentioned)
- Brief mention of miscarriage

The Love in Ashford Falls series continues with Abbey and Jude's story in Hidden Vows!

Continue reading for a first look.

Prologue

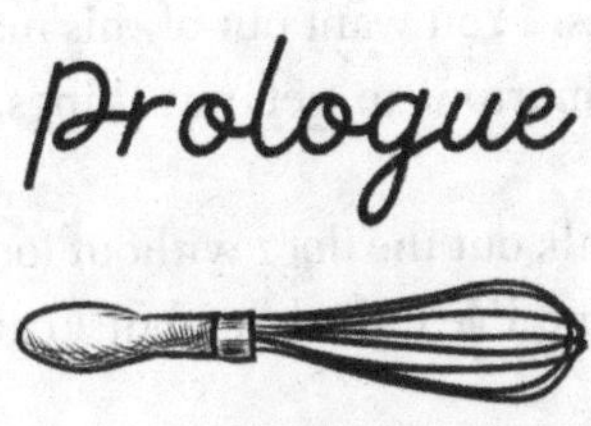

ABBEY

"You asshole!" I shout, shoving at his chest.

"I told you we were too young! That we rushed this! You're only eighteen!" Jude shouts, just as loudly.

There's something in his eyes, but I'm not clear-headed enough to analyze what it is. He's broken something inside of me, and I don't know if I'll ever be able to get it back.

"That doesn't make it better! That doesn't excuse it." I turn away, pacing toward the front door of our apartment—our home. "How could you do this?" My voice is so quiet now; all the fight drained from my body. Slowly, I turn back to him, tears welling in my eyes. "I never thought you could do something like this to me—to us."

"Abbey—" His voice cracks on the single word. He steps forward, reaching for me, but I don't let him touch me.

"No. You don't get to touch me right now." Jude flinches, and I wipe frantically at my face. "I don't know how we fix this." My voice is so quiet and I desperately fight to hold back the sobs building in my chest.

I can't look at him, not with the pain etched across his face.

What right does he have to be in pain?

My eyes fall to the floor. If I keep looking at Jude I'll break, and I don't feel safe doing that here, not after what I've just discovered.

Squaring my shoulders and with a conviction I don't fully feel, I meet his eyes. "You want out of this marriage, you got it. I'll come back tomorrow to get my things. Please don't be here."

Somehow, I walk out the door without looking back at him. It's the hardest thing I've ever done, but I can't stay—not after this.

Jude may have been telling me for weeks we made a mistake getting married, but I never thought he was capable of hurting me. I never thought he'd go to these lengths to prove me wrong, but maybe I don't know Jude like I thought I did.

Stumbling out the back door of the building, I look around, trying to figure out where I should go. The person I want to talk to most is my mother, but going to my parents' house means seeing my father, and I know he'll gloat about my failed marriage.

The need for my mother's comfort far outweighs the dread of seeing my father. She'll let me cry and scream and feel whatever I need to feel without judgment or comment, and that's what I need more than anything else.

Still refusing to look back at the building that's been nothing but comfort since I first walked through the doors, I steel my spine and walk toward the street.

Maybe the long walk will help me figure out how this happened.

ALSO BY
Erin Graves

The Love in Ashford Falls Series

Shuttered Hearts

Unexpected Love

Hidden Vows

Forever in Stonebridge Hollow Series

Three Months Yesterday

Standalone Novellas

Nine Holidays Falling

Holiday Haven

ABOUT THE
Author

Erin Graves writes small town contemporary romance novels with a lot of heart and a touch of spice. She's a wife, cat mom, author, and sometimes crocheter. She was born and raised in Maryland and now lives in Pennsylvania with her husband and two cats. She started writing in high school but stopped when she thought she could never be a published author. Fifteen years later, her first novel was published.